Her gaze swept over his face. Even in the dim light, his features were strong and manly.

"I'm not sure what's going on in that head of yours, but it doesn't look good." Kyle's voice remained low.

Admitting that she was weighing the pros and cons of kissing him probably wouldn't help. Not in the least.

His eyes were intently searching—Skylar worried he might actually be able to figure out what she'd been thinking.

And yet...the longer his gaze held hers, the thinner the air between them became. The warmth of his hand against her back radiated across her skin.

"I want to kiss you, Skylar," he whispered. "I don't think I've ever wanted anything so much. But I—"

She pressed her lips against his, silencing whatever reason—likely a good one—they shouldn't do this. She knew they shouldn't but...

He wanted to kiss her. More than anything.

And if she wasn't so caught up in the feel of his lips on hers, his soft groan when the kiss deepened, she'd have told him that she knew exactly how he felt. If there was one thing she'd wish for, it was this: she wanted to kiss Kyle Mitchell until she couldn't remember why it was a bad idea.

* * *

TEXAS COWBOYS & K-9S

W9-BVW-403

Dear Reader,

Welcome back to Granite Falls, Texas. Kyle Mitchell has just returned from serving overseas but he is in no hurry to get home. He knows his homecoming might be awkward due to the lingering bitterness between him and his older brother, Hayden.

But before he can even think about heading home or his brother, he has to honor a promise he made to his fallen best friend. It's this loyalty and honor that make Kyle such a wonderful hero. Yes, he's handsome and a cowboy and he loves dogs and babies—but he's a good man. The sort of man Skylar and her girls need in their lives.

When Kyle arrives with the stray dog her husband had adopted while serving overseas, Skylar's spirits are lifted. Jet, the dog, brings smiles and laughter from her girls—something there's not enough of. It seems like every time Skylar finds her footing, the world seems to knock her back down. But Kyle's job offer—in the faraway town of Granite Falls—seems too good to be true. Could this be a fresh start or is she only setting herself up for more heartache and disappointment?

Until then, happy reading!

Sasha Summers

Their Rancher Protector

SASHA SUMMERS

If you purchased this book without a cover you should be aware
that this book is stolen property. It was reported as "unsold and
destroyed" to the publisher, and neither the author nor the
publisher has received any payment for this "stripped book."

HARLEQUIN®
SPECIAL
EDITION™

Recycling programs
for this product may
not exist in your area.

ISBN-13: 978-1-335-40801-3

Their Rancher Protector

Copyright © 2021 by Sasha Best

All rights reserved. No part of this book may be used or reproduced in
any manner whatsoever without written permission except in the case of
brief quotations embodied in critical articles and reviews.

This is a work of fiction. Names, characters, places and incidents
are either the product of the author's imagination or are used fictitiously.
Any resemblance to actual persons, living or dead, businesses,
companies, events or locales is entirely coincidental.

This edition published by arrangement with Harlequin Books S.A.

For questions and comments about the quality of this book,
please contact us at CustomerService@Harlequin.com.

Harlequin Enterprises ULC
22 Adelaide St. West, 40th Floor
Toronto, Ontario M5H 4E3, Canada
www.Harlequin.com

Printed in U.S.A.

Sasha Summers grew up surrounded by books. Her passions have always been storytelling, romance and travel—passions she's used to write more than twenty romance novels and novellas. Now a bestselling and award-winning author, Sasha continues to fall a little in love with each hero she writes. From easy-on-the-eyes cowboys, sexy alpha-male werewolves, to heroes of truly mythic proportions, she believes that everyone should have their happily-ever-after—in fiction and real life.

Sasha lives in the suburbs of the Texas Hill Country with her amazing family. She looks forward to hearing from fans and hopes you'll visit her online: on Facebook at sashasummersauthor, on Twitter, @sashawrites, or email her at sashasummersauthor@gmail.com.

Books by Sasha Summers

Harlequin Special Edition

Texas Cowboys & K-9s

The Rancher's Forever Family

Harlequin Western Romance

The Boones of Texas

A Cowboy's Christmas Reunion
Twins for the Rebel Cowboy
Courted by the Cowboy
A Cowboy to Call Daddy
A Son for the Cowboy
Cowboy Lullaby

Visit the Author Profile page
at Harlequin.com for more titles.

Dedicated to the hardworking volunteers
at the local animal rescue and animal shelters
(SA Pets Alive here) for taking care of all the fur-babies
until they find their forever home.

Chapter One

Skylar disentangled baby Greer's chubby little fist from her long dark hair. "You've got a handful of Mommy's hair, don't you, baby girl?" She smiled down at her six-month-old, holding her against her chest in a thick cotton baby wrap. "Look at you, smiling."

Greer smiled, cooing softly as Skylar carefully untwined her hair from her daughter's tiny fingers.

"Momma, Momma." Four-year-old Brynn was half skipping along the dirt driveway back to the house. "Look." She pointed at the rising dust down the country road. "Someone coming?"

Skylar paused, shielding her eyes from the bright West Texas sun. Frank's home was a good distance from town and, other than the mailman, they didn't get many visitors. Since they'd just walked down the gravel drive to pick up the day's mail, she knew George wouldn't head out this way again until tomorrow. "I don't know, Brynn." She continued to bounce and pat Greer, her eyes narrowing as the dust cloud grew closer and closer. She brushed aside the unease sliding up her spine. *There's no more bad news left to fear.* Chad was already gone. It had been almost a year now, but there were times she woke up, drenched in sweat, reliving the day the uniformed casualty notification officer arrived on her doorstep to tell her of Chad's passing as if it had just happened.

A large blue truck crested the dirt road, slowing.

"Who that?" Brynn asked. "Who, Momma?"

"Probably someone passing through." Smile in place, she realized her other daughter, Brynn's twin, was nowhere to be seen. "Where's Mya?"

"Don't know." Brynn shrugged, spinning on her heel. "Picking flowers."

Picking flowers—by the mailbox. The mailbox by the road… The road with the big blue truck heading this way. Heart in her throat, she forced out, "Stay here" to Brynn. Holding Greer tightly to her chest, she sprinted back down the gravel drive to her daughter—happily picking wildflowers.

By the time Skylar had reached Mya, the truck had come to a stop. It didn't matter. Her heart was hammering away, thundering against her rib cage. "Mya." She placed her hand on her daughter's shoulder.

Mya turned, holding out the bouquet of flowers she'd picked. "Ma."

Skylar took the flowers with shaking hands. She was okay. Thankfully, the driver had been paying attention. *I should have been paying attention, too.* She pulled her daughter in for a hug, waiting until her heartbeat eased and there was enough air in her lungs for her to breathe before she leaned back to point at the truck. "Careful." She spoke the word slowly, her daughter's eyes watching her mouth as she formed the word.

Mya nodded, her eyes widening when she spied the truck. She grasped Skylar's hand tightly and pulled her back up the path to where Brynn waited.

The truck drove a few feet forward, the whir of the electric window followed by a deep voice. "Excuse me? Are you Skylar Davis? I'm looking for the Davis homestead?"

"Who wants to know?" Considering how few visitors they had, she couldn't help being suspicious. Folk didn't head out this way for no reason. Thirty miles down a dirt road with nothing but tumbleweeds, cacti and the occasional roadrunner for company wasn't exactly a scenic drive.

"My name is Kyle Mitchell." He put the truck in Park and turned off the ignition.

Skylar squinted. With the sun at the man's back, she couldn't make out much beyond his size. A big man, spare and fit…and walking this way. "You can stay off my property, Kyle Mitchell. Whatever you're selling, I'm not interested."

"No, ma'am." But he'd stopped moving. "I'm not here to sell you a thing." He pulled off the tan cowboy hat he'd been wearing. "I...I knew your husband."

The ache in her heart still had sharp edges, edges that felt raw and exposed at his words.

"Chad," he went on, staying right where he was. "I'm sorry, Mrs. Davis. Chad and I were good friends."

She nodded stiffly.

"He asked me to bring you something." He held his hand out, toward the truck. "He felt strongly about it."

It was the last thing she'd expected to hear... After everything she and the girls had been through, she needed something good. They all did.

"What's the holdup out there?" Her uncle Frank opened the glass front door, the squeak of the rusty hinge reverberating in the air. "My puzzle get here?"

"Unca," Brynn mumbled, tugging on her hand. "Get grumpy."

"Hold on, Uncle Frank," Skylar called out.

"Why?" Frank yelled. "What am I waiting on?"

"We have a visitor."

"Who?" His voice rose, his slow footfalls echoing down the metal ramp that led into the small wood frame house. "Who are you? What business do you have here?"

Brynn took Mya's hand and, together, they ran

to the small wooden clubhouse Skylar had built for them. They tended to do that when Frank was around—the only thing consistent about her uncle's temperament was how erratic it was.

"Uncle Frank, he's a friend of Chad's." She ignored her uncle, more curious about what Chad had given this man to deliver to her than her uncle's temper.

"Is that so?" Frank's snort was loud. "Interesting you show up now? Chad's been dead a year now."

"Yes, sir." There was an edge to the man's voice. "I was on active duty."

"Was?" her uncle asked. "You wash out or something?"

Skylar shot Frank a look. "Uncle Frank." She crossed the hard-packed earth that made up their front yard and handed her uncle his beloved newspaper. "Here."

He snatched the paper, but never stopped looking at Kyle Mitchell. "You here for a handout?"

"No, sir. Chad asked me to come." The man shifted from one foot to the other. "I won't keep you for long."

"You won't keep *me* at all." Her uncle shook his head and lumbered slowly back up the metal ramp and into the house, letting the door slam shut.

"I didn't mean to cause trouble." Kyle Mitchell ran a hand over his head.

"That?" Skylar forced a laugh. "He's having a good day today." Sad, but true. Greer's soft coo drew her attention down to her heavy-lidded daughter. It was almost nap time. There was no way she'd put Greer down inside, not when her uncle was in a snit. Instead, she went back to bouncing, gently patting Greer's little back in what she hoped was a soothing rhythm. "Did you serve with Chad?" She took a step closer to him, then another.

"Yes, ma'am." Unlike her, he didn't move. "I'd like to think he was one of my best friends."

Chad had been an avid letter writer. Most of them recounted his days—as if he was journaling all the things he thought and saw and did. A lot of the details had been unremarkable, likely censored so she wouldn't worry, but she'd treasured each and every one nonetheless. Chad's words gave her a view into the world where he was and kept him close. But the name Kyle Mitchell didn't ring any bells.

When she reached the rotting wooden post, the wind rattling the gate hanging from one chain, she could finally see the man who had driven from who knows where to find her. For Chad.

"I know you," she said, her voice going thick. Pictures. Chad and this man. So many pictures. "But he called you—"

"Needle." He shrugged, grinning. "Yeah. Not the best nickname."

But fitting. At least Chad thought so. If there was one person her late husband had mentioned in each and every letter, it was Needle. Needle was the spotter to Chad's sniper—his eyes, his right-hand man, and his brother. According to Chad, Needle could get them anywhere, calculate the perfect target distance, talk down a potentially hostile situation, *and* sew up any size hole in their field uniform. Chad had said the only time he'd felt at peace were the times he and Needle were staked on a roof somewhere, beneath the stars, talking about home and family and friends. She'd heard about this man for years. Now here he was. Emotion welled up, too strong to ignore. "I knew it wasn't your real name but…"

"Might as well have been." He nodded, still smiling. "I would have called first—"

"Nonsense." Without realizing it, she'd closed the distance between them. "You're welcome. Anytime." This man had saved Chad's life more than once. Chad swore Needle—Kyle—was his guardian angel.

"I appreciate that. He showed you all off enough that I feel like I know you and the girls. Whenever he'd get a new picture, he'd pass it around." His gaze wandered to the wooden clubhouse. "The girls are bigger now, of course."

Even though she knew how proud of his girls Chad was, it was still nice to hear. She'd sent pictures often, to make all the things he'd missed out on a little easier. "And getting bigger every day." Sometimes, she wished she could slow time down— just a little. "He never met Greer." The lump in her throat made it hard for her to finish. "I know he'd have doted on her just as much as the other two." She

stared up at the man, at ease now. This was Needle—
rather, Kyle Mitchell. Live and in person. And here.
She didn't know why it made her happy, but it did.
"I'm going to have to work on calling you Kyle."

"It's good to meet you, Skylar," he said, holding
out his hand. "Face-to-face, that is."

"It's nice to meet you, too, Kyle." She shook his
hand. "Where are you from?"

"Granite Falls—it's part-ways between San An-
tonio and Austin." His gaze bounced to the top of
Greer's head.

"You're a long way from home." A good seven
hours from home.

"I came here first." He glanced back at the truck.
"Wouldn't have been able to rest until I'd done what
I promised."

Greer fussed a little so Skylar started walking,
slowly, toward the girls' clubhouse. He followed,
a small smile on his face as she hummed, patted,
and bounced. "She fusses and fights against falling
asleep," Skylar explained.

He nodded.

"I guess you could say she's stubborn." She smiled
at Kyle. "Like her father."

"He was that," he agreed, his eyes shifting her
way.

While she'd received a nicely typed letter signed
by important people, she knew very little about her
husband's death. For the most part, it didn't matter.

But there was one thing she needed to know. "You were with him?" She ignored the waver in her voice.

His nod was stiff. "Not when he went out but… when they brought him back on base."

It was enough. "Thank you." She covered his hand with hers. "It helps to know that someone who cared about him was with him until the end." The stark sadness in his eyes was an all-too-familiar sight. It had taken her a long time to look her reflection in the eye without fighting back tears.

"If I could have brought him back to you, I would have." He had a hard time meeting her gaze then.

"I know." She did, too. "Chad told me you were the reason he'd stayed alive as long as he had. I have no doubt you'd have done the same—if you'd been there that day."

His jaw muscle clenched tight but he didn't say a word.

"Do you want to come inside?" Her uncle would raise a commotion, but she didn't care. It was warming up and a glass of lemonade would do them all some good.

His brows rose. "You sure that's a good idea?"

"I'm sure." Frank Kline could be charming. Growing up, Skylar had only seen pictures of her uncle. He'd always cancelled right before every holiday or family gathering. But Skylar knew about him. Her mother had told her all about how easy it had been for her sweet-talking younger brother to get out of all the mischief he'd caused—no matter how big or small. He was all sincerity and charm, her mother had said, until he got what he wanted.

That was the Uncle Frank Skylar had met in the hospital. A kind, caring, soft-spoken man—ready and willing to help in her time of loss. It was only after she'd moved home with him that she remembered what her mother had said. By then, she had no place to go. For the girls, she'd had to make peace with that. "Whether you come in or not won't change the fact that my uncle is a grumpy old man."

"It's not just me." He turned, pointing at the truck. "I've got Chad's present."

Right. The present. She'd been so surprised to realize who Kyle Mitchell was that she'd almost forgotten why he was here. She peered at the open window of the truck.

Kyle whistled and the brown head of a dog appeared in the window. One ear was cocked upright, the other lay flat. "Chad didn't want him left behind."

Just when she thought her emotions were in check… But now, her throat officially closed off. Her heart thumped, heavy and aching, as the dog jumped through the window and trotted, slowly, cautiously, toward her with its head stooped. "Are you Jet? You are, aren't you?" Skylar asked, kneeling in the dirt and holding out her hand. "Is that you?"

Jet's stub of a tail kicked into overdrive and he made a low grumble-whine in the back of his throat before rolling onto his back.

"That's Jet all right. He's a good dog," Kyle said. "Sweet—too sweet for his own good."

She nodded, rubbing the dog's stomach. "I know all about you, too. Chad said Jet was in a pretty sorry state when he found him? Said he was skin-and-bones, treated poorly, and begging for food."

"Pretty much. Chad couldn't take it." Kyle chuckled. "He snuck Jet a treat and that was it. The dog followed him around like a shadow."

She cradled the dog's head in her hands, staring into Jet's timid chocolate-brown eyes. "He sure loved you." Once Jet had appeared, there'd been a difference in Chad's letters. He might have saved the dog from starving, but Jet had given Chad something good to focus on.

Skylar was incredibly grateful for the dog and Needle. They'd given Chad the support and love he'd needed when she couldn't. She'd always hoped Jet would come back with him once his tour was up—that Needle and Chad would laugh and share stories over a dinner she'd cooked for them. That's what she'd wanted. Her husband back. The future they'd always talked about. Hope and love and joy.

Instead, her days consisted of making the best of things and putting on a brave face for her daughters...

Jet rolled over, stood up and leaned forward to sniff Greer, sound asleep in her front pack. He whimpered, his tail going even faster, and his head cocking to one side.

"Momma?" Brynn's voice was soft, almost breathless. "Who that?"

Skylar turned, holding out her hand to her daughters. "Brynn, Mya, come meet someone special."

Kyle Mitchell had been dreading this—all of it. He'd known coming face-to-face with the woman Chad had loved and acting like it wasn't his fault that Chad was dead would be a challenge. He hadn't known how much.

He'd taken one look at Skylar Davis and his words were stuck in his throat.

He'd seen pictures of her before. She was pretty—more than pretty. But this woman was harder than the woman in the pictures. Sadder, too.

Because she'd lost her husband.

"Brynn. Mya." Skylar stood and waved the two little girls forward. "This is Daddy's friend, Mr. Mit—"

"Kyle." He squatted in front of the girls. "Who are you?"

"Brynn." The little girl pointed at her chest. "That's Mya." She put her hand on the other little girl's shoulder. "We twins."

"I can see that." The only difference between the girls was their hair. Brynn's was longer, Mya's cut at her jawline. Looked like Brynn was the talker of the two. He remembered Chad saying Mya was the funny one. Maybe she was just shy around strangers. One thing was certain, they were the cutest things he'd ever seen. Even cuter than their pictures. "This is Jet."

Jet was basically circling the girls, tail wagging and trembling with excitement, so happy he didn't know what to do. Which was a good thing, since Jet belonged to Skylar and her girls.

"Jet." Kyle patted the ground at his side.

Jet ran up, ears drooping, and sat, his gaze bouncing between the girls.

"Nice?" Brynn asked.

"Very." Kyle nodded. "Right now, he's trying not to give you dog kisses. And lots of them."

"Why?" Brynn asked, smiling at the dog. "Kisses good."

"You can pet him," Kyle said. "He wants to be friends."

"Momma?" Brynn asked.

Skylar nodded. "Help Mya."

Brynn took Mya's hand but Mya pulled away, shaking her head.

"No?" Brynn asked.

Mya shook her head again.

Skylar knelt between her daughters, one hand steadying the sleeping baby against her chest. "Mya. It's okay. Jet is a nice dog." She ran a hand over Jet's head, earning a look of pure adoration from the dog. "Dog." Skylar slapped her hand against her thigh and then made a snapping gesture. "Dog."

Mya nodded but she didn't make a move to touch Jet. Or say a word.

"She scared," Brynn said, the hand holding her sister's tightening. "Lots."

Kyle nodded, watching the exchange. "Looks like she's got you to help her with that." Being the second of three sons made him an expert on sibling diplomacy. Granted, neither of his brothers were shy like Mya, but he was all too familiar with translating the long silence of one brother for the other.

Mya slipped behind Skylar's legs, content to hide. Brynn wasn't hiding. She was almost as excited about petting Jet as Jet was. Her little face lit up with the sweetest smile as she slowly reached her hand out toward the dog.

Jet couldn't take it. He dropped to the ground and rolled over again, his tail stirring up a mini dust storm from all his excitement.

Brynn thought it was hilarious. Mya was smiling, too.

"He's a silly dog," Kyle said, rubbing Jet's stomach. "But he's a good friend." Exactly what Chad had wanted for his girls. He'd hoped Jet would give his little girls some comfort and love. Kyle only wished he could have gotten Jet to them sooner.

Brynn sat, her legs stretched out in the dirt, while Jet tummy-crawled closer and closer—until his nose was pressed against one of her legs.

"Jet," Brynn said, giggling. "Nice dog."

Jet decided that was an invitation to move a little closer to rest his head in Brynn's lap and stare up at the little girl.

"Hi," Brynn said, pointing at her chest. "I Brynn."

Jet continued to stare up at her.

The two of them together? Pretty damn adorable. Kyle used to tease Chad about how much he was like his dog—they were easy to love and impossible to ignore.

"How about that cold drink now?" Skylar asked, taking Mya's hand and standing. "Come on, Brynn, you can bring Jet."

"Unca?" Brynn asked, not moving from her spot.

"Uncle won't mind." Skylar tried to sound convincing, but even Kyle wasn't buying it. "It's not every day we have visitors."

Probably because they lived in the middle of nowhere. He was familiar with West Texas but there were none of the rugged buttes and landforms of the picturesque Old West films here. Instead, there were thickets of mesquite trees covered in thick purple-tipped thorns. The little groundcover was an occasional patch of scrub grass intermixed with abundant flat-leaf prickly pear cactus, covered with near-invisible hairlike thorns. A quick appraisal told him if it wasn't covered in dirt, it was pointy to the touch.

"How long have you lived out here?" he asked, following Skylar and her children to the door.

"Awhile." She glanced his way but didn't add anything more. "Frank?" She opened the door and peered inside. "Uncle Frank?"

"In the kitchen making my own lunch," Frank answered, clearly irritated. "Why is he still here?

Why are you still here?" He gestured with his half a sandwich.

"I invited him in, Uncle Frank," Skylar said. "It's hot outside, too hot for conversation. Kyle, this is my uncle, Frank Kline. Uncle Frank, this is Kyle Mitchell."

Her uncle made a grunting sound, scowling at Jet.

"What can I get you?" Skylar asked, skirting around her uncle to get into the small kitchen. "Water? Lemonade?"

"We're out of beer," Frank said, shooting Skylar an accusatory look.

"It's a little early for a beer, but thanks." Kyle smiled, taking care not to react to his surroundings. Nothing about this made sense. The place was tiny and, while clean, in need of some serious repair. Why was Skylar here? Chad's death would have left her entitled to some money. Not a lot, but enough that she shouldn't have to be here. Where did they sleep? From where he stood, all he could see was one bedroom.

"It's never too early for a beer," Frank snapped, grabbed his plate, and stomped to the back of the house—where a door slammed shut.

"Water would be good," Kyle said, inspecting the far wall covered in brightly laminated posters. Most of the pictures were hands, making various signs... Sign language.

"Use my cup, Momma," Brynn said, sitting on

the floor and patting the spot at her side until Jet lay down, leaning against her. "Jet. I like you."

Mya headed into the kitchen, tugged on Skylar's pants, and tapped three fingers—fanned wide—to her mouth. Kyle glanced back and forth from Mya to one of the posters. According to the illustrations, Mya had made the sign for water.

"I'll get you some water, too." Skylar smiled, stooping to kiss her daughter on the head.

Mya tapped her fingers against her lip and pulled her hand back.

He glanced at the posters again. *Thank you.* That was the sign for thank you.

"You're welcome." Skylar filled a pink plastic cup with water and gave it to Mya. "Ice?" she asked him.

"I won't say no." He nodded. Even inside, it was warm. From the looks of it, the small window unit was working extra hard to crank out enough cold air to cool the room.

Skylar pulled a teal-and-peach cup from the cabinet, added ice and water, and handed it to him. "Brynn wanted you to use her cup."

Kyle eyed the cup. The outside was clear, the inner plastic teal. But between the clear plastic and the teal was an ocean scene—complete with plastic fish and glitter and shells that moved when he tipped the glass to drink. "That's some sparkly cup."

"Princess," Brynn said. "Princess cup."

He held the cup out. "It does look like a princess cup."

Brynn nodded, her expression so serious he couldn't help but smile.

"Brynn likes princesses," Skylar said.

"What about Mya?" he asked, sitting in the kitchen chair she indicated.

Mya was sitting on the floor beside her sister, sipping water from her pink cup—her big brown eyes fixed on Jet.

"Mya likes llamas and horses," Brynn said, lying on the floor beside Jet.

Mya sat her cup down and lay down, too, closing her eyes when Jet wedged himself between them—making little grunts of happiness. Mya didn't open her eyes but she was finally grinning.

Skylar's gaze collided with his and they exchanged a smile. She reached behind herself to unbuckle the reverse backpack thing that held baby Greer.

Kyle thought it looked kind of like a kangaroo pouch. *Pretty handy.*

"Mya like llamas and horses and baby cows, too." Skylar eased the straps free, smiling down at the sleeping baby. "What do you think Greer will like, Brynn?"

Now that Greer was free of her pouch, she looked awfully small. Kyle didn't have much experience with babies, but he hadn't imagined they'd be so... tiny. He hadn't noticed the crib in the corner until Skylar slowly bent forward to place the tiny Greer inside.

He was sizing up the house all over again. Did they all sleep here? In the living room? If that's what it was called. It was more like one room, the only separation between the kitchen and living room was the seam where the linoleum ended and the brown carpet began. Carpet that was frayed and stained. Try as he might, he couldn't help but notice the buckling linoleum countertops, the water stain on the ceiling, and a whole slew of things that needed fixing. "Do you all stay here?"

He had more questions than that. A lot of questions. But it was a start. Delivering Jet wasn't the only thing Chad had asked of him. Kyle had promised to make sure Skylar and the girls were taken care of—always. He was pretty sure Chad wouldn't have been happy about this. Any of it. He sure as hell wasn't.

Skylar must have caught his not-so-subtle inspection of the house because she said, "We stay in the trailer behind the house."

He felt like an ass. "Sorry. I didn't mean—"

"It's okay." She stretched her arms and shoulders. "More water?"

"Please." He stood, wanting to get a glimpse of the trailer Skylar and the girls called home and dreading what he'd find. He peered through the blinds covering one of the windows on the back wall. Other than a rusted-out truck and a pile of metal and car parts, all he could see was a travel trailer. A travel trailer that listed forward at an odd angle, rust stains and plywood covering part of the roof.

Well, hell.

He'd hoped this visit would be quick. The plan had been simple. Get Jet to his new home, make sure Chad's family was okay, and head for his family ranch in the Hill Country and get to living. But now? Chad would never forgive him if he drove away and left Skylar and the girls here. Hell, he'd never forgive himself. *I let you down once, Chad. I won't do it again.*

Chapter Two

"Want something else? Coffee?" Skylar whispered. Since the girls had dozed off, they'd managed to keep their voices to a low murmur—even if that had kept conversation to a minimum.

Kyle shook his head, his long legs stretched out in front of him. He sat, all hunched up, making the 1970s'-style yellow-padded linoleum chairs look doll-size. "I'm good."

"Won't your family be missing you?" She took a sip of her water. "I'm sure they'll be happy to have you home. Eager for a reunion with your kids? Wife?" The last thing she wanted to do was keep the man from his family.

"No wife." He shrugged, cleared his throat. "No

kids. My family doesn't know I'm back. I'll get there when I get there." His gaze swept over the child-friendly sign language posters the pediatric audiologist had mailed to them.

Considering they were the only things hanging on any of the walls, they were hard to miss. Frank had grumbled about it, complaining about her making holes in the drywall, but she'd put them up anyway. Mya had had some words when she lost her hearing, but she was shy about using them. So Skylar did her best to give Mya access to every communication avenue available. Once Skylar had a job and reliable day care, Mya could have cochlear implant surgery. *Like finding a veterinary-tech job that could provide enough money to pay for childcare, a place to live,* and *set money aside for the surgery was easy...*

She glanced back at Kyle Mitchell—who was carefully studying the posters, the muscle in his jaw working.

"Is your family from these parts, originally?" Kyle asked, softly.

She shook her head. "I think my uncle moved out here about three years ago."

He looked at her, one brow raised.

"I was confused, too." Skylar laughed. "It's not exactly the sort of place you dream about retiring to." But it was the perfect place to disappear. Her uncle had never come right out and said he was hiding from someone, but Skylar suspected as much.

"You said it, not me." The corner of Kyle's mouth cocked up. "Can I ask why?"

"I only know what he's told me." She shrugged. "Sometimes, that's not as straightforward as you'd think." Like when he'd convinced her that she should put him on her bank account in case something happened to her. Chad had just died, Mya had been in the hospital, she was into her third trimester with Greer, and she'd been so close to coming apart that she'd never stopped to consider possible consequences. Never in her wildest dreams could she have imagined her uncle would empty her account. He'd bet it—*all* of it. And lost. *Everything.*

"Skylar..." He hesitated, his fingers tapping on the tabletop. "Are things, well, are you and the girls okay here?"

She stood, clearing the cups and fidgeting in the kitchen until the sharp sting in her eyes and the lump in her throat were manageable. "Why wouldn't we be?"

He sort of unfolded himself from his chair, carried Brynn's princess cup to the counter and slid it to her. "Instinct." His eyes met hers. "Hasn't failed me yet."

She searched for some sort of neutral yet reassuring answer. When that didn't work, she stood there, staring into his eyes. "You have one blue eye and one brown eye." How had she not noticed that?

He nodded, a small smile on his face. "Chad said you were a veterinary technician?" He glanced at the girls, now an overlapping pile of dog and little girls, and smiled. "You work at a clinic out here? Somewhere?"

She started washing the cups, careful to avoid direct eye contact. "No." She hadn't worked since Mya got sick. Not that he needed to know her sorry tale. He'd come all this way so the girls could visit Jet. For some reason, it was important that he not think of her as...needy or vulnerable or trapped. Worse, that she'd lost everything because of her own naivety. This was her fault, after all.

"I guess it's hard to find work out here?" he asked.

"You could say that. Flat Brush doesn't have a clinic but the vet from Amarillo comes through every now and then. Which is fine, since we don't have a pet." She washed and dried their cups. "I know the girls would love it, seeing them with Jet..." She broke off, then shook her head. "It would be one more thing for me to take care of."

He nodded, his fingers tapping on the countertop now. "What about—"

"What the hell are you still doing here?" Frank boomed, throwing open his bedroom door so hard it crashed into the wall.

She winced. "Uncle Frank, the kids—" But it was too late.

Greer started wailing immediately.

Brynn woke, sniffling and disoriented, working herself up quickly, too.

Even poor Jet looked ready to hide.

Mya slept on, blessedly unaware of the chaos that had erupted.

"Can't a man get any peace and quiet in his own house?" her uncle barked, covering his ears for added production value. "Why don't you take the girls outside? Or to your trailer?"

She couldn't risk running the AC if it wasn't absolutely necessary, it had to last. Frank knew that. He also knew that Skylar wouldn't snap back at him because of Brynn. Brynn was so sensitive, more so since Mya had lost her hearing. It was up to her to keep things calm for the girls. If that meant walking on eggshells and swallowing her anger, she would. Sometimes that was easier than others.

"What can I do?" Kyle asked. "To help?"

Skylar didn't hesitate for long. If she didn't calm Brynn, Mya might wake up. The two of them had that twin connection. If Brynn was crying, Mya would cry. And once Mya started, she had a hard time stopping. "Can you get the baby? She'll be fine if you just pick her up." Skylar hurried to Brynn, knelt, drew her daughter close, and pressed playful kisses all over Brynn's face. "Hey, sleepyhead. Did you know you were taking a nap with Jet? He was making doggy snores, sleeping right there, between you and Mya."

"Jet?" Brynn wiped the sleep from her eyes. "I did?" she sniffed, her breath wavering. "Where Jet?"

"There." Skylar loosened her hold so Brynn could

see the dog. He'd returned to his spot beside Mya. "See?" She wiped the tears from Brynn's cheeks.

Brynn nodded, smiling. "Silly."

"He is silly," Skylar agreed, tickling her tummy.

Her uncle sighed loudly. "I don't want that damn dog—"

"Frank," she said.

"That dog needs to get out of *my* house. Visiting hours are over." Frank took up his spot in his recliner, picked up the remote, and turned on the television. "It's too loud."

It wasn't. Not anymore. Brynn was calm and Greer... She wasn't crying either.

Skylar glanced over her shoulder, all the while cradling Brynn in her lap. She didn't know what she'd expected but it wasn't the image in front of her. Little Greer wide-eyed and silent, staring curiously up at Kyle. Kyle, his well-muscled arms holding Greer, wearing the exact same expression. Wonder, uncertainty, and, possibly, fascination. There was something about seeing her tiny baby cradled against the expanse of Kyle's rock-hard chest that stirred an ache inside.

Being out here, in the middle of nowhere, with no one to talk to—no one invested in her girls—wasn't easy. She exchanged letters with some of the moms from Fort Pendleton, but it wasn't the same. From birthdays to teething to first steps to meningitis, she'd weathered it all on her own. And she was fine; she was. But for a split second, she didn't feel fine. She felt…lonely.

Enough. She was a Marine's wife. She had to be tough. It was the job.

Skylar drew in a deep breath, pressed a kiss against Brynn's head, and eased her daughter from her lap. "How about we get some juice and cookies and go have a picnic in the clubhouse?"

Brynn popped right up then, all smiles. "Okay, Momma."

"Not my cookies." Her uncle pointed the remote at Brynn.

"No, Unca." Brynn shook her head, her smile vanishing.

Skylar glared at her uncle. He had no right to intimidate Brynn. Not now. Not ever. "Just get the yummy ones, Brynn."

Frank must have picked up on just how close she was to putting him in his place because he took one look at her and turned all his attention to the television.

She hadn't realized that Kyle was next to her until he spoke. "Mya's a sound sleeper."

"You would be, too, if you couldn't hear a thing. She's deaf." Her uncle sighed again, shaking his head. "What the hell do you think all those posters are poking holes in my walls for?"

"Uncle Frank." Skylar counted backward from five. It was true. Mya was deaf. But the way he spit it out was almost accusatory. Like it was a personal affront to him that Mya had lost her hearing. Like the stupid thumbtack holes were single-handedly depreciating his home's value. "Kyle is my guest. He came a long way so the girls and I could meet Jet. Please be considerate—"

"Considerate, huh? What about me? No one ever asked me if I was okay having a damn dog in my house, Skylar. Some dog you know nothing about, too. What if he bites one of the girls? Did you think about that?" he huffed. "Don't you sass me about being considerate."

According to her uncle, *he* was never the problem. Everyone else *was*. She'd gotten used to it. Being as isolated as they were, she didn't have much choice. But Kyle was watching, narrow-eyed and tense, which made it impossible to pretend her uncle's behavior was acceptable.

"How about I take Jet outside?" Kyle offered. "Maybe Brynn could help? Jet loves to play fetch."

"Thank you." Skylar attempted to smile but she was pretty sure it didn't work. "Brynn, do you want to go out with Jet and Kyle? Maybe you can show them the clubhouse."

"I wake Mya?" Brynn asked. "Gentle?" Brynn knew her twin so well. If Mya woke and Brynn was gone, she'd panic. Since Mya had lost her hearing, she'd become even more dependent on Brynn.

"Gently." Skylar nodded, reaching for Greer. "I'll take her. She probably needs a change anyway." Watching Kyle's fascination give way to panic—

like her baby girl was a ticking time bomb—almost made her laugh. She was pretty sure a dirty diaper couldn't compare to what he'd seen on a tour in Afghanistan.

"Oh. Right." Kyle handed Greer over with the greatest care. What was it Chad had called him? A gentle giant? She could see it now.

As soon as Greer saw her, her baby girl cooed and kicked her little legs.

Kyle chuckled. "She knows who you are."

Frank grumbled something about missing his shows followed by the increase of the television volume.

Real subtle, Frank. Skylar risked a glance Kyle's way. The poor man had had no idea what he'd be driving into today. "I'm sorry," she whispered.

He frowned. "*You* have nothing to apologize for." He had more to say; she could tell. But whatever it was, the slight shake of his head and the compressed line of his lips told her he was holding back.

"Mya," Brynn murmured, drawing all eyes. Brynn knew her sister couldn't hear but old habits were hard to break. Mya had been a precocious two-and-a-half-year-old, always watching and learning and laughing. Meningitis hadn't just taken her daughter's hearing; it had taken Mya's confidence, too. To Skylar, that was the worst of it. "Mya." Brynn bent over her sister, using her eyelashes to give Mya butterfly kisses against her cheek.

Mya grinned, but her eyes stayed shut.

Brynn added pats and tickles and hugs and, before long, Mya was sitting up, smiling ear to ear. When Mya saw Jet sitting beside her, staring at her with big brown eyes, Mya looped her arm around the dog's neck and gave him a hug. Jet rested his head on top of hers, making that little contented grunt that was the equivalent of a cat purr.

The simple show of affection, her girls and their father's rescued dog, tugged even harder at Skylar's heart.

"Outside?" Brynn said, pulling Mya up.

"Daw?" Mya asked.

Brynn nodded. "Outside." She pointed.

Mya took her sister's hand, patted Jet and headed for the door.

"Thanks for taking them out. I'll change Greer, get some cookies and juice boxes and be right out— okay, Brynn?"

"'Kay, Momma." Brynn nodded, already leading Mya and Kyle outside.

"Why is he hanging around, Skylar?" Frank was up and out of his recliner, hovering over her as she laid Greer in the portable crib that also served as a changing table. "I don't like him. I don't trust him. He's after something."

"Frank." She swallowed, focusing on her daughter—on giving Greer the smiles and attention she deserved. But once Greer was changed and secured back into the front pack, she faced her uncle. "He's here for the girls, because Chad asked him to come.

And whether or not you like it, this is our home, too. That's what you said, remember?" She hadn't meant to add that last bit. It was a dig, and they both knew it. He'd said all sorts of things to get her to do what he wanted. But there was no point in stirring him up—he'd never back down or see what he did as wrong. He honestly believed he'd been trying to better their circumstances. It had never occurred to him that betting Chad's death gratuity money could result in a loss. Not just a little bit, all of it... Everything she had to live on and provide for her children.

But the damage was done. Her uncle was scowling. "You want him to stay so you can get him to feel sorry for you, fine by me. Get him upset over the sad state of Chad's widow, needing a handout."

She brushed past him, grabbed the package of cookies and three juice boxes from the refrigerator and headed for the front door.

"No one is keeping you here," Frank barked. "You don't like living under my roof—you go find yourself someplace else to live. Go on. How're you going to make it with three mouths to feed?" He shook his head. "It's my retirement check that supports you, don't forget that."

Don't say a word. Don't respond. But the way he'd treated Kyle, the way he'd spat out Mya's deafness, the way he'd looked at her as if *she* was ungrateful... It was too much.

"How can I forget, Uncle Frank? Every time Greer needs diapers or baby food, you remind me how much we are taking from you." She summoned as much courage as she could. "But don't you forget that *you* spent all the money Chad had left for me and the girls. We have *nothing.* We can't leave. You know that. You did that. I promise you as soon as we can go, we will." She turned, proud of herself— until she saw Kyle Mitchell standing in the doorway.

Kyle Mitchell had grown up in a verbally combative family. Not when his father was alive. No, he had only golden memories of that time. But when his mother had remarried… Well, there wasn't much he liked to remember after that. The one good thing that had come from all the yelling and door slamming and words that left gaping wounds and ever-lingering self-doubt was Kyle's ability to shut down his anger. He'd vowed never to let anger overtake reason. No excuses.

But right now? It was a struggle.

It hadn't taken long to see how stressed and exhausted Skylar was. How could she not be? Not that she let on, she was too proud. And, dammit all, he understood.

But this man was her *family.* Skylar's words were stuck on repeat, cycling through his mind and threatening his vow to keep his temper under control. What this man had done to his niece—to children? Kyle's stomach roiled at the idea of such a betrayal.

He saw red.

The defensive tilt of Frank Kline's head, the challenge on the man's face, wasn't helping Kyle with the whole control-your-temper thing.

"Cookies," Skylar said, the word brittle and forced—enough to make him stop imagining how gratifying it would be to knock that look off Frank Kline's face.

"Good." He cleared his throat and tried again, hoping for a little less menace this time. If he were looking at Skylar, he might be able to manage it. "Good."

She all but herded him outside. Her light brown eyes remained fixed on his face until she'd pulled the door closed behind her.

He drew in a deep breath, crossing the near-rotten wooden porch to grip the railing. If Skylar could keep it together, he could, too. Another deep breath.

Behind him, he heard Skylar walking down the metal ramp. His gaze trailed after her, across the dusty patch of dirt and cacti and weeds that acted as the yard, to the girls' clubhouse. "Cookies," her singsong declaration reached him. She stooped and disappeared through the door of the clubhouse.

As clubhouses went, it wasn't much of one. Sheets of plywood with rough-cut holes for windows and a door. He ran a hand along the back of his neck, his gaze sweeping the horizon. None of this was right. His grip tightened on the railing. By now, he shouldn't be surprised at the evil man was capable of. But this sort of betrayal, by her own family, was far worse. It was personal.

"Kyle?" Brynn called out, her head peeking out of one of the windows. "Jet cookie?"

Jet stuck his head out, almost like he knew what Brynn was asking and was waiting for an answer.

Kyle smiled. "Maybe one. Careful, or he'll try to eat them all." His grip on the railing eased and he trotted down the metal ramp to the clubhouse. He could be angry later, when he was alone. Right now, he was going to have some cookies. He stooped, peering inside the clubhouse. "Hmm."

"It's cramped." Skylar smiled, bouncing Greer—who was free from the reverse backpack thing—on her knee. The girls sat on a wooden child-sized outdoor bench against one wall. Jet sat in the middle of the clubhouse, intently watching as the cookie bag was passed. "We'll make room," Skylar said, scooting her lawn chair over just enough for him to sit on the packed dirt ground.

"Cramped, huh?" he asked.

"Come in, come in." Brynn waved him inside.

"Yes, ma'am." He sat, his long legs stretched out through the front door so as not to take up all the room. "I like your clubhouse."

"Momma made." Brynn was all smiles. "Princess house."

"I thought so." He accepted the juice box from Skylar. "Veterinary tech, kid-juggler, and builder. Sounds like you're handy to have around."

Skylar smiled, though she was having an extra

hard time meeting his gaze. "The girls and I went walking and found some old wood—"

"An' a snake," Brynn added.

"And a snake." Skylar nodded.

"It tried to bite Momma," Brynn said, shuddering.

"But he didn't bite me." Skylar patted Brynn on the head. "And I took care of that snake."

"With a shovel." Brynn's eyes went round. "Bye, snake."

Kyle burst out laughing then. "Bye, huh?"

Skylar cooed at Greer. "Mommy's not going to let those bad ol' rattlesnakes anywhere near her baby girls."

Kyle watched the exchange, his admiration for the woman growing. "You found the wood, took care of the snake, and then what happened?"

"Momma carried it, mostly." Brynn pointed at the plywood overhead, then the walls. "Mya and me helped." Her little finger tapped some smaller boards, quite proud of herself. "We all worked real hard."

"It was hard work." Skylar smiled. "But we did it all on our own, didn't we?" She was facing Mya, her fingers and hands moving, each action clear and intentional.

Mya nodded, pointing at her chest. "Me, too."

He smiled and gave both the girls a thumbs-up. "Good job."

Mya smiled. Brynn smiled. And Skylar…was staring at him. *Interesting.* As soon as he'd caught her, she'd looked away. But she'd definitely been staring. Too bad he didn't know what she was thinking. Right now, he had so many questions, he was damn near bursting with them. But something told him he needed to be careful with her. For someone who didn't have much, pride was something she couldn't afford to lose.

"You get lonely out here?" he asked, before he'd thought through what he was saying.

"With this crew?" She shook her head.

"I'm sure they keep you busy. I was talking friends?" Or someone special? But then he paused and asked, "Do you have a car?" Surely, she did. Surely, she had one thing that was just hers—something she could pack up the kids in and take for a drive, a little getaway?

A one-shoulder shrug. "Only Frank's." Her brows rose. "It's a clunker."

Brynn laughed, making a horrible groaning-cranking sound. "Like that."

"That doesn't sound normal." He chuckled but was having a hell of a hard time finding the humor in all of this. She was stuck—in every sense of the word. When was the last time she'd had time to herself? Seen someone other than her asshole of an uncle? Had a view that wasn't downright…depressing? She was strong, he got that. But even the strongest of people needed a break now and then. He knew that firsthand. He had an idea. "Is there a place to eat in town?"

"There's three restaurants. A Dairy King. Flat

Brush Bar-B-Que Café. And… I never remember the other place but Frank loves it—"

"Dairy King or the café it is." He had no interest in setting foot in any place that man frequented. It was childish but he damn well didn't care. "You up for it?"

Skylar's eyes went round—that's where Brynn got it from—and her lips parted in surprise. "Umm…"

It wasn't the first time he'd noticed Skylar was a beautiful woman. Her shirt was threadbare from washing and her jeans had frayed patches, but *she* was beautiful. Her eyes, too. So much to see in those golden-brown depths. Intelligence. Caution. The total love she had for her girls…

"That's very nice of you but we'd just delay your homecoming." Those eyes of hers seemed to be searching his face—looking for something.

"I'll leave tomorrow. It's too long a drive to start now." Whatever plans he'd had were no longer relevant. He had no idea what to do about Skylar's situation but leaving her here, like this, was wrong. He couldn't do it. He wouldn't. And he still hadn't broached the idea that Jet was supposed to stay here but he knew that wasn't going to go over well. He'd figure it out. He just needed more time. "You and me and the girls for a fun night on the town."

Mya interrupted then, waving her hand before patting Jet on the head. "Who?"

"Jet," Brynn repeated, looking for help. "Momma."

"Right." Skylar held out her hand. *"J."* She swung

her pinkie in a J shape. *"E."* Her hand fisted. *"T."* She tucked her thumb between her pointer and middle fingers. Then she pointed at the dog and said, "Jet."

"Jeh." Mya nodded.

Brynn nodded. "Yup. Jet." She smiled, Mya smiled—and now he was smiling, too.

Kyle held his hand out. *"J?"* He copied what Skylar had done.

Mya watched.

"E." He made a fist.

Mya stood, using her little hands to correct his thumb placement.

"Thank you." He winked at Mya, earning him a little nod and a sweet smile in return.

"Thank you." Skylar showed him the sign. "Though she does a pretty good job of reading lips."

"Thank you," Kyle signed to Mya. *"T?"* His mind blanked so he wiggled his fingers then shrugged.

Mya took his hand, tucking his thumb into place before stepping back to nod. "'Kay?"

Kyle studied his hand, doing his best to mentally file what he'd learned for later use. "Okay." For a first attempt, it wasn't so bad. Mya was happy. So happy she climbed into his lap and leaned back against him, giggling when Jet decided to give her a thorough head-to-toe sniffing.

He stared down at the top of Mya's head, doing his best to ignore the memories and emotions crowding in on him. He was back home. He was safe. Mya and Brynn, Greer and Skylar were safe. From bombs and attacks anyway. He drew in a deep breath. Some things were best left in the past. Locked up, tight.

Right now, his mission was getting Skylar to agree to have dinner with him. He wouldn't get all of his questions answered, but he might get some. As it was, he was struggling with the idea of leaving Chad's family here. *Chad.* He owed it to him to do right by Skylar and the girls. Now all he needed was to figure what, exactly, that meant.

Chapter Three

Skylar poured cereal into the girls' bowls and added milk, smoothing Mya's hair.

"Is Jet coming?" Brynn asked, scooping up some cereal. "We can play ball."

"Kyle said they'd come see us before they left." Skylar shot a glance at her uncle's closed bedroom door. After his meltdown last night, it was probably best if he stayed in his room.

Once he'd heard she was going out for dinner, he'd immediately started complaining about the expense and the hassle and how he was too tired to go out. When she'd explained she and the girls were going with Kyle, he'd blown up. Not only had he called her ungrateful and selfish, he'd dared to suggest that she was willing to do *whatever it took* to get Kyle Mitchell to take them with him when he left. Of course, he'd followed that up with an assurance that no man wanted to take on three kids to raise—and she was kidding herself if she thought anything different.

Skylar had done her best to let his nastiness roll off her back. She'd changed Greer, packed a few things into Greer's diaper bag, and left. She'd heard thumps and yells all the way to Kyle's waiting truck—he probably had, too—but it hadn't stopped her.

She wanted to go. For the first time in… Well, she couldn't remember the last time she'd done something she *wanted* to do.

But by the time Kyle had moved all the car seats into his truck, corralled the girls while she'd changed Greer's diaper again, and endured Brynn's made-up nonsense songs for most of the drive into town, she suspected he was regretting his invitation.

Or not. She hoped not.

It had been a long time since she'd had a dinner she hadn't cooked. It had been even longer since she'd had a conversation with another adult. An actual conversation. Chad had been right—Kyle was easy to talk to.

For her, last night had been like a minivacation. It was amazing how much easier dinner was when she had help with the girls. She'd even managed to eat while her food was still warm. When they got back home, she'd ushered the girls straight to their trailer—before Kyle was able to get a glimpse into the space she shared with her girls. They'd managed to avoid talking about Frank or the uncomfortable conversation he'd walked in on so, silly or not, she'd wanted to end the evening on a high note.

And it had.

Until she was in bed, tossing and turning and worrying about what would happen when Kyle left…with Jet. The girls would be devastated. It wouldn't matter that she'd told them, over and over, that Kyle and Jet were leaving. It was going to hurt. All of them.

Enjoy the time you have. That's what her mother would have said. Good advice for a soldier's wife. But not an easy concept for four-year-olds.

She glanced at the clock for the fiftieth time this morning. For as much as she dreaded their leaving, she couldn't wait for them to get there. She liked Kyle. Liked spending time with him. When the roar of an engine and crunch of rubber on gravel finally announced Kyle's arrival, she was smiling just like her girls.

Mya turned in her chair to peer out the window, then clapped her hands. "Jeh."

Skylar smiled. The girls were excited over the dog. She was excited about Kyle. After her uncle Frank's tirade, there was a flair of panic. Was that okay? To be excited over Kyle Mitchell? Or maybe it wasn't about *him*? Maybe she was just excited about having someone to talk to? Kyle was knocking on the door before she'd figured out the answer. But the questions lingered—so did the odd mixture of exhilaration and dread and anticipation she'd woken up with.

He is leaving. She reminded herself. *Today.* As nice as his visit had been, he'd leave and life would return to normal. *Enjoy the time we have.* What else could she do?

"Kyle?" Brynn asked, slipping from her seat to run to the door.

"Hold on, Brynn." Skylar stopped her daughter then shook her head. *Really, who else would it be?*

Brynn stopped in front of the screen door and waved at Kyle. "Hi." She rocked back and forth on her feet. "Momma said wait," she explained.

Skylar was laughing when she opened the door. "Morning."

"Good morning." Kyle's jaw was covered in stubble, his eyes a little puffy...but he still managed to be alarmingly attractive in his tan cowboy hat.

"Rough night?" she asked, stepping aside.

"I don't sleep much. Dreams…" He shrugged. "I'm good."

She didn't push. "How about some coffee?"

"Is it a good idea?" He didn't move. "Jet and I can hang out here."

Because of her uncle. "Okay." She swallowed. "The coffee offer still stands."

He nodded, his gaze meeting hers. "I'll take it."

That was all it took to get her answer. *Him.* She was excited to see *him. Oh.* And now that she knew that, there was no stopping the surge of heat to her cheeks.

"Where's Jet?" Brynn asked, stooping to see between Kyle's legs.

"He's here." Kyle nodded, smiling down at her. "Ready for a game of fetch—even has his ball."

"Can I play with Jet, Momma?" Brynn pleaded.

"Let me get Greer cleaned up and we'll all go out. Okay?" Skylar saw Brynn's shoulders droop a little.

"I don't mind," Kyle whispered, his hand warm against her arm.

"You and Mya go on with Kyle. I'll be right out." Hopefully, he hadn't heard the slight waver to her voice.

"Thank you, Momma." Brynn raced to the table. "Mya." She grabbed her sister's hand and tugged, waiting impatiently for her twin to climb down from her chair. They giggled all the way out the front door.

"I'll hurry," Skylar said.

Kyle gave her a little salute. "It's fine. They're good girls. I can keep them in line." He followed her girls down the metal walkway and into the yard.

Skylar lingered in the open doorway long enough to see Jet and the girls' reunion. All the bouncing and laughing made Skylar happy. Really happy. They needed more of this—all of them. Laughter and joy and playtime… *Someday.* It was a promise to herself and the girls.

She filled a plastic travel mug with coffee before she retrieved Greer from her high chair, changed her diaper, and carried the baby and Kyle's coffee outside.

Skylar always knew the instant Greer saw her sisters. Her little legs started kicking and her arms bounced. To Greer, there was no better form of entertainment than watching her sisters. "They are lots of fun," Skylar agreed, holding on to one of Greer's hands. "You'll be running after them in no time."

"Thank you." Kyle took the coffee. "I'm not sure who's wearing who out? The girls or Jet?"

"He should sleep on the trip home." She glanced his way. "What time are you thinking of heading out?"

He took a sip of his coffee. "No rush."

Which made her happier than she should be. The longer he stayed, the harder the goodbyes would get. As much as she wanted him to stay—*Wait. I want him to stay?*

"You okay?" he asked.

She nodded, her gaze pinned on the girls. While Brynn was handing the ball to Mya to throw, she was doing her best to calm herself down.

Kyle was a friend. She didn't have many of those. People had friends; it was natural—human even. There was nothing wrong with her and Kyle becoming friends. The man had been Chad's best friend, after all. Kyle was here because of the near brotherhood that he and Chad's friendship had forged. How many times had Chad told her about Kyle going above and beyond in the name of friendship? He was true-blue, Chad's go-to, someone he'd counted on to get things done.

Why was she letting Frank twist friendship into something…*else*? Something sordid.

She was a widow. With three children. And nothing to offer. Her uncle was right about all of that. But she would never use her body to get what she wanted. That her uncle, of all people, could suggest such a thing was both horrifying and infuriating. Then again, that was what Uncle Frank always did: agitate. He was very good at it.

She sighed.

"Skylar?" Kyle asked, turning to face her, his eyes on the travel mug he held. "I have a question." He looked at her then.

She nodded, meeting his gaze—and ignoring the odd tightening at the base of her stomach. "Did you want milk? Or sugar?"

"No. The coffee is good." He shook his head. "I know of a job. I mean, our local veterinarian was looking for a new tech not too long ago." A now useful bit of information his mother had relayed in one of her regular letters. "Plus, we're looking for someone to help out with the dogs and the cattle and such. At my family's ranch. We raise cattle and my brother is part of a nonprofit that helps place retired or discharged service dogs with families. Lots of animals."

Skylar blinked, her gaze falling from his as the tightening at the base of her stomach gave way to something cold and hollow. "What?" Frank's words from last night echoed in her mind. *The sad state of Chad's widow, needing a handout.*

He cleared his throat. With the sun beaming down, his eyes were momentarily distracting. His blue eye was brilliant under the wide Texas sky. The other was a deep copper. *Both lovely.* "A job," Kyle went on. "There's a cabin on the property. I think it's only two bedrooms but it might work, for now." She didn't miss his quick glance at the trailer or the way his jaw muscle tensed.

She swallowed. "No, thank you." *Needing a hand-out...*

He recovered, but not before she'd seen his mouth fall open and his brows climb into his hairline. "No? You don't want to think about it?"

She shook her head.

"Can I ask why?" The words were gruff.

"I could ask you the same thing." She glanced at him. "You don't know anything about my qualifications or my experience. Why offer *me* this job?" Because he would go above and beyond to get things done, like honoring his word to Chad.

His jaw was clenched hard now.

"I know you mean well, Kyle, but you don't know me." She cleared her throat. *The sad state of Chad's widow, needing a handout.* She wasn't sure what bothered her more: that Uncle Frank was right or that Kyle Mitchell saw her that way. Sad. Pathetic. Needy. Maybe she should be mad at herself for believing someone would see her in any other light.

Whatever the reason, she was mad. And…hurt. "It's important that I make my way—without a *handout* or sponging off someone's pity."

"Skylar, hold on." He held his hand up, stepping closer.

"You've honored your promise to Chad, and I thank you for it. I think it's best if you leave now."

He was staring at her, struggling with what to say next.

She stared right back, daring him to contradict what she'd said but knowing he couldn't.

"Momma?" Brynn giggled.

Brynn, Mya, and Jet were staring at them. No, not at them—at their feet. Skylar stared down at the pile of dog toys at their feet.

"Throw one." Brynn clapped her hands. "Jet wants to run."

"He's fast." Kyle crouched, picking up one of the rubber balls and giving it a good throw.

Skylar smiled at the surprise on her daughter's faces as the ball continued to sail through the air. Kyle had a good throwing arm. Jet was sprinting after the ball as though his back legs were spring-loaded.

She glanced at Kyle. What was she doing? She didn't want to stay here. She didn't want the girls to grow up this way. But accepting Frank's help was exactly how she'd wound up here. Frank was family. Kyle was… Kyle was someone Chad trusted and sent to check on them. But that didn't mean she should uproot the girls in the hopes that things would be better? Did it? Her stomach churned and twisted until it was in knots.

His gaze locked with hers. "Give me a minute. Please, Skylar."

No. Don't do it. Don't listen. If she did, he might say what she wanted to hear.

"I didn't offer you the job out of pity." He took his time, considering his words. "I offered you the job because he's got you in a corner. I don't mean to speak ill of your kin but...I'm not sure he has your—or the girls'—best interest at heart."

She pressed a kiss to the top of Greer's head, but she didn't argue.

"The way I see it, it's going to be hard to get ahead here. No car. No job." He didn't know why, but the bastard was trying to make sure Skylar had no other option. He ran a hand along the back of his neck. "The job offer is a way to get you out of here, to give you options...and a real chance at independence." He swallowed, seeing her posture get stiffer and stiffer, and knew he was pushing it. "And...and there's grass where I live. Green grass."

Skylar was so surprised she laughed.

He could breathe a little easier. "I've only spent a day with you all but we've known each other for years through Chad. That's why I care about what happens to you. This has nothing to do with pity."

He was doing a piss-poor job of explaining things. "Do you understand?"

Skylar was staring up at him. "I guess."

"That's a start." He glanced at the house. "Unless there's something keeping you here?"

"He's the only family I have left." Not that she sounded happy about it but, still, it explained a few things.

He nodded.

"We stayed in base housing for a while but when Mya got meningitis, I had a hard time knowing which way was up. Frank just showed up—out of nowhere—when I needed help. And he was great... I know that's hard to believe, but it's true." She sighed. "We lost our base housing so he said we could stay with him until we found a place. I brought Greer home from the hospital, thinking all this was temporary." She shrugged. "Then there was no money for a house or Mya's surgery or...anything."

That knocked the air from his lungs. That Frank Kline had taken her money was bad. But money for surgery. For Mya? He'd taken Skylar's nest egg—her security and her future. Kyle wasn't sure what to say. Not out loud anyway. Mentally, he was working through a long list of insults. Frank Kline was an asshole. A selfish son of a bitch. A thief. A soulless bastard... And so much more. "What kind of surgery?"

"Cochlear implant. If she's a candidate." Skylar watched the girls smother Jet with hugs and pats and approval—the ball safely retrieved. "She's doing well, picking up signs, and she has Brynn. But they start kindergarten next year. I want that to be as easy as possible for her, you know?" The longing in Skylar's voice triggered his protective side. Skylar was a good mother. A damn good mother. All she wanted was to take care of her kids.

His attention returned to Mya, Brynn, and Jet. To look at them now, it was hard to believe Mya ever had reservations about Jet. They were fast friends now—all three of them. The girls were covered in dirt and Jet kisses, but they were grinning from ear to ear. Those grins were familiar. Chad's grin. "How old was she when she got meningitis?"

But she knew what he was asking because she answered, "Chad died right about the time she got sick. The twins were almost three."

She'd lost her husband, dealt with Mya's illness, and had a baby, and the only support she had cleaned out her bank account and treated her with a total lack of respect? "A lot of people would have buckled under that sort of pressure."

"I didn't have a choice." She held Greer close, stooped to pick up the ball, and offered it to him.

He threw the ball, mulling over Skylar's words. As soon as Jet tore off after the ball, Mya and Brynn were clapping and squealing. A simple pleasure that brought so much joy. After everything they'd been through, didn't they deserve some joy? "You have a choice now, Skylar. Not a handout. A job. If you want it."

She was frowning when her gaze locked with his.

"I can see you're still skeptical so I have a few things that might help," he said, grabbing Greer's little foot when the baby cooed and flailed her arms at him. "Greer wants to hear what I have to say."

"Oh, she does, does she?" But Skylar was laughing again.

"Austin is about forty-five minutes away. The Texas School for the Deaf is there—so are a whole slew of specialists." He only knew this because he'd spent the night researching on his phone.

"I'm listening." Skylar shook her head.

"And your own place." He kept talking to Greer, her gooey grin so damn adorable he didn't care that he was making faces and acting like an ass. "Green grass."

"You mentioned that one." She sighed.

"Chad wanted you to keep Jet." He looked at her then.

"He did?" She blinked, several times. "Of course, he did. He wrote stories about Jet in his letters—just for the girls."

He waited until the knot in his throat eased enough for him to go on. "Frank seems less than enthusiastic over Jet."

"But he'd be welcome on your ranch?" she asked.

"I'll even build him a doghouse myself."

"I'm sure the girls would help." She eyed the clubhouse.

He could picture it. He wasn't sure he'd get a lot

of help, but it'd be fun nonetheless. "Plus, my mom would love having the kids around. She only had boys so, these three? She'll be making them princess dresses before Christmas."

"Kyle." She took a deep breath. "You make it sound so easy. But there's a lot of us. Stuff. Car seats…" She broke off, a frown returning to her face.

"What?" he asked, turning in the direction she was looking. The car seats sat on the ground where he'd left them the night before.

"Frank left." She glanced to the house, back at the girls, her frown growing.

"He left? And didn't tell you?"

"He does that sometimes." But she was blinking harder now.

"Talk to me, Skylar. Let me help." If she didn't give him something to do, he might just go after Frank Kline and teach him a lesson or two.

"It's just, normally there's enough food in the house when he takes off like this. And I'm low on diapers." She glanced his way, blinked again, then drew in an unsteady breath.

Like this? Meaning this wasn't the first time Frank had left her, stranded, in the middle of nowhere. At the end of his last tour, he'd decided to live the rest of his life without violence. But he was willing to make an exception for Frank Kline. "I'll take you into town." He let go of Greer's foot and clasped Skylar's shoulders. "We can get the girls an ice cream." He was having a hard time breaking eye contact.

Under the morning sun, her eyes were brown and gold with flecks of mossy green. The longer he studied them, the more pronounced each hue became. Her lashes were long and thick. If he had a romantic bone in his body, he'd have said her eyes were mesmerizing. But he wasn't a romantic so beautiful would have to work.

"Thank you. For everything." She was breathing harder than before.

"You're welcome." His hands slid from her shoulders, the rapid thump of his heart echoing in his ears. "Besides, the drive in will give me time to come up with something else."

"Something else?" She stooped, picked up the ball Jet had dropped at her feet, and offered it to him.

"Another reason—*the* reason—for you to come with me." He cleared his throat and threw the ball. "Take the job." He was selling her hard and they both knew it. What choice did he have? If she didn't come with him, he was stuck in Flat Brush, Texas, for who the hell knew how long. He'd told Chad he'd make sure his family was okay. They weren't—not here. But it wasn't just about keeping his word to Chad now. Skylar deserved to have an ally—to have someone on her side, someone to listen to her, support her, and help her succeed. He wanted to be there for that. For her. If she needed more time to make up her mind, he'd wait.

"Okay." It was a whisper, so soft he wasn't sure he'd actually heard it.

"Please tell me that was an okay about the job—not the ice cream?" He smiled down at her, holding his breath until he heard her answer.

"Okay about the job. I'll take the job." Louder this time. Determined. Like she'd made up her mind. "And the ice cream, too."

"Yes, ma'am." He knew this was the best thing for her—for all of them. Not just Skylar and the girls, but for him, too. Having them around reminded him of the joy to be found in even the little things. Playing fetch with Jet. Cookies in clubhouses. Nonsense songs in the car. And the way the sun bounced off the green specks in Skylar's beautiful eyes.

Chapter Four

As soon as she said it, she'd committed. Even though a laundry list of all the things that could go wrong began scrolling through her head, it wasn't enough to make her change her mind. It didn't matter that this was the only home Greer had ever known. Kyle's home was close to the resources Mya desperately needed. It didn't matter that they'd be starting over, completely on their own. They were already on their own—with the added bonus of Uncle Frank's mood swings and lies.

Her gaze swept the mostly dirt yard, watching her girls laugh as Jet bounced back and forth between them—the ball still in his mouth.

One thing was certain. If they could be happy here, they'd be happy...

"Where are we going?" Skylar asked. "The name of the town?"

"Granite Falls," Kyle said, tipping his cowboy hat back on his head.

"Granite Falls." She pressed a kiss against the top of Greer's head.

"It's off the Colorado River—we have a creek that runs through the ranch. We're lucky, too, since drought can hit the Hill Country pretty hard." Kyle took in their surroundings. No matter how hard he tried, it was clear he wasn't a fan of Flat Brush. "Well...nothing like this. It's nowhere even close to this."

"No." She had to laugh. "It'd be hard to top this."

Kyle's smile was warm and natural.

She liked that about him—he was up-front. Chad had said as much. Needle—Kyle—kept things on the level and always honored his word. It was a quality she'd all but given up on out here.

"So." Kyle nodded at the trailer. "We hauling it along?"

She eyed the listing trailer and shook her head. "It's Uncle Frank's." If she took it, he'd likely accuse her of stealing. And while she didn't think he'd ever put her behind bars, she'd never thought he was capable of what he'd already done. *Better not test him.* "I guess I should start packing." Packing. As ridiculous as it was, she didn't want him to see where she and the girls slept. The trailer was... Well, it wasn't like she'd had options.

"I know I sprung this on you." His forehead creased. "There's no rush. On my part." But the glance at Frank's house suggested otherwise.

She said what he was thinking, "I'd like to be gone before he gets back. No knowing when that will be so…" She shrugged. "The last thing the girls need is another one of his episodes."

"We can all pitch in?" he offered. "The more hands, the better."

She almost said no. *Pride cometh before the fall.* It was something her mother used to say, followed by several disapproving tongue clicks. Right now, she could almost hear her mother's voice in her head— and the tongue clicking, too. But that didn't make it easy for her to say, "Yes, thank you."

"Girls," she called out, giving them her brightest smile. Change was hard, no matter how old you were. But this was good change—a necessary change. It was up to her to make this an exciting adventure versus something unknown and worrisome. "I have some wonderful news."

Mya grabbed Brynn's hand and pulled her across the patch of dirt, Jet at their heels.

"What, Momma?" Brynn asked.

Mya stared up at her expectantly.

"Well, we are going to go with Kyle and Jet to his ranch where it's green and pretty." She paused, looking to Kyle for reassurance.

"It has hills and a creek and, when you're a little older, we can go swimming by the waterfall not too far from our ranch." Kyle nodded. "We have horses and cows and more dogs, too."

Brynn was wide-eyed. "More dogs?"

Skylar did the best she could with sign language, keeping it simple. "Go with Jet and Kyle." She finger spelled Kyle's name, then placed her hand on his arm. But he'd turned toward Mya so her hand landed square in the middle of his chest. His very hard and well-muscled chest. His T-shirt was soft— soft enough that she could feel just how hard and well-muscled his chest was. "Kyle," she repeated, fully aware of how odd she sounded.

"Go?" Mya repeated.

Skylar nodded, removing her hand from Kyle and clearing her throat. "Go home with Kyle and Jet."

Mya stared up at Kyle.

Kyle squatted in the dirt before Mya, his hat casting a shadow over him and Mya, no less huge but far less intimidating. "Please, come," he said—and signed—then pointed between all of them and did the sign again.

Mya smiled and nodded.

But Skylar hadn't moved beyond the fact that Kyle had used sign language. "Do you know sign language?" she asked, trying not to stare down at the man making her little girl smile.

"No." He stood, winking at Mya. "But I figured I better learn."

The sting in Skylar's eyes was sharp and sudden.

"You did?" There it was again, that tight—breathy voice that didn't sound a thing like her.

Those mismatched eyes fixed on her face. Whatever he was looking for, he was in no rush to find it. Eventually, he nodded, the tightening of his jaw muscle leaving her puzzled over what he might be thinking.

"Now?" Brynn asked, pulling on her hand. "Go now?"

The little hand frantically tugging on her was just what she needed to stop overanalyzing Kyle Mitchell and start dealing with the herculean task of moving while avoiding as much embarrassment as possible. "First, we need to pack up our things. From our room and the big house."

"Okay." Once again, Brynn grabbed Mya's hand and, together, they sprinted across the dirt and weeds toward the metal door of their travel trailer.

"What can I do?" Kyle asked, watching the girls disappear into the trailer—their excited giggles audible in the quiet of the place.

If she sent him into the house and Uncle Frank came home, there was a high likelihood that her uncle would use his right to shoot a trespasser. He might not actually shoot Kyle, but threaten and wave his pistol around and make more drama than any of them wanted to deal with. But sending him into the trailer meant revealing just how deplorable her sleeping conditions were.

"The sooner everything is packed, the sooner we

can get on the road." Which was true. It wouldn't take long. She wasn't exactly sure what had happened to the boxes of things she'd had from Fort Pendleton but there wasn't much to pack. Uncle Frank had said something about a rental storage unit and not being able to pay the bill and the things had been donated to a thrift shop before she'd known about it.

Luckily, she'd kept—and hidden—the few things she'd deemed worth anything. The laptop was old and out here there was no internet, but it held pictures and videos she treasured. Besides her photo albums, the quilt her mother had passed on to her, and every note and letter Chad had written to her, were the shoes and clothes that hadn't been stored and lost with the contents of the storage unit.

She grabbed several black plastic yard bags from the dilapidated shed and headed toward the trailer, Kyle at her side. It was when they reached the door that she paused. There was no way to talk away the reality of her world. No way to make light of it…but she wanted to.

"Well." She cleared her throat. "It's not the Ritz." With a smile glued in place, she cradled sleeping Greer close, and took the three steps up and into the trailer. "Here's a bag." She handed the trash bag to Brynn.

"Room for our boxes, too?" Brynn asked, holding her treasure box—a shoebox they'd decorated with glitter and pictures cut out from cereal boxes and newspapers and magazines.

"Of course." Skylar nodded. She'd never questioned what made her daughters choose the items they put in their treasure boxes. It didn't matter if it was a flattened metal bottle lid, a shiny copper washer that looked like a magical ring, a special rock, and every toy they'd collected from the cereal boxes Skylar bought them whenever they were in town, if it fit in the box and they wanted it, into the box it went.

She risked a glance at Kyle then—and regretted it. He was doing his best to keep a blank expression but there was no denying his shock.

He was well over six feet, so he'd had to hunch to come inside. Now that he was inside, he was still hunched over. A hailstorm that had come through had left holes in the ceiling. Uncle Frank said the place looked like it had been shot up—not that he'd offered to do anything about it. But Skylar had found a few boards and a somewhat weatherproof tarp and done the best she could to keep the elements out.

During the day, the window air-conditioning unit stayed off, so now that the trailer was full, it was rapidly getting miserably hot.

"Kyle." Brynn waved. "See my treasures?" She held out her box, so proud it tugged at Skylar's heart.

"That's something," he said, his voice as sweet and soft as ever.

Skylar took a deep, wavering breath. "You can show him later, Brynn. Let's get all of your and Mya's clothes into one of these bags."

Kyle took his cue from the girls. When he saw where their clothes were, he helped fill their trash bag up. The child-sized sleeping bags were rolled up and stowed away, revealing the outdoor-patio-furniture cushions she'd bought to place on top of the plywood and upturned milk crates she'd wired together for a bed. Between the snakes and mice and scorpions, she'd had to come up with some way to keep the girls off the floor. At the time, she'd felt accomplished. Now…she felt like a horrible mother.

You do the best you can with what you have. Another saying her mother had used over and over again. One she'd used herself, over and over, since the day Chad had died.

When that was done, Kyle helped her collect the odds and ends that belonged to Greer. Her crib was the only piece of actual furniture they owned so she was extra careful taking it apart, putting each bracket and rod and pin into a baggie for safekeeping. Kyle used some straps from the toolbox on the back of his truck to secure the pieces in place for their trip.

She didn't let him help with her things though. She couldn't. Instead, she told the girls to help him put everything in the truck. Not that it took very long. She'd just folded up her last pair of jeans when the three of them came back inside.

"She going to be okay in that?" Kyle asked, nodding at Greer in the thickly padded carrier. "In the heat?"

Skylar nodded. "We're done." She held the half-full bag in her hand.

"That's it?" He eyed the bag.

She nodded. "And that." The plastic tote with the computer and letters and quilt.

He grabbed the tote. "Nothing else?" He was staring around the trailer again, his jaw getting more and more rigid.

"Bye-bye," Brynn said. "Bye, roof that Momma fixed. Bye, beds that Momma made. Bye, squeak-squeak air ditioner."

Mya imitated Brynn, waving as she spoke.

"Yes." Skylar nodded. "Bye-bye, squeaky air conditioner." She followed them down the steps and, with a deep breath, she closed the door to the trailer. Were they really leaving? Was this truly the last time she'd ever step foot in that horrible little trailer? If she didn't have such faith in Kyle—faith that Chad had instilled—she'd never agree to such a thing. But it *was* Kyle. So she'd hold on to that faith and know that they were going on to bigger and better things.

"Let's go," Brynn said, spinning. "Let's go to Jet's home."

"We will." Skylar smiled. "But first we need Mya's posters and your princess cup."

"Oh, right, Momma." Brynn's eyes went round.

It didn't take long to remove the laminated posters from the wall. Carefully, she rolled each one up, slid a rubber band around it, then gave them all to

Kyle—who packed the posters, sippy cups, and her few utensils into another trash bag.

"All that's left is the portable crib inside Frank's house." Skylar stood, hands on her hips, to look around. "Just let me change Greer first?" She was already unwinding Greer from the front pack and laying her onto the waterproof pad when she glanced his way. "I'll be quick," she said, noting how rigid his jaw muscle was.

He nodded. "That's everything?" He didn't sound so sweet and soft now. If anything, he sounded upset.

Skylar finished changing Greer, watching her tiny daughter yawn and smile before her little eyelids drifted shut. Another look at Kyle told her he was struggling. "Girls, can you take Jet a bowl of water, please?" She reached for one of the empty plastic margarine tubs she used for leftovers and filled it with water. "I bet he's thirsty."

"'Kay, Momma," Brynn said. Mya nodded.

They each took one side, walking with painstaking care out the door and to the ramp.

Skylar watched as they sat, one on either side of the dog, while he drank water. "You're angry?" she asked. "The trailer? I know it's not much."

"Not much?" His voice was brittle.

"It was the best I could do, Kyle." She was torn between apologizing and feeling defensive. "We had no—"

"Angry with you?" He looked incredulous. "How could I be angry with you?" He shook his head, tipping his hat back before resting his hands on her shoulders. "Skylar, I have nothing but respect for what you've done here. You've made a home for these girls out of… Well, you've done miracles."

His praise rolled over her, leaving only relief. "I wouldn't go that far."

"I would." He was staring at her again, that same slow exploration that put that lump back into her throat—the lump that made her sound not like herself. "Chad would be proud of you."

The stinging was back, ten times stronger than before, making her blink. "He would?" she whispered.

With a deep sigh, he pulled her into his arms. "He would." His voice was deep and thick and gruff. "At the risk of sounding condescending, I'm proud of you, too."

It had been so long. So, so long. She couldn't remember the last time she'd been held close. For the last year, all of her hugs had been from her girls. Sweet, tight little hugs that filled her heart with love and gratitude. But being held this way was an entirely different thing. She melted into him, soaking up his strength and giving in—for a few moments—to the urge to let him support her.

Yes, he was big and handsome and muscular and she was fully mindful of all those things. But, for now, it was the way they breathed together that she focused on. Him and her. Sharing space. She shut out everything else until the thud of his heart was solid against her chest and the sound of his breath echoed hers. Thump-thump. In and out. Solid and strong. She buried her face against his chest, pressed her hands against his back, and welcomed the comfort he offered so freely.

The roar of blood in his ears slowly eased. Kyle could only hope Frank Kline didn't decide to head home before they were gone. If he did, Kyle wasn't sure he could be held accountable for his actions. Bad people existed, that was a fact. But this was a sort of willful negligence that Kyle couldn't wrap his head around. Skylar and her children. *Little* children. *Innocent and dependent and precious.*

And yet, Skylar had found a way to give her girls smiles and a playhouse, laughter and a home. She'd been strong and done what needed doing for her girls.

He couldn't think about the roof of the trailer. He couldn't think about the makeshift beds the girls had been using. He couldn't think about the rotting camp cot Skylar was clearly using for her bed. Or the rusty air-conditioning unit that looked like a fire waiting to happen.

Those things were over now. If he'd had any doubts about pushing this move, they no longer existed. She had to get out of here. The girls had to get out of here. They deserved so much better. They deserved a good life. And they would have one—in Granite Falls. *With me.*

It was up to him to pull himself together, to help make this transition easier. If he was tense, they'd pick up on it and he saw how hard Skylar was working to make this move into something fun and exciting. One bark or scowl or snap and he'd mess that up.

Better to think about the woman in his arms—the smart, resilient, tough, and beautiful woman in his arms. The longer she held on to him, the more firmly he held on to her. It was stupid to think he could somehow hug away the last year and however many months she'd been stuck out here but it was all he could do. He held her until the hell she'd been through became secondary to his far less noble reaction.

It wasn't as though he hadn't noticed Skylar was a woman. He had. A damn beautiful woman, at that. But, to him, she was Chad's widow. She belonged to his best friend. And, until now, he hadn't been pressed up against her very womanly form and, now that he was, there was no denying how good she felt to him. Soft and warm. She fit all too well against him. Her hands pressed against his back, keeping him close, and sending conflicting signals along each and every one of his nerve endings.

Yes, this was nice and it felt good to have her in his arms but he was here as a friend—for a friend. That's all. Friends didn't get distracted like this. He shouldn't lean into her, note the scent of watermelon and soap, savor the brush of her breath through the cotton of his shirt, and he sure as hell needed to control the urge to bury his nose in her hair...

Stop this. All of this.

It took more effort that he'd expected to ease her away from him. Mostly because he didn't want to put space between them. *And that is exactly why I have to put space between us.*

"We should go." He made the mistake of looking down at her—looking into her eyes. Light brown and flecked with gold. Damn beautiful. His chest grew uncomfortably tight. *Stop. Now.*

She nodded, looking up at him with the same wariness he was feeling. "We should." She nodded again, cleared her throat and went to scoop baby Greer up. She walked him through the portable crib breakdown, hastily scribbled a note on the tablet stuck to the dented front of the refrigerator and turned to face him.

"For Frank?" he asked, suspecting the answer.

"I wouldn't want him to panic." Her gaze fell from his. "I can't leave without saying something. It's not…right."

There was a whole lot about this situation that wasn't right. After everything Kyle had heard and seen, he was pretty sure ninety-nine percent of the problem was Frank. He might not give a damn about Frank or his feelings, but that didn't apply to Skylar. She was leaving a note to have the closure she needed to move on. He could respect that.

With a final glance around him, he followed Skylar outside—eager to get on the road. Jet, Mya, and Brynn were still sitting together in the shade. He made sure everything was secure in the truck bed, adding a few tie-downs in case the wind picked up, then buckled the three car seats into the back. It was tight, but they all fit.

"Where's Jet going to sit?" Skylar asked, peering into the backseat.

"He'll find a spot." Kyle shrugged. "He always finds a way."

"We have that in common, I guess," Skylar said, smiling at the dog.

"I think we're good so whenever you're ready?" He walked around the truck as he spoke, tugging the straps and making sure his tailgate was secure—doing pretty much anything he could to stop himself from appreciating that smile. "We'll stop in town for ice cream."

"Can I run into the bank?" she asked. "I know there's not much but I'd like to take what I have." She secured baby Greer into the middle car seat carefully.

Kyle nodded. "Of course." If it was hers, she should take it with her.

"Okay, girls." Skylar turned, clapping her hands together. "Who's ready to start our adventure?"

He heard the slightest waver to her voice and placed a hand against her back. This couldn't be easy. Sure, this was hell on earth but there were no surprises here. Leaving? Starting new in an unknown place with strangers and with her daughters in tow… She was trusting him a hell of a lot and he wasn't about to let her down. Not after everything she'd been through.

He and Chad had had to trust one another to stay alive. It was that trust that Chad had counted on. He'd died knowing Kyle would come here and do what needed to be done—no matter what. Chad had been family—a brother. As such, Skylar and the girls were family. Family looked out for one another. It was that simple.

"I like your truck," Brynn said, smiling as Skylar buckled her car seat. "It's sooo tall." She held her hand up high.

"That high?" He smiled, watching Skylar so he could buckle Mya in.

Mya held the buckle out and pointed to what went where, then patted him on the hand when he was done. She gave him a thumbs-up. "Good."

He gave her a thumbs-up then signed and said, "Thank you." He'd downloaded an app on his phone last night hoping to pick up on a few basic words. *Please*, *thank you*, *come*, *go*, *dog*, *mother*, *sister*, *baby*, and *water*. So far, that was it. Hopefully, it'd be enough for now.

Mya grinned and patted his hand again.

Jet peered into the truck and looked at Kyle.

"I know," Kyle said. "Here." He pulled his sleeping bag from the tool chest mounted inside his truck bed and placed it on the floorboard behind Skylar's seat. "You good?"

Jet jumped up, spun in a circle one way twice, back the other way three times, then flopped down.

Mya and Brynn thought this was hilarious.

"He good," Brynn said.

Mya blew Jet kisses.

For a second, Kyle stared into the backseat of his truck. It was one thing to know Skylar and the girls needed an exit strategy and a whole other thing to realize *he* was their exit strategy. For a minute, the enormity of what was happening rushed in on him. It was a lot to take in—and a whole lot of responsibility.

It's the least I can do... If it wasn't for him, Skylar wouldn't be in this situation. She'd have Chad with her right now.

"Okay." Skylar sounded excited. "Here we go."

They closed the back doors of his crew cab truck and took their seats up front. That's when he saw her hands were shaking. Not just a little bit either. A whole hell of a lot.

"Need a minute?" he asked, his voice low.

She shook her head but didn't look at him. Instead, she tucked her hands between her legs, took a deep breath, and closed her eyes.

He didn't push it, since he figured he'd pushed enough. He put the truck in gear and backed down the dirt drive and out onto the dirt road. It was so dry, the truck kicked up a cloud of red dust in their wake. A quick glance in the rearview mirror showed the twins staring out their windows, fascinated by the passing mesquite trees, barbwire fences, tumbleweeds, and cacti. Hardly a scenic view but they seemed happy enough.

Skylar's tension eased a little more with each mile he put between them and Frank's place.

The dirt road opened up onto the two-lane country road that would take them into town, ice cream, and a trip to Skylar's bank. He was in no hurry but he got the feeling she was. It was almost like, now that they were leaving, she couldn't wait to be gone.

"Are you a cone or milkshake fan?" he asked, hoping to ease into conversation. It'd be a hell of a long drive to make in silence.

"Me?" Skylar asked, turning his way. "I'll be honest. I'll take my ice cream any way I can get it." She smiled.

"That's a good answer." He nodded.

"You?" she asked, glancing into the backseat and waving.

"I'm a malt man, myself. Easier to enjoy while driving." He glanced in the rearview mirror again. Mya and Brynn were making signs at each other.

"A malt?" She sighed, resting her head against the seat.

"Don't tell me you've never had a malt." He frowned her way.

"Okay, I won't tell you." She smiled.

He chuckled. "You're missing out, Skylar." He glanced her way, a little thrown by the way she was watching him.

She blinked, her gaze falling from his.

He turned his attention back to the road, the only

sign of life was a buzzard perched atop a large, gnarled mesquite tree along the side of the road.

"You said it's green?" she asked. "Granite Falls?"

"Yes, ma'am." He chuckled. Had she read his mind? Or had the look on his face given him away? Chad had always said his face was an open book. Which got them into trouble on more than one occasion. "You'll see soon enough."

Twenty minutes later, they reached Flat Brush. It was, without a doubt, one of the saddest little towns Kyle had ever seen. Its main street was mostly vacant boarded-up storefronts with For Sale or For Lease signs in the windows.

"The bank is just up there and on the right." Skylar pointed. She turned to look at the girls. "They've dozed off—"

"I can stay in the truck with them? Keep the air conditioner blasting?" Kyle offered. "Might be a little easier than unloading and loading and trying to take care of business?"

She held her purse close. "Are you sure?" Her gaze darted to the backseat. "If Greer wakes up—"

"Then I'll get her out of her car seat and tell her my life story. Guaranteed to put her back to sleep in no time." He pulled into a visitor spot in front of the bank and put the truck into Park. "Or, we can go in with you."

"Something tells me your life story would be anything but boring, Kyle Mitchell." She shook her head, that gaze still pinned to his face. "Are you sure? I already feel like you've done so much for us."

He realized what was bothering her then. It was there, on her face. As much as it stung to see it, he understood. She'd been living with Frank Kline too long. "You don't owe me a thing, Skylar. Just so we're clear. I'm not planning on turning this against you in the future or lording it over you. Okay?"

She nodded.

"I mean it." He met her gaze, willing her to believe him.

"I know." It was a near whisper. "Chad believed in you. That's all I need to know. I guess... I'm so grateful." Her voice wavered and she swallowed.

He had two choices: hold her close and let her cry or tease away the emotion. Since they were sitting in the bank parking lot, he decided the latter was the best way to go. "You're grateful now? Just wait until you have your first malt."

Skylar was so surprised, she didn't quite cover her mouth in time to muffle her laughter. Not that Kyle minded. He liked the way she laughed. Free and easy, like Brynn or Mya. When she laughed, she wasn't carrying the weight of the world on her shoulders. "I'll hurry," she whispered, climbing out of the truck.

He watched her go inside, still smiling, and glanced in the rearview mirror. Jet sat up, yawning, his head cocked to the side. "Keep it down. We don't want to wake up the girls." He reached back and scratched Jet behind the ear. "What do you think?

How do you think Hayden's going to react? You'll like Hayden. He gets along better with dogs than people." *People change.* It did happen. He'd changed. It had been years since he'd spent any real time with his brother. Hayden was a father now, newly married, and, according to their mother, happy and… mellow. The mellow part was hard to believe but…

I need to cut Hayden some slack. He'd been a kid, a kid trying to protect his little brothers from their lying ass of a new stepfather. Kyle and John hadn't wanted to see the sort of person their stepfather really was, not until they'd learned the hard way. In the end, Hayden had been right but a rift had formed between the three brothers that time and perspective could heal—at least that's what Kyle hoped. Since there wasn't a damn thing he could do about it until he got there, Kyle hadn't let himself dwell on how he'd be welcomed home. And all of his worry about coming home had taken a backseat once he'd pulled into Frank Kline's driveway. But now that he'd set them all on a one-way path forward, little things like his big brother's and mother's reactions, the state of the bunkhouse he'd offered to Skylar, and if there was a position open on the ranch mattered.

"Now's the time to find out." He sighed, shook his head, and pulled his phone from his pocket to call home.

"Hayden Mitchell." His brother's voice was brusque.

"Hey, big brother. It's Kyle." He cleared his throat. "I'm home, stateside."

"You're home? That's great, Kyle. Mom will be over the moon. I'm pretty damn happy, too—"

"Well, you might not be after I'm finished." He drew in a deep breath and laid it all out there. Chad, Jet, Skylar, the girls, Frank's place, the bunkhouse, the job with Buzz and helping out at the ranch, and their imminent arrival. "I should have called. I should have asked. I just… I had to get them out of there, Hayden. I had to." There was long, extended silence. So long, Kyle worried they'd been disconnected. "Hayden?"

"The bunkhouse was wiped out in a tornado so they might have to stay in the main house for a bit— no problem. But your place made it." Hayden cleared his throat. "Mom and Lizzie will be happy having little ones under the roof. And Weston will love having someone to play with."

Lizzie—the wife he'd never met. Weston—the nephew he'd never met. *Lots of changes.* But maybe that was the best way for them to move on.

"As far as a job? Pretty sure Buzz is still looking so this will make his day. He'd probably pay her pretty well, too. But, even if he's found someone, you know we always need help with the animals here on the ranch." Hayden paused. "You're doing right by Chad."

Kyle stared out the front windshield, words rising up and sticking in his throat until they formed a hard lump. Doing right? As far as he was concerned, it still wasn't enough—it would never be enough.

Chad died because of him. Skylar and the girls had suffered this way because of it. He couldn't undo the grief and hell Skylar had shouldered since Chad's death, but he'd do his best to share her burden moving forward. He owed it to Chad. "It's the least I can do," he ground out.

"You headed this way now?" Hayden asked.

"Still in Flat Brush." He saw the bank door open, saw Skylar headed this way…saw her face. "I don't know if we'll get there tonight or tomorrow."

"Probably best if you find a place along the way to overnight. Kids that young need to move a bit." Hayden chuckled. "Or they get downright ornery."

"I'll call when we're an hour out," he said. "I gotta go."

"Okay… Kyle?" Hayden paused. "I'm glad you're home. It'll be good to have you here."

Kyle let out a slow breath. "I'm looking forward to it." He hung up about the time Skylar opened the passenger door. "What's wrong?"

Her face was beet red, her jaw locked tight, and there were tears on her cheeks.

"Frank." She shook her head, her jaw working. "I… I… He's been lying this whole time." She shook her head, sniffing hard and doing her damnedest to hold back the tears.

"But you're okay?" he asked. He didn't give a damn about Frank.

"Better than okay." She nodded. "I've been getting

monthly benefits checks from the military this whole time, Kyle. This whole time. And he never told me."

Kyle stared at her.

"I should have known, I guess… After all the lies he's fed me but it never occurred to me. I'd only ever had a little bit, in savings. We'd opened up a joint checking account when we first settled… Because, I never learn." She was shaking her head now. "Today…I saw there was money in the checking account and asked about it. The bank associate told me it was the regular monthly deposit, as always…" Those brown eyes were huge and flashing. "I asked for the last six months' statements." She smoothed the papers she'd crumpled. "I didn't know. I didn't know we were getting a monthly payment all this time… But he did. All that money… I don't know how he's managed to spend it or how he could live with himself when Mya… Mya…" She broke off, staring blindly at the papers. "I let this happen, Kyle. I did…"

"You didn't do anything except put your trust in family. Your top priority was your girls, as it should be. There was no way of knowing he'd do…well, this." Kyle's grip tightened on the steering wheel as he took a few seconds to imagine knocking Frank Kline on his ass. It was pretty damn gratifying. Once that was done, he shook his head and turned to her. "Well, he's never going to get another penny from you, Skylar."

"He certainly is not." There was a snap to her

voice. "I closed the account and took what was left." She shook her head. "The nice woman gave me the Military Affairs number so all I have to do is stop payments until I get an account set up in Granite Falls."

He smiled. "Sounds like a plan. Now you can finally start saving what you need for Mya."

Skylar nodded, her chin crumpling slightly before she reined in her emotions. She straightened, drew in a deep breath, and spoke calmly. "Yes. Yes, you're right."

"How about we go celebrate?" he asked, resisting the urge to take her hand in his. He started the truck, backed out, then made a left and headed down the street toward the large red-and-white Dairy King sign. "Going in or drive-through?" he asked.

She glanced in the backseat. "They're sleeping. We don't need to get ice—"

"Oh, yes, ma'am, we do." He pulled into the drive-through. "Two chocolate malts," he told the girl in the window. "Large."

Chapter Five

Greer wasn't happy. At all. She was wailing her little lungs out and there was no stopping her. "I'm sorry," Skylar said to Kyle, for the third time.

"She's just letting you know her opinion on things." He grinned, staring out the windshield. "We're almost to the next town. How about we stop, get some dinner, and maybe look at getting a couple of rooms for the night? Let the girls stretch their legs a bit?"

Skylar frowned. "Dinner sounds good."

Greer's volume steadily increased but Kyle seemed unruffled by it. Still, Skylar was relieved when they spied a family-friendly looking café with an outdoor dining area where Jet might be welcome. He pulled in, parked, and helped get the girls free and clear of their seats, making sure Mya and Brynn took hold of her hands. Skylar ignored the sudden ache his thoughtful gesture caused. Instead, she watched as he lifted Greer from her seat. Greer stopped wailing immediately. She was still red-faced, with tears on her cheeks, but she gurgled and smiled up at Kyle as if he'd hung the moon and the stars in the sky just for her.

"Greer Rose." Skylar couldn't help but laugh. "I know Kyle is a nice man and you feel just horrible for giving him a headache, don't you?"

Greer turned, smiling and cooing some more.

"She sure knows her momma's voice," Kyle chuckled. "She lit right up."

Skylar was pretty sure her baby girl was far more enthusiastic over being freed from her seat— by Kyle—but she didn't point that out. She knew Greer would start crying once she was returned to her car seat but there was no way to manage all three of them without it. "I'll get her seat," she offered.

"I can carry her." He was wearing that awed expression again—the one that made her insides go a little too warm and soft for her liking.

"I don't want the girls to be a bother." She meant it.

"If it was a bother, I wouldn't have offered." He adjusted Greer in his arms and headed toward the front door of the restaurant. "Let's see if they're dog friendly." He held the door open.

Skylar slipped the strap of Greer's diaper bag onto her shoulder, and steered the girls inside. Jet followed behind, staying close and behaving himself. Inside, the floor was covered in peanut shells and country music poured from the tinny speakers. It was early so the dining room was mostly silver-haired. All eyes turned their way and conversation all but came to a stop when they walked in. But one look at Kyle with Greer and her girls turned the senior diners' curiosity into warm welcome.

The waitress assured them Jet would be no bother as long as he behaved himself, instead of sitting outside. Kyle gave his word and the woman showed them to a large booth in the corner. Jet, on the nervous side, hurried under the table and lay across Skylar's feet.

"We eating, Momma?" Brynn asked. "I'm hungry. Mya is hungry, too." She pointed at Mya and rubbed her tummy.

Mya nodded.

"Me, too," Kyle said, bouncing Greer just enough to keep her entertained.

Skylar read over the menu quickly. As kind as Kyle was being, he'd run out of patience once Greer got cranky for her dinner. "Macaroni and cheese?" she asked, pointing at the picture on the child's menu for Mya.

Mya's smile was all the answer she needed.

"Can I have this, Momma?" Brynn asked, pointing at a piece of pie.

"That's dessert, Brynn." She smiled.

"Special 'casions." Brynn nodded, looking very solemn for a four-year-old.

"Dessert is for special occasions only?" Kyle asked, regarding his menu.

"Yes," Brynn said. "Only special 'casions."

Skylar stared down at her two daughters. They never asked for much and always appreciated what they got. Was dessert asking too much? Considering the surprises her day had revealed and the adventure they were on, Skylar was pretty sure dessert was in order. "Well, maybe tonight is a special occasion," she said. "Maybe, *after* you eat some macaroni or a grilled cheese we should get some pie."

Brynn's eyes went owl-like. "Really, Momma?"

Kyle chuckled, peering over the menu at her. "I'm pretty excited about the pie, too."

Skylar tapped Brynn's nose, then Mya's nose with her finger. "Really." She pointed at the picture for Mya. Mya, however, shook her head and pointed at the macaroon cookies. "Okay." To Mya, there was nothing better than cookies, of any kind, and milk. And Skylar was just fine with that.

For the first time in over a year, she had some spending cash. She'd done her best not to touch the small nest egg she had in savings; it was earmarked for Mya—it had been a source of hope when things got rough. But now, she could breathe. Never in a million years could she have imagined she was getting a monthly payment. Because Frank had made sure of that. But not now. Not anymore. It wasn't a lot, but it was *something*. More than she'd had in…a long time. Not enough to make her independent, of course. But a start. If her daughters wanted dessert, they were getting dessert.

They ordered their dinner and Greer started to fuss, so Kyle went out to the truck to get her car seat. Once she was bibbed and buckled in, she devoured her bowl of rice cereal, had a couple of bites of pureed squash baby food, and several ounces of formula.

"Better?" Skylar asked, carefully wiping the remnants of Greer's dinner from her face.

Greer cooed, offering a toothless grin.

Kyle was laughing.

"What?" Skylar asked, giving Greer a quick once-over.

"Oh, nothing." But he was still laughing.

"Kyle? What is so funny?" Skylar turned, waiting for an explanation.

"You. The faces you make when you're feeding her." He winked at Mya and Brynn. "You kind of squish up your face and open your mouth and eyes real wide."

Skylar stared at him. "I do?"

Brynn nodded. "Yep."

"It's…" Kyle shook his head, his smile something to see. "It's sweet."

Skylar's embarrassment melted away. "Oh." She

liked Kyle Mitchell and she *really* liked Kyle Mitchell when he was smiling.

Their food was delivered and Delores, the waitress, went on and on about the girls. "They have some of their momma and their daddy." Delores looked back and forth between Skylar and Kyle. "Daddy's hair and Momma's smile."

"Thank you," Skylar responded, ignoring Kyle's choking sound.

"It's not every day we have such a sweet family in." Delores leaned forward to gaze at Greer. "Cute as a button." She made a silly face at the baby. "You let me know if you need anything now, you hear?"

"We will, thank you." Skylar smiled her thanks then turned to see Kyle, red-faced, but recovering. "I figured it was easier to say thank you than to offer up a whole convoluted explanation of who we were to each other and why we were traveling together. The food would get cold."

"Can't argue with that logic." He nodded. "Caught me off guard is all."

The food was delicious. It helped that she didn't have to cook—or worry about the cleanup. It also helped to know she could pay their own way.

But, mostly, it helped to have another set of hands. Frank had always barked and glared and sighed until he carried his dinner to his room—complaining the girls were all *fussy and bad for the digestion.* But not Kyle. When Mya patted his hand and asked for help putting the straw into the top of her kiddie cup, he did so without hesitation. When Mya dropped her fork, he got her another one. And when Brynn announced that she'd eaten all of her macaroni and cheese and she wanted pie, he readily agreed.

Skylar happily accepted a bit of Mya's coconut macaroons with a light coconut frosting as well as a bite of Brynn's apple pie. "They're both so good," she declared, regretting her decision to stick to decaf coffee.

"Kyle's pie is, too," Brynn said, giving Kyle's cherry pie a look. "Kyle, will you share with Momma, please?"

Kyle nodded. "Of course." He scooped up a large bite of pie and held it out to her. The pie wobbled. If she took the fork, chances were the pie wouldn't make it to her mouth and the gooey cherries would wind up all over the twins. Instead, she leaned forward, mouth open, and let him feed her.

She sat back, the sweet tang of cherries filling her mouth. "Mmm," she murmured, chewing and nodding.

For a few seconds the fork didn't move. Kyle didn't move... He seemed entirely focused on her mouth.

She grabbed her napkin and wiped. First, she'd made faces feeding Greer. Now she had cherry pie on her face... But the napkin was clean. When she glanced his way, he'd gone back to eating his pie—like nothing had happened.

Nothing *had* happened.

"Which is best, Momma?" Brynn asked.

"Oh." Skylar looked back and forth between the plates, smiling at each of them. "That's a tough one." But her gaze stopped and hung on Mya. "Mya?" she asked. "You okay?"

Mya nodded, even as her lips seemed to plump. She opened her mouth and stuck out her tongue, making a face. It looked swollen, too.

"Momma, what's wrong?" Brynn asked.

Skylar reached across Brynn and pressed a hand to Mya's cheek. "I'm not sure." She handed Mya her water. "Sip, baby." She signed "water," but Mya shook her head and turned away, her little hands pressing against her throat as her breathing grew labored. That was when Skylar started to panic. "Mya?"

"Is she allergic to anything?" Kyle asked, his forehead creased and his jaw clenching tight.

"No." She frowned. "Not that I know of." But both of them were staring at her plate. "She's never had coconut before."

"Delores!" Kyle slid from the booth. "Where's the closest medical clinic or hospital?"

"Everything okay?" Delores asked. "It's just a hop, skip, and a jump down the road. Can't miss it. On the right." She saw Mya then. "Oh, land sakes… You go on. Just go."

Skylar didn't hesitate. Somehow, she and Kyle managed to get the kids and Jet into the car. Somehow, they made it to the tiny community hospital not two blocks away.

Kyle barreled out of the truck and freed Mya from her car seat.

"Go, please, go," Skylar pleaded, watching as he carried Mya, running, into the hospital before she hurried to get Brynn unbuckled and Greer's car seat out of the back. Jet jumped down and followed along, looking more agitated than usual.

"Is Mya okay, Momma?" Brynn asked, holding tightly to her hand. "Momma?"

"She will be okay." Skylar squeezed her hand. She had to be. She could not lose her daughter. She would not.

Inside, the small hospital waiting room was empty. No Kyle. No Mya. No nurse at reception. No one. Skylar swallowed down the urge to call out. Brynn was on the verge of tears—hearing her mother yell wasn't going to help. She crossed the lobby, her heart in her throat, and pushed the Emergency Room button. The doors swung wide and the silence ended.

"You Mom?" a nurse asked, waiting for Skylar's nod before she continued. "Mya's oxygen levels are a little low so we're giving her some oxygen."

Skylar followed the woman to a curtained partition.

"We are going to give her a shot of epinephrine," the nurse said. "It will alleviate the swelling of her airway. She's breathing but it's hard work."

Skylar nodded, the sight of her daughter's blue-tinged face almost breaking her. "Hurry, please." She was at the bedside, smiling down at Mya. "Hi, baby girl. It's going to be okay." In that moment, she hated that Mya couldn't hear her. She hated staring down at her daughter and knowing there was nothing she could do to make this better. It was painfully familiar.

She was vaguely aware of Kyle saying something before he took the handle of Greer's car seat from her hand. "Skylar?" Kyle's voice was low and soothing. "We'll be in the waiting room." He took Brynn's hand. "We will be right outside." He was already leading them away.

She nodded, but focused on Mya, on taking hold of her little hand.

She heard someone clear his throat, and the room suddenly came into sharp focus.

"I have the epinephrine here. This might burn," Dr. Wilson—according to his name tag—said seconds before giving Mya an injection.

Mya's reaction confirmed it was not a pleasant experience. She reached down, pressing one hand to her thigh. But, since her throat was swollen, Mya's cries were garbled and weak, making it even harder to breathe.

"Mya." She leaned forward, resting her daughter's hand against her cheek and pressing a kiss to each one of the fingertips.

Mya stared up at her, her chin quivering and her lips wobbling. "Ma," she croaked.

"I love you," Skylar said, making the *I love you* sign with her other hand. "It's okay." *Please, please let her be okay.* She bent forward to kiss her forehead. "It's okay."

Tears streaked Mya's cheeks but she nodded.

The room seemed to hold its breath but, within minutes, Mya's oxygen level went from ninety-three percent to ninety-eight percent and climbing.

"Good." Dr. Wilson nodded. "We'll watch her for a bit, get some steroids in her system, and make sure there's no worries about relapsing."

"Thank you." Now that Mya was out of danger, Skylar needed a good, long cry in the bathroom sometime soon.

"I'll write up a scrip for the steroids for you to fill tomorrow," Dr. Wilson said, patting Mya's leg before slipping through the curtains. "If she keeps improving, we'll send you on your way this evening. But let's give it an hour or so."

Skylar nodded.

"I'll get you a chair," the nurse said. "And you can stay, if you'd like."

"Yes, please. I'm not going anywhere." She smiled down at Mya—who was no longer blue or puffy— and pressed kisses all over her face. "I'm staying right here." She tapped Mya's nose.

Mya smiled up at her. "Brynn?"

"You want your sister?" Skylar asked, signing "Brynn" and "come."

Mya nodded.

"I'll get the family," the nurse offered. "We're empty so I'll open up this side so there's room for you all."

"Thank you." Skylar nodded. "Thank you for everything."

Kyle held the door of the hotel suite open, Greer's car-seat handle gripped in one hand and Jet's leash in the other. It was only a suite in the barest sense of the word. The kitchenette was separated by a paper-thin partition wall—and no door. But a large basket sat on the table. There was fruit, muffins, mini pies, and some coloring books and crayons. Everything they'd need to make it through the night and breakfast in the morning, too. *Damn thoughtful.*

"We sleeping here?" Brynn asked, skipping into the room. "It's so big."

Kyle gave the small kitchenette another look—through Brynn's eyes. Compared to Frank's hovel and the trailer she'd shared with her mother and sisters, the space was clean and open and somewhat spacious. Not big, by any stretch of the imagination, but better than what Brynn had come to expect. A hard knot formed and sat low, heavy and hot in the pit of his belly.

He couldn't help but think of Chad. Again. Tonight, Chad had weighed on him. What would he have done or said to Frank? How would he have handled tonight's ER visit. From helping out at the dinner table to carrying Mya into the hospital to the simple innocence of Mya's smile. He was missing this, all of it. And it tore at the wound on his heart.

"Just for tonight." Skylar brought up the rear, holding on to Mya's hand. "I still can't believe Delores did this."

"Delores and the Senior Supper Club." Kyle smiled, nodding at the basket and watching Skylar's wide-eyed reaction. "I'm not surprised. Something like this happens in a small town and folk step up to help out. Especially when kids are involved."

"It's beyond generous. I'm so grateful." There was no doubting Skylar's sincerity. "I never expected this. All of this." She began inventorying the room, heading through the kitchenette to the bedroom beyond. She flipped on the bedside lamps, peered into the bathroom, and generally took in the lay of the land. "Is this what Granite Falls is like? A small town?"

"And proud of it. They don't take kindly to folk coming in, putting in chain stores, or making big changes. No, thank you. But they're good people. Like this." Kyle set Greer's car seat on the foot of one of the beds and unbuckled the grinning baby. "Are you smiling at me?" That smile. She had Chad's smile.

Greer kicked, animatedly blowing little bubbles.

"That means yes." Skylar glanced between Greer and him. "She's taken with you."

Kyle decided not to point out that, other than Frank, Greer's world was made up of the people currently in this room. He preferred thinking Greer *was* taken with him, that he was the cause of all her smiles and coos and excitement. No one had ever seemed this happy to see him. It was gratifying as hell. "What's not to like?" he teased, picking up Greer and cradling her close. "Now that I know I won't drop her or break her, I think I've got this baby thing down."

Skylar laughed. It didn't last long and she sounded tired, but it still counted. "Glad to hear it." She covered her yawn with the back of her hand. "Can I ask you to keep an eye on her while I bath the girls? I'll get a bottle ready for you."

Greer made a high-pitched happy sound that had Jet cocking his head to one side.

"Translation?" Kyle asked, glancing at Skylar.

"She said she'll be very good and drink her bottle and not spit up on you or expect you to change her diaper." Skylar opened the trash bag containing the girls' belongings and started rifling through the contents.

"All that, huh?" Kyle bounced Greer a little. He wasn't sure how it was possible to be so captivated by something so tiny and inarticulate, but he was. Every single time he scooped her up, he was struck by the slightness of her weight. The perfect little fingers that happily clasped on to his—which were giantlike in comparison—all the while with her grinning a toothless grin. The wisp of a curl on the top of her head only added to the whole elfin appearance.

No, not elfin. She was too cute. More like a wing-less fairy. Dainty and sweet and doll-like.

"Bath time." Skylar directed the girls into the bathroom. "We'll hurry, Kyle."

"Don't rush on my part." He offered Skylar a re-assuring smile. "Jet and I will keep a close eye on Greer."

"Thank you." Skylar's gaze lingered on his face—almost disbelieving—before she pulled the door around, leaving it cracked in case he needed her.

You did good, Chad. Kyle smiled as he laid Greer on the bed. *Your girls are precious. And Skylar...* Well, Skylar would have made him so damn proud. *He* was proud of her. The thought struck him fast and hard in the throat. He had no right to feel *any-thing* for Skylar. She was Chad's wife... Off-limits. *Get your head straight.*

Kyle didn't know how she'd managed to raise the girls under those conditions—not just raise them but find ways to make them happy. No small feat when they'd had nothing but dirt, cacti, a crappy air con-ditioner, and leaning travel trailer while being be-holden to a man who'd made a habit out of leaving them on their own to fend for themselves.

That was the part Kyle was struggling with the most. How could Frank Kline look himself in the eye? How could he live with himself, knowing he'd put his needs and wants ahead of these children? Not to mention stealing from Skylar.

"He's a right old bastard," Kyle said, using a happy

singsong voice. "But you and Brynn and Mya and your momma won't have to worry about mean old grumpy Uncle Frank ever again."

Greer cooed and kicked out, grinning up at him.

Jet rested his chin on the edge of the bed, ears perked up, eyes fixed on Greer.

"I know." He scratched Jet behind the ear. "She's something, isn't she?"

Jet's tail thumped but he never took his eyes off Greer.

"She's yours now, Jet." He kept on scratching. "You and I, we need to keep an eye on her. And her sisters." And Skylar, too. Though something kept him from saying as much out loud. It had been less than forty-eight hours. Surely feeling this…connected to a person wasn't normal? Granted, the circumstances were highly unusual but still.

By the time the girls were bathed and in their pajamas, Skylar was drooping. She kept a smile on her face and a cheerful tone to her voice but it was taking effort. He left them long enough to collect Greer's portable crib and a few needed baby supplies, then returned to find the twins in one of the big beds— heavy lidded and yawning.

He glanced at Mya. She seemed just fine. All smiles. All pink cheeked and smiling. It was almost like their trip to the ER hadn't happened. *But it had.*

"Sleep tight and tomorrow we go to Kyle's home," Skylar said, pressing a kiss to Brynn's forehead.

"Our home?" Brynn asked, yawning.

"Yep." Kyle nodded, setting up Greer's portable crib.

"More doggies?" Brynn asked.

"And cows and horses, too." Kyle stood and smiled at the girls. "And my nephew, Weston, will be good company for you two to chase around. He's a little younger than you but he'll love having some play-mates."

"Go Kyle?" Mya asked, her voice soft.

Skylar used her hands as she said, "Yes. We're going to Kyle's house in the morning." Then she pressed a hand to Mya's forehead. "Okay?"

Mya nodded. "Good."

Skylar leaned forward and pressed a handful of kisses against Mya's temple. "Sleep." She smoothed the hair from her daughter's face and tapped her nose. "I love you." She held up her hand. Both Mya and Brynn did the same. Kyle made a mental note of that sign, too.

"You want to take a shower?" he asked. "I'll keep an eye on them."

"No." She peered down at Greer, smiled and changed the baby's diaper in record time. "I'm fine."

You're not fine. He stood, staring down at her. "You're not going to convince me that you'll get any sleep tonight so I figure we should take shifts watching Mya? That way you're not beat and we're both somewhat upright tomorrow?"

Skylar stared up at him, frowning. "Kyle…" She drew in a deep breath. "Mya's my daughter. It's my job to take care of her, not yours."

He nodded. "True." And it was. "But that doesn't mean you can't take help now and then." He shrugged.

"You've been helping more than enough." There was a slight edge to her voice then. Frustration? Irritation? She busied herself putting Greer into the crib, patting the baby's back until Greer's breathing steadied, then carried the near-empty bottle into the small kitchenette beyond the half wall partitioning off the bedroom.

Had he been pushing too hard? If he hadn't pushed, she wouldn't be here…and Mya wouldn't have wound up in the ER. No, they'd still be stuck on Frank Kline's property with no hope of getting out and no knowledge of the money Frank had been stealing each month. Maybe he had been a little too pushy but, dammit, he'd had no choice. And he didn't regret it. He followed her, not sure what to say, but knowing something needed to be said.

"I'm sorry," she whispered. "Today… I didn't know. Coconut… I should have known." She shrugged, struggling to keep her voice steady. "It's just…" The way her shoulders drooped did him in. "Mya—"

"Is one tough little girl." He didn't think as he pulled her into his arms. "Tough and sweet and fine. She is, Skylar. She will be." His hold was loose—easy enough for her to pull out of. "Now we know. No coconut. Ever." The *we* slipped out easily enough but the guilt that followed was near crippling.

Her laugh broke on a barely muffled sob. That sound, so garbled and raw, seemed to open the floodgates. With her arms tight around his waist and her face buried against his chest, she started to cry. Not a few tears. No, these were bone-racking sobs that demanded he hold her close for as long as she needed. They were hard and ragged, rolling over her until Kyle was certain she'd cried herself out. But the tears kept coming, just as desperate as when they'd started.

Deep down, he knew she'd been holding back. Her girls were her everything, and she'd never let her emotions go unchecked this way for fear of upsetting them. But how long had this been bottled up inside? All the fear and anger and grief? *Too long.* After what happened today, she'd more than earned herself a good cry.

He rubbed her back, the sound of her struggle forming a vise around his chest. The grief in her tears twisted down the clamp, pressing in on him. "It's okay now, Skylar. Let it out."

"I—I—I'm f-fine…" Her long indrawn breath was ragged.

"You are." He smiled in spite of himself. "But even if you weren't, for a bit, that'd be okay, too. You tell me if you want me to let go?"

She nodded, her tears making the front of his shirt wet.

He kept rubbing her back, in long, slow strokes. He didn't know if it helped her or not but it was helping him. There were times his guilt over Chad's death damn near brought him to his knees. Like now. If he'd been more careful, done his damn job, Chad would be here and Skylar wouldn't have been shouldering the weight of...everything. It was his fault she'd suffered like this for so long; the least he could do was give her a shoulder—or a shirt—to cry on. After seeing where she'd been living and what she'd been dealing with, he should feel guilty. *Dammit.* As long as he didn't think about Frank Kline, everything he'd done, or Skylar and the girls' prior living conditions, he could keep a cool head. But now that he was thinking about all of those things, he had to find a way to talk himself back into being the cool, calm presence she needed.

"Even the strongest people need a break now and then. It's not a sign of being weak—it's part of being human," he murmured against her temple. "As far as I'm concerned, you're a badass."

She shook her head but didn't say anything.

"Look at your girls," he insisted. "You put those smiles on their faces. You found a way to keep them entertained and positive and with enough imagination to turn that leaning wooden shack into a playhouse—"

"Hey," she interrupted, peering up at him with red-rimmed eyes.

"I was teasing." He smiled. "You're missing the point here."

"Oh?" She didn't seem fazed by the fact that she was still holding on to him—or that there was barely any space between them.

But he was. And it had him reeling. The moment her gaze met his, the tightness and pressure in his chest gave way. And having Skylar, in his arms, soft and warm and all woman, was something he hadn't prepared himself for.

Focus. Not on the unnerving reaction Skylar was causing. No, on being here for Skylar and the girls. *Focus on honoring Chad's last request.* Chad— who expected him to take care of the family he left behind, not get blindsided and want more than he should. How could he not? Skylar was a strong, beautiful woman who had his heart thumping in a way he didn't recognize.

"Thank you, again." Her gaze swept over his face before she rose on tiptoe and kissed his cheek. "You're a good man, Kyle Mitchell."

Whatever Kyle had been thinking vanished and all that remained was Skylar, the softness of her lips and the desperate longing throbbing in his chest. For a moment, maybe a couple of seconds, the space between them sparked—pulling them closer and tripping up the too-quick beat of his heart. If he tilted his head, he could kiss her... And, right or wrong, there was no denying that's exactly what he wanted to do.

Chapter Six

Skylar wasn't sure which was worse: blubbering all over Kyle Mitchell's shirtfront or the overwhelming comfort she found being in his arms. Wrapped up in his strength. His scent. His warmth. Like her own human security blanket. It had been a long time since she'd felt so at ease. So long that she couldn't remember when that last was, let alone how good it felt... Before Mya's illness. Before Greer's birth. Before Frank showed up. Before Chad's death. Her heart twisted, tighter and tighter until the tears threatened to start all over again. Staring at his chest was a far safer alternative to staring into his concerned eyes.

No. Enough. Kyle had just called her a badass. A real badass wouldn't cry like a baby. *Correction.* Greer had never pulled the sort of fit she'd just had. Even though she knew Kyle was a good man, she couldn't shake the lingering fear that—at any minute—Kyle would realize he'd made a cataclysmic mistake and return them to Uncle Frank's doorstep.

"I really am fine now." She didn't sound *fine* but at least her voice wasn't shaking anymore. Not that she was in any hurry to lose the comfort Kyle was offering up. Right or wrong, she wanted to hold on to this—to him—for a few seconds longer.

"Fine. Good," he murmured, his voice deep and rich and soft.

The more her tears receded, the harder it was for Skylar not to pick up on things that she shouldn't be noticing. Things like the way his scent tightened her stomach. How the slight press of his hand on her back seemed to urge her to arch into him. The brush of his every breath against her temple. The rapid thump of his heart beneath her cheek. The bunch and shift of his back muscles beneath her fingers… And the sheer breadth of his chest beneath his soft cotton T-shirt—a T-shirt that clung to his rock-hard pecs and was currently wet with her tears.

He was a soldier. Of course, he was strong. She drew in a deep breath. But the rest of it? The tightness and urges and…all of it? Well, she was pretty sure those were not the things he'd hoped to inspire when he'd offered her a shoulder to cry on. Maybe holding on to him was a bad idea. *Maybe?* Holding on to him was definitely a bad idea. "Kyle?" She cleared her throat, her gaze locked with his.

"Mm?" The sound was a rumble. Deep and gruff and…

She blinked, horrified to realize her gaze had wandered to his mouth. His mouth, which was so close. *What is wrong with me?* "I think you're right," she said, forcing herself to let go of him. "I think it's been a long emotional day and it's getting to me." That was the only reason she was noticing all the ways Kyle Mitchell was manly and…handsome.

He immediately let her go and shoved his hands into the pockets of his jeans. "It was one hell of a day."

She managed a smile. "Thank you, again, for everything." She shook her head. "There are times when words just don't get it right, you know? *Thank you* is a nice enough term but it's not enough to express how grateful I am to you—for *everything.*"

"*Thank you* works." He smiled.

"Well, still…" She swallowed against the tightness of her throat. Handsome also didn't get it right. Kyle was more than handsome. He was… *It doesn't matter.* What mattered was how good he'd been to them. Above and beyond good to them. She headed back into the bedroom, suddenly panicked by the distance between her and Mya. She leaned forward, mentally chastising herself for leaving her daughter alone.

"It's only been five minutes," Kyle whispered. "She's okay, Skylar."

"I know. She's going to be fine." She smoothed the hair from her daughter's face, her features smooth in sleep.

"Here," Kyle said, dragging the chair from the corner next to the bed.

"Thank you." She sat, smiling up at him. "I'm pretty sure Chad never imagined you'd wind up saddled with us…and *everything*."

"Saddled, huh?" He shrugged, sitting on the still neatly made bed. "Chad was like a brother to me. Hell, we were closer than I am with the two brothers I have."

She heard the edge to his voice and asked, "You're not close?" Being an only child, she had no frame of reference. As a mother, seeing Mya and Brynn together made her heart happy. Not only were they sisters, they were the best of friends. If she'd had any siblings, she'd like to think they'd have been close like that.

He sighed. "I don't really know them anymore. When I left things were…complicated."

"Which is code for…" She stopped herself. "It's none of my business. I'm sorry." At the same time, she didn't relish arriving someplace loaded with tension. There was a chance the girls wouldn't immediately take to their new home. Add two hostile men to the mix and this could all go horribly wrong in a matter of minutes.

"No. I've made peace with it." Kyle ran a hand

along the back of his neck, something she'd seen him do a time or two when he was tense or frustrated. "I owe my older brother, Hayden, some apologies for being…difficult."

She frowned. Kyle? He'd been nothing but solicitous with her and the girls. "I'm having a hard time imagining you as difficult."

"Oh, I can be." He chuckled.

She shook her head. "What did you do?"

"I didn't listen to him when he told me our stepfather was a piece of…" He glanced at the bed and her sleeping daughters. "He wasn't a good guy. Our stepfather, Ed, I mean. Thinking back, I realize how hard I was on Hayden when he was just looking out for his little brothers." He sighed. "At the time, it felt like he was trying to fill our father's shoes—taking charge and holding us accountable for our actions while Ed let us do pretty much whatever we wanted. And once Ed picked up on the tension brewing between us brothers, he used that to convince us Hayden was being unreasonable because Hayden was jealous of him and taking it out on us." His smile was sad. Reflective. "Ed just wormed his way in. He'd known how to spin the sweet talk and lay on the charm. He and Hayden went toe-to-toe the moment Ed walked in our front door." He ran his hand along the back of his neck again. "All Hayden was trying to do was keep us from buying into a man who damn near bankrupted the ranch and left a mess behind."

"Left?"

"He passed on a few years back." He ran a hand along the back of his neck.

Skylar studied Kyle. The regret wore on him, it was plain to see. "Sounds like a straightforward apology will clear the air."

His gaze shifted her way. "You think so? Seems too easy."

She stared at Kyle for a long time, taking care with her words. Words, she knew, held power. "Chad said a lot of things about you, Kyle. One of them was that he hoped you'd find a way to fix whatever is broken between you and your brothers." Maybe that was not exactly how Chad's letter had read but she didn't feel comfortable reciting it word for word since Chad had been a little more explicit about Kyle needing to get his head out of his ass and making things right with his family.

One eyebrow rose sharply. "He said *that*?"

"Something like that." She couldn't hold back her smile.

"Sure." But he was smiling again, too. "Chad always cut through the bullsh— Uh, stuff." He winced. "I keep forgetting about the girls."

That was the thing about Kyle that kept Skylar off-balance. He was censoring his language for her daughters—aware enough to take their impressionable little minds into consideration—without being asked. It mattered, even though they were sound asleep.

That belly-tightening thing was happening again. The unnerving warmth, too. She drew her legs up, wrapping her arms around them, and rested her chin on her knees. It didn't help. Sure, he seemed perfect—especially after everything he'd done. But he wasn't perfect—no one was. Maybe she should focus on his flaws over his many, *many* assets... If she could find something, anything, about him that would dim his appeal, that was a good thing. As it was, she found everything about Kyle Mitchell a little too appealing.

"What?" he asked.

I'm staring. At him. She shook her head.

"That's some look." He frowned.

"No." She shook her head, her nerves stretched taut. "I... It's late and I'm beat." True, but not exactly a brilliant diversion.

"Okay." He glanced at his watch. "You want first watch?"

She should argue. Mya wasn't his responsibility.

"Or second?" He was watching her. "You can't stay up all night, Skylar. And if you try to and then fall asleep, you'll kick yourself. If we split this up, we'll both get at least three hours."

He sounded so rational. Like sitting up by her daughter's bedside wasn't the least bit out of the ordinary. "Are you—"

"I'm sure," he cut her off. "First or second watch?"

She glanced at Mya. She was tired but there was no way she'd sleep—not yet. "First."

He nodded. "I'm gonna shower." He grabbed the canvas backpack he'd carried in and headed for the bathroom.

Jet, who'd been lying between the portable crib and the girls' bed, lifted his head and stared at the closed door.

"He'll be right back," she said, smiling as his ears drooped and his tail started wagging. She uncurled from the chair and held her hand out. "You're a sweet thing, aren't you?"

Jet stood and hurried to her chair, leaning against it and staring up at her.

"You knew my Chad." She ran her hand over the dog's head. "And he loved you." Knowing Chad had something to love and comfort him had eased some of her worry. "Thank you for taking care of him. You and Kyle."

Jet rested his chin in her lap, his tail still thumping and his eyes closing as she continued to stroke his head over and over.

"And thank you for looking out for Mya today." She rubbed behind Jet's ears as she spoke.

Jet yawned, stretched, and flopped out on the floor by her chair.

"You've earned a good night's sleep, too." She rested her head on the back of the chair, turning her attention to Mya. Sleeping. Breathing easy. Relaxed.

The bathroom door opened, and Kyle came out. He wore some gray cotton athletic shorts and a white undershirt—entirely acceptable attire. And yet, to

Skylar, the cotton clung and hugged the angles and ridges of Kyle in an entirely unacceptable way.

"You've made a friend." He nodded at Jet, then ran a towel over his close-cropped hair.

She nodded, not quite capable of speech. Because, really, the white cotton undershirt was basically molded to Kyle's chest. *That is some chest.* A chest she was not going to stare at. *No staring at any part of Kyle from now on.* Her gaze returned to Mya and she swallowed. "He's the sweetest dog."

From the corner of her eye, she saw Kyle hang the towel over the rod in the closet before flopping onto the bed. If she turned her head to the left, she'd get quite an eyeful of Kyle Mitchell. But she wasn't going to turn her head. She was going to watch Mya.

For two hours and fifty-seven minutes, she watched Mya breathe. Every few minutes, she'd lay her hand on her daughter's chest or feel her face for any hint of fever. And when that was done, she'd relax a bit—soothed by peace and quiet—plus Kyle's occasional snore.

Two hours and fifty-eight minutes later, Kyle yawned, rubbed his hands over his face, and sat up. "We good?" he whispered, yawning again.

She nodded.

"Give me five minutes." He stood, headed into the bathroom, and returned minutes later, patting his face. He looked wide awake. "Cold water."

"That explains it." She was not feeling wide awake. She could only imagine what she looked like. She changed into her worn white cotton nightie, washed her face, and hurried from the bathroom to the bed.

He chuckled softly. "You good?"

She yawned. "Yes." It hadn't occurred to her to go to the other side of the bed. She'd been too tired to think about anything but sleep… But now that she'd burrowed in, she realized she wasn't just wrapped up in sheets and comforters, she was wrapped up in Kyle. The pillow beneath her head was very definitely, and most pleasantly, Kyle scented. Hopefully, he hadn't noticed the way she'd turned into the pillow. *Hopefully.* Her gaze darted his way…

He'd seen it. But she wasn't sure what to make of his expression. The way his jaw was locked. The slightest flare of his nostrils. It had the stomach-tightening, warm tingly thing kicking into overdrive.

"Get some sleep, Skylar." Kyle's voice was low. "I'll keep her safe. I promise you."

She nodded—Mya would be fine. Her heart was clipping along at an unnaturally fast pace not because she was worried about Kyle watching over Mya—she knew he'd keep them safe. No, her heart was reacting to Kyle. And there was nothing safe about it.

Kyle stifled a yawn with the back of his hand. Between this heightened awareness he had with Skylar and the nightmare waiting for him when he did doze off, sleep had been patchy at best. He couldn't do a thing about the nightmare—there was no getting rid of it. But he could try harder to fight what was happening with Skylar. She was Chad's wife. Chad, his best friend. The one he'd left to die alone… That, right there, should bring all thoughts of touching and kissing Skylar to a complete stop.

No such luck.

Kyle kept his eyes on the road, his fingers tapping out the beat of the music playing softly through the truck speakers. Until he'd spied the thirty-miles-to-Granite-Falls sign, he hadn't realized just how concerned he was about his homecoming. Not that he was going to let on that he was concerned, of course. So far, the girls—and Skylar—seemed excited about reaching their destination. He'd been doing everything he could to keep that excitement front and center.

All through breakfast, he'd shared stories about growing up on the ranch. It'd been a solid reminder of how idyllic his childhood had been. As he told them about bottle-feeding a stray calf and climbing hay bales and picking peaches right off the tree to eat and playing in the creek behind the house, skipping rocks and counting turtles, he felt a tug deep in his chest. He was going home. For Mya's sake, he spoke slowly, acting things out, even using pen and paper to draw pictures for her. She liked that best of all, laughing at his sorry attempt at a turtle.

They'd packed up, picked up Mya's medicine and

headed down I35 then over to highway 281, which was a straight shot to Granite Falls.

"It's so green," Skylar said for the fiftieth time. "And all the flowers."

"They must have had a wet fall and winter to get the wildflowers blooming like this." He was pleased Skylar and the girls were seeing his home at its best. Either side of the highway was lined with waving bluebonnets, dancing black-eyed Susans, and the vibrant red, orange, and yellow blooms of the Fire-wheel. "Nothing like seeing the wildflowers in full bloom. I'm partial but, to me, there's no place pret-tier."

Skylar smiled at him. "I bet it's good to be home?"

He nodded. It would be. His conversation with Hayden had been short and to the point but, luck-ily, there'd been no hint of animosity. If anything, Hayden had seemed legitimately pleased to hear from him. It gave him hope that Skylar was right. Once he'd apologized for being a stubborn-ass kid, he and Hayden might be able to start fresh.

He passed the exit for Granite Falls, drove a few more miles, then off onto the farm-to-market road that led to the ranch.

"How long has it been?" Skylar asked. "Since you were home last, I mean?"

He paused, racking his brain. "At least…four years." He frowned. "Too long." He glanced her way. He'd cho-sen not to see his family while she'd lost hers.

Skylar was studying him, without judgment—

more considering than anything else. "If there's anything I can do, let me know. Even if it's just talking. I'm a good listener."

He smiled. "I appreciate that." And he did, too. Between the falling-out with his brothers and then Chad's death, it had been hard to open up to people. Easier to stand on his own two feet. But Skylar's offer felt different. "Ditto. If you ever need a sounding board, I mean."

Skylar nodded.

"Are we there, Momma?" Brynn asked from the backseat. "We home?"

Kyle chuckled. "Almost…" He stretched out his words, the gate to the ranch in sight. "Almost…" He turned, the gravel crunching under his tires. "Now."

"Now?" Brynn repeated, clapping her hands. "We here!"

Kyle nodded. "All the way down the bumpy road. Tell me when you see a house." It might have been his imagination but Skylar seemed to sit up, too. Nervous or excited? He wasn't sure. But a sideways glance showed her hands clasped, tightly, in her lap. He understood. Oh, so well. He was thankful for the girls then—thankful he had little eyes watching and taking cues from him.

In the rearview mirror, he saw Brynn leaning one way then the next, staring out the windows with wide eyes and an equally wide smile. He saw the house first, but he waited.

Brynn's inhale and squeal, followed by her cheery,

"I see it! I see it! I see it, Kyle!" She was clapping. "Mya." She patted her sister's arm. "Look." She pointed out the window.

Mya nodded as she stared, wide-eyed, at the house.

"It's… That is your home?" Skylar asked, a mix of shock and apprehension. She cleared her throat. "It's much larger than I'd imagined."

It was impossible for him to see it as anything other than his childhood home. He supposed it was large but the previous generation of Mitchells tended to have lots of children. His parents stopped at three. At the moment, he was thankful for the extra room. Losing the bunkhouse made housing options for Skylar and the girls tricky, but his place should work. It was rustic, no denying, but still a step up from where they were coming from. If Skylar wasn't agreeable to it, then they had the option of staying here.

"I should have told you earlier but I didn't want to upset you or make you change your mind about coming. Hayden told me the bunkhouse was lost to a tornado. There's plenty of room so you don't need to worry about a thing, I promise." He smiled at her, hurrying on to add, "My home is away from the main house. It's pretty cool—one of the original structures on the ranch. They call them dogtrot, or breezeway houses. It's been built onto, of course, so there's plumbing and electric and all the modern amenities of home. No outhouses required."

"I see what you did there, Kyle, but you didn't distract me." Skylar's gaze fixed on him, a tiny crease forming between her brows. "Your house?"

He nodded. "My place is like an old-time duplex. I'll keep to my side—you won't even know I'm there." Which was a bit of an exaggeration.

"I didn't mean that." She shook her head. "I didn't think we'd be taking up space in your home. I'd imagine you'd like some peace and quiet and privacy and—"

"Skylar," he interrupted. "I'll have my own room. That's more privacy than I've had in a few years." He grinned. "Besides. You might need an extra hand now and then." He broke off, realizing his mistake the minute her jaw locked up. "If you're okay with that?" He hoped like hell he'd smoothed things over. "Hayden says there's room in the big house."

The crease between her brows deepened.

"I should have told you." He shook his head. "I'm sorry."

"Yes, you should have…" Her sigh was resigned. "But I think I understand why you didn't. I accept your apology—as long as you don't keep anything else from me. Deal?"

"Deal." But it took effort to say the word. He was already keeping something from her and he was pretty sure knowing he'd played a part in Chad's death wasn't something she could forgive. And even if he was going to tell her, he wouldn't do it now. She and the girls deserved to settle in before he pulled the rug out from under her again. He swallowed hard.

"You pick where you want to stay, Skylar. It's up to you." He peered at the girls in his rearview mirror. "But if you stay at the big house, I'll be bored with all my peace and quiet and privacy and come looking for some company."

She rolled her eyes, but she was smiling. "Well, hanging out with my girls will definitely keep you from being bored."

He chuckled, relieved. In the last couple of days, a bond had been forged between the two of them and, now that he was parking in front of his family home, he was surprised how reassuring it was to have her at his side.

"Breathe," she said, patting his hand. "They're your family. Whatever happened is in the past. You have a chance at a fresh start here, Kyle."

He caught her hand in his, giving it a squeeze. As brief as the touch was, it left a thousand tiny prickles playing along the end of every nerve. "We both have a chance."

She swallowed, her big brown eyes locked with his, as she nodded. "Thanks to you."

He blew out a long slow breath, hoping to chase off the electric current running along his hand and the knot rising up in his throat—a knot that grew rock-hard the moment the front door opened. All at once, his mother, brother, and a woman who had to be his brother's wife, Lizzie, were on the front porch. The urge to bail out of his truck and hug his mother and brother close was damn near overpowering. He'd been through some shit. Some ugly, nasty, burned-into-his-brain things he'd come to terms with. It had been this—the fear of losing his family—that he'd never been able to accept. After all the ugly, nasty things, he knew how dark and lonely life could be. That wasn't the life he wanted.

"Welcome home," Skylar said, resting her hand on his forearm. "They look happy to see you." She paused. "You look happy to see them."

"I am." But he couldn't move. He could only sit and stare.

If Greer hadn't erupted into a mass of tears and wailing, he'd probably have remained rooted in his seat, worrying over what to say and do. *Little Greer to the rescue.* He was out of the truck, opening the back door, and unbuckling Greer before he'd thought to let Skylar handle it. In a way, soothing Greer would soothe him. Besides, nothing galvanized a group of adults like a baby needing comfort.

"Oh, poor darling thing." His mother was instantly at his side. She stood on tiptoe, wrapped her arms around him and pressed a kiss to his cheek. "I'm glad you're home, son. So glad. Now let's get this little sweetheart taken care of, shall we?"

"Thanks, Mom." He smiled down at her. She looked just the same as he'd pictured her. All smiles, bright eyes, and warmth. "It's good to be home." And it was, so much that his chest grew heavy and ached all at once. He shifted Greer, still crying, so that she was upright against his shoulder—patting her back with a steady rhythm—the way he'd seen Skylar do.

"Who is this tiny thing?" his mother asked, immediately transfixed by Greer.

"This is Greer," he said, holding the baby so his mother could see her. "She's the youngest. Brynn and Mya are in the…"

"Right here." Skylar stood, holding on to her girls' hands. "This is Mya." She wiggled Mya's arm. "She's deaf and learning sign language so we do a lot of charades. And this is Brynn."

"That's me. I hear," Brynn said. "And I can talk."

"And you're all adorable. Just adorable." His mother was all smiles. "You must be Skylar?"

"Yes, ma'am." Skylar let go of Brynn and held out her hand. "Skylar Davis."

"Jan Mitchell. Please, call me Jan." His mother shook her hand. "It's so good to meet you and your girls, Skylar. This is my son Hayden and his wife, Lizzie." She smiled. "And Weston, who's turning two next week, will be up from his nap soon. He will be so happy to have some playmates."

Kyle watched Skylar and the girls—not wanting the reunion with his brother to be a big deal. In a way, he wished they'd had a chance to get all the awkwardness out of the way without an audience.

"It's nice to meet you," Lizzie said, her gaze bouncing his way. "You, too, Kyle." She had no qualms closing the distance and hugging him and Greer. "It's good that you're home."

He chuckled.

"Hayden's been pretty nervous," Lizzie whispered, then stepped back. "Can I help with anything? Or anyone?"

But Kyle, still bouncing Greer, was looking at his big brother. Hayden? Nervous? About what? He was the one who'd messed things up, not Hayden. He was the one who'd pushed back, no matter what Hayden said or did. Why was Hayden having such a hard time making eye contact and looking so uncomfortable?

"Can I take her?" his mother offered. "If that's all right, Skylar?"

Skylar nodded. "I'm sure Kyle would appreciate it. She's getting a little too attached to him."

The comment caught him off guard. *Kyle would not appreciate it.* He was perfectly fine with Greer getting attached to him since he was pretty damn smitten with her. Not that he said a thing. He nodded, carefully shifting Greer from his arms to his mother's—and instantly feeling exposed and vulnerable.

But his big brother was studying him, almost hesitant, and Kyle didn't see much point in delaying. He stepped forward, hand outstretched, and the damn lump in his throat all but closing off his windpipe. "Hayden."

Hayden surprised him by pulling him into a hug. Not some one-armed man hug, but a real hug. The sort of hug that added more pressure to his chest and made the lump in his throat razor sharp. "You good?" Hayden asked, still hugging him. "You home for good?"

Kyle nodded, whatever words stuck on the other side of the lump.

"I'm glad." Hayden released him just as quickly.

"How about we all have some lunch?" their mother said. "Afterward, we can look into getting everyone settled. How does that sound?" she cooed, smiling down at Greer. "Are you hungry, little one?"

Greer blew bubbles in response.

"Need help bringing things in?" Hayden asked. "I remember, babies come with a lot of…stuff."

She glanced at the truck bed, uneasy. "No." She spoke quickly. "Not really. I can get Greer's bag." Her gaze met Kyle's.

He glanced at the truck bed, wishing he knew what was troubling her. "I'll get it, Skylar." He nodded.

"There now, see. Let the boys take care of it and we'll get these little ladies fed, shall we?" His mother was cooing as she spoke, so caught up in Greer that she didn't pick up the way Skylar stiffened.

"I'm hungry, Momma," Brynn said, cementing Skylar's fate. "Jet is hungry, too."

"Okay," Skylar said, smiling down at her daughters. "Let's get something to eat."

"I'll bring Jet along, Brynn," Kyle said, smiling at the little girl's thumbs-up.

With a final glance at the truck, Skylar followed

his mother and Lizzie into the house. Leaving him and Hayden alone.

"You look tired," Hayden said, giving him a once-over.

"Last night was a little rocky." He shrugged, heading to the rear of the truck. "Come on, Jet," he called, giving the dog's back a reassuring pat. He and Jet went around to the side of the truck bed and he reached in, when he figured out what was bothering Skylar.

"Smart." Hayden eyed the trash bags. "Keep things dry. The rest of their things coming later on with movers?"

Kyle paused, considering. "She wouldn't thank me for telling you, but this is everything those girls have in the world. Right here."

Hayden's eyebrows rose but he only nodded.

"This is a good thing, for her." Kyle swallowed. "For all of them. Thank you for letting me—"

"There is no *letting* you do anything, Kyle." Hayden ran a hand over his face—a familiar gesture that almost made Kyle smile. "This is your home. If you want Skylar and her girls here, then they're more than welcome." He cleared his throat. "I know what you're doing would mean the world to Chad."

"To Chad, *they* were the whole world." Kyle's gaze bounced from his brother to the truck bed and the girls' meager belongings. He didn't know what the hell he was doing but he was trying. He had to, didn't he? Somewhere along the road, it'd become more than honoring the promise he'd made to Chad. He was invested now—in Skylar and the girls. Knowing they were safe and happy mattered to him. *They* mattered to him.

Chapter Seven

"I can't get over it," Skylar said, leaning against the back-porch railing, a spring breeze lifting her hair and cooling her neck.

"Over what?" Kyle asked, handing Mya a pink crayon. He sat, holding a large box of crayons, while Mya and Brynn lay on the porch, lost in the pages of the coloring books Delores and friends had provided with the care package from the hotel.

Skylar wasn't sure which was prettier: the rolling green fields dotted with vibrant wildflowers or Kyle, cross-legged and attentive, and her girls. She smiled and stooped to pat Jet on the head. "How beautiful it is here."

Kyle nodded. "And green?" His eyes met hers.

When Kyle smiled, it lit up his whole face. "I think I mentioned that a time or two."

"Did you?" She shrugged, shooting him a smile. "I don't remember."

Kyle's gaze dipped to her mouth just long enough for her breath to waver.

"I'm taking it, things weren't so green where you came from?" Jan asked, looping some yarn around her knitting needle.

"No, ma'am." Skylar turned her focus on Greer—not Kyle—who was still sleeping peacefully in Weston's hand-me-down infant bouncing seat, before returning to the peaceful view. "Not green at all."

Jet yawned, stretched, and glanced at Sierra and Charley—Lizzie and Hayden's dogs, already snoozing on the porch. Charley and Sierra weren't in the least bothered by a new dog's arrival, but Jet was still reticent. So far, he'd ventured a few sniffs and circled the other dogs a few times—before promptly returning to her, the girls, or Kyle.

Skylar understood the feeling. While everyone had been more than welcoming, she couldn't quite shake off the too-good-to-be-true vibe of it all. She couldn't help feeling that, at any minute, something would come along and snatch all of this away. Life had been so difficult for so long, it was hard to let go of the knot of doom twisting her stomach.

"Green," Brynn said, holding up the crayon. "Pretty pretty green."

"Exactly." Skylar nodded, then crouched by Mya.

"Green." She pointed at the crayon, then made the sign for *green*.

Mya nodded. "Gree," she repeated, her voice thick. She made the sign.

Skylar nodded, gave her a big smile, then kissed her forehead. "Perfect."

"She can speak?" Jan asked.

"Some. She lost her hearing about eight months ago after catching meningitis. For a while, I thought we might lose her, too." She stroked the curve of her daughter's cheek, giving Mya a wink. "But Mya is tough stuff."

"Like her momma," Kyle added, offering Skylar a brown crayon.

Skylar sat on the porch, took the crayon, and leaned forward to color with Brynn—while taking care to avoid making eye contact with Kyle. "I'll take that as a compliment."

"It was meant as a compliment." There wasn't a hint of teasing to his voice.

She glanced at him—that crooked grin of his—then back at the coloring book. For a minute, the lines and details of the princess dancing with woodland animals became blurred and wobbly. But, after a few blinks and the cold nudge of Jet's nose against her side, she snapped out of it. With any luck, she'd manage to ignore the uptick of her heart rate and the swirl of warmth in her belly caused by Kyle's crooked smile.

It wasn't the first time she'd been thrown by her

reaction to the man. Initially, she'd tried to write it off as gratitude. After all, he was the first person to show her true kindness in so long. But now, other things were getting to her. Like the deep timbre of his voice. The earthy scent of him that lingered on Greer's onesies when he'd held her close. The way the corners of his eyes crinkled when he smiled—how it made his whole face smile. He was handsome, that was plain to see. And then…there was his body. *I need to get a handle on this.* On the heart thumps and tingles and warmth and all the things she shouldn't be feeling.

"Blue?" Brynn asked, holding out the powder-blue crayon. "Like sky."

Skylar took the crayon and leaned back, once again staring out at the landscape, mesmerized by the natural beauty and depth of color from the land below to the endless sky overhead.

"An' Kyle's eye. One of 'em," Brynn said. "Momma." She tugged on Skylar's T-shirt until she had her mother's attention. Sure enough, Brynn was holding up a deep blue right by Kyle's face. "See?"

Skylar nodded.

"All the boys have brown eyes," Jan said, her knitting needles continuing to clack. "Kyle is special. One brown, one blue. As bright and blue as the Texas sky."

Kyle rolled his eyes then. He made sure to make a production out of it, too, so Mya was in on the joke.

Brynn and Mya giggled—which was all it took to

make Skylar smile. If there was one thing her time with Uncle Frank had taught her, it was to enjoy the little things.

Jan Mitchell was laughing, too, the clicking of her knitting needles paused. "Now that's a happy sound."

Kyle's rich chuckle ignited a rapid-burning fuse down the length of Skylar's spine.

"What's so funny?" Hayden asked, coming out the back door with an adorable sleepy-eyed little boy on his hip.

"I'm assuming Kyle was making faces, at my expense." But Jan wasn't reproaching him, she rolled her eyes—the same sort of eye roll that had started the gigglefest, thanks to Kyle.

But Kyle was up now, regarding his nephew with a mix of trepidation and affection. "He's a handsome little cowboy."

Weston hugged his father, pressing his cheek against Hayden's shoulder.

"This is Uncle Kyle," Hayden said. "He's big and scary-looking, but he's not so bad."

"Kyle's not scary," Brynn said, her face squished up in confusion. "Kyle is nice."

"You heard her," Kyle said, winking at Brynn. "You can't argue with that."

"Mr. Hayden is teasing Kyle, Brynn," Skylar explained. "Being silly. Like you and Mya. Kyle and Mr. Hayden are brothers."

"Oh," Brynn said, staring back and forth between

the two men. "Who's that?" she asked, her eyes locking on Weston.

"This is Weston," Hayden said.

At the sound of Brynn's voice, Weston had straightened. Now he was leaning forward, craning around Kyle to see the girls.

"Down," Weston said, patting his father on the chest. "Down, Da."

"Down, please?" Hayden asked.

Weston nodded, still staring at the girls.

Skylar sat watching the three of them. The girls stood, setting aside their crayons, to stare at the toddler. Weston, tall for almost two, stared right back.

"Weston." Kyle crouched between the girls. "This is Brynn." He put his hand on Brynn's shoulder. "This is Mya." He put his other hand on Mya's shoulder. "Girls, this is Weston."

Mya looked Skylar's way then, a little furrow forming between her brows.

"Weston," Skylar said, slowly, spelling his name. She paused, deciding on an easier sign, and repeating it several times for Mya.

Mya nodded. "'Kay."

"What was that?" Kyle asked.

"A sign for Weston." She showed him. "This is the sign for *w*. And this is *boy*. Easier than spelling it each time."

Kyle nodded, making the sign.

Mya was quick to correct Kyle's thumb placement but, once he got it, she gave him a big smile and patted his arm.

"Thank you," Kyle said, signing, "Thank you" at the same time.

"Here." Brynn handed Weston a crayon. "Color with us?"

Weston held the crayon but didn't move.

"Come on." Brynn sat, patting the spot beside her. "Come sit, Weston. Color, too."

Weston sat beside Brynn, watching her color.

"Brynn's my little mother, always taking charge," Skylar offered up. "She's used to helping Mya."

"She's a good sister." Kyle nodded, watching the children.

"Had you two met before this week?" Jan asked, her knitting needles still paused as her attention bounced between Skylar and Kyle.

Kyle shook his head.

"Sort of," Skylar said, then laughed. "Maybe not in person. Chad was a letter writer." And she'd read them all to the girls. She wanted them to know their father in some way. "Needle, that's Kyle, was mentioned often. He always had Chad's back." He still did—why else would she and the girls be here?

Jan sat back. "I am so sorry to hear you lost your husband." She swallowed. "The hole in your heart heals some but you'll never stop missing them."

Skylar nodded, tucking her brown crayon back inside the box of crayons.

"Wanna color?" Brynn asked, pushing the coloring book closer to Weston.

Weston grinned, leaned forward, then scribbled all over the page.

Brynn sat back and frowned. "Momma."

"Weston is young, Brynn," Skylar explained. "He might not be able to color in the lines yet."

Brynn held up the coloring book. "Nope. He can't, Momma." She sighed, closed the book, and set it aside, looking disappointed. It was so precious, Skylar had no choice but to laugh. So did the other adults on the porch.

"He does like to play ball," Hayden offered.

"Like Jet?" Brynn asked, standing and taking Kyle's hand. "Can we?" she asked, looking up at Kyle for an answer.

Skylar's heart rose up and lodged in her throat.

Kyle glanced her way, surprised—but not displeased. She could see it in the crinkles at the corners of his eyes. One light brown, the other vibrant blue. *As bright and blue as the Texas sky.*

She nodded and swallowed hard.

"Let's go." Kyle took her hand. "Mya?"

Skylar stood again, and leaned against the porch railing as the girls, Weston, Hayden, Kyle, and all three dogs ran back and forth after the various tennis and rubber balls being tossed in all directions. Between the barking and whistles and laughter, it was clear they were having a good time.

"That right there? That laughter? There is no

sweeter sound." Jan went back to knitting. "I can still remember when it was my boys running around, chasing our old hound dog Old Ben. My boys were pure mischief so it was a good thing that dog had the patience of a saint."

"In the few days he's been with us, Jet has made himself right at home with the girls." She smiled when Jet trailed after Mya, content to be her canine shadow in all the chaos.

"He wasn't your dog?" Jan asked, her needles still clicking.

"No. He was Chad's. He'd adopted him when they were deployed and he asked Kyle to bring him to us." And Kyle had—without giving it a second thought.

Lizzie opened the back door and walked onto the back porch to join them. "Sorry for not coming out sooner. I had to make a few phone calls for work."

"What do you do?" Skylar asked, waving at Brynn.

"I'm the art teacher for Granite Falls High School." Lizzie smiled, sitting in one of the wicker rocking chairs with a sigh. "There's an art show next week and, with Weston's birthday, I'm trying to get everything lined up ahead of time."

"It's the first time we've ever had anything like this in Granite Falls and it's all thanks to Lizzie," Jan explained. "Hayden stole her away from the big city and a big, fancy job and we're all glad he did."

Lizzie smiled at the woman. "I am, too."

"How long have you been married?" Skylar asked, the affection between the two women obvious.

"Ten months," Lizzie said. "I came to adopt Sierra and wound up stranded."

"Thank goodness," Jan interjected. "I always say, things have a way of working themselves out the way they're supposed to. You were supposed to put that smile back on Hayden's face."

Lizzie was staring out at the man in question with pure adoration. "Lucky for me, Hayden came with Weston. Without Weston, it would have been a harder sell to get me to stay here." She laughed.

Skylar grinned. "He is adorable."

"Isn't he though?" Jan shook her head. "The spitting image of my boys. He'll grow up tall and handsome, just like his daddy, you just watch."

Skylar wasn't sure what to say to that. This was all so new that it was hard to wrap her mind around everything that happened the last few days. The fact that this was home now? It was going to take some getting used to.

"Let's get him out of training pants and talking in complete questions, first." Lizzie smiled at Skylar. "Your girls are precious. I don't know how you manage all three of them on your own."

"Chad and I were married six years." Skylar glanced at Greer, who was still sleeping. "But I think, in that time, he was home maybe four months so I guess it's just the way it's always been." Until now, she hadn't really thought about it. "Kyle's been very helpful, Mrs. Mitchell, stepping up without being asked. You raised him right." Mothers needed to hear that sort of thing from time to time. "It's kind of him but I don't want to get too comfortable with it. Relying on his, or your, kindness that is."

She and the girls needed to find their place here. So did Kyle. He'd been gone a long time and, in that time, he'd let relationships go untended. Now he was back, his focus needed to be on those things—on his life—not on being readily available for her. No, she'd managed just fine on her own with Uncle Frank. *We will manage just find on our own here.*

Greer chose that moment to gurgle-squeal, announcing her newly awake state with gusto.

Skylar unbuckled the seat and lifted Greer, smiling as her tiny daughter stretched and wriggled. "Hello, sweetheart." She spoke softly, smiling as Greer reached up for her hair. "Did you sleep well?"

Greer's toothless grin was the best answer.

"I appreciate you being independent and all," Jan said. "Your Chad wasn't blood, but he was Kyle's brother and that makes you family. He protected my boy more times than I'd like to think about, watching over him." Her gaze locked with Skylar's. "I'd like to do the same for you and your girls."

Skylar was so taken aback, she was speechless. Speechless and on the verge of tears. The warmth and sympathy on the older woman's face tugged at some long-forgotten memory of her own mother… "I need to change her," she murmured, carrying Greer inside before she made a scene.

* * *

Kyle heard the thump of the back door and glanced up in time to see the look his mother and Lizzie exchanged. Seconds later, Lizzie was hurrying across the yard to his side.

"I'll help out here if you want to go check on Skylar?" Lizzie nodded in the direction of the house.

"She okay?" He frowned, searching the wraparound porch.

"I don't know. Your mom was being very sweet about all of us being family, through Chad, and Skylar sort of ran inside with Greer to change her diaper." Lizzie paused. "We both feel terrible, Kyle. We didn't mean to upset her."

"No." His chest clamped down hard. *Family. Through Chad.* He ran a hand along the back of his neck. "After losing so much and being on her own so long… I imagine this is a lot to take in."

"Go on," Hayden said. "Make sure she's okay. We'll keep wearing the dogs out." He winked as all three children chased after the dogs, laughing.

With a quick nod, Kyle was across the yard and up the steps, patting his mother's shoulder before heading into his childhood home. There was no sign of Skylar in the cavernous great room or the open kitchen. He headed down the hall and peered into each room, coming to a full stop when he found Skylar standing in the middle of Weston's nursery, holding Greer.

"Skylar?" he asked, softly.

She shook her head but didn't look at him.

While he wanted to respect her boundaries, he couldn't leave her if she was upset. "Hey," he murmured, softly, almost coaxing, as he came around to stand in front of her.

She kept her eyes on the ground. She held Greer facing outward, gently bouncing the wide-eyed baby.

Greer saw him and started kicking, her little hands fluttering, and an excited coo filling the air.

Kyle chuckled. "Now that's the sort of welcome a man could get used to."

Skylar sniffed. "You shouldn't." She sniffed again, brushing past him to lay Greer on the changing table.

Kyle watched her, her words a gut punch, waiting for her to say more.

Silence filled the room—save for Greer's gurgles and squeaks—while Skylar changed the baby's diaper. But when Greer was changed and she was snapped into the onesie that made Greer look like a tiny pink-and-white bumblebee, Kyle couldn't take it.

"Skylar—"

"No, stop, Kyle." She rested her hand on Greer. "I forgot, okay? I forgot what it's like to have a...a family. People who say nice things and do nice things and...*care*."

He stepped closer, wanting less space between them until he could figure out what to say.

"But I know that, just like that—" she snapped her fingers "—it could all be gone. All of it. Everyone is being so nice and welcoming and...and I can't...I

can't stop thinking it's not real. *You're* imaginary—
it's the only thing that makes sense. I mean, look at
you. And all you've done." She shook her head. "And
this has to be a dream which means I'll wake up at
Frank's and—"

"You're awake." He caught her hand. "You and
Greer and Mya and Brynn are never going back to
Frank's." His voice was a little too gruff so he cleared
his throat.

Her light brown eyes darted to him then back to
the carpeted floor.

He placed her hand on his chest, hoping she
wouldn't pick up on how out-of-control his heart
rate was. "I'm real."

"I don't want to rely on…anyone. To be…needy."
She pressed against him, then gripped his shirtfront.

"I know." *Needy* wasn't a word he'd use for Skylar.
Still, he wished she'd rely on him—a little.

"I'm strong. I don't cry or get emotional. I hold it
together." She sniffed, her gaze blazing up at him.
"But I've cried more in the last few days than I have
in…years."

Even with tears on her cheeks and a red-tipped
nose, she was so damn beautiful she took his breath
away. "Maybe you finally felt safe enough to cry?"
If she needed to cry, then he'd hold on to her until
she was done.

She was staring at him now, studying his every
feature. "Safe…" She swallowed, her voice a whisper. "Is what's happening here safe?" The way her

gaze lingered on his mouth and the slight parting of her lips had him holding his breath.

He knew what she was asking. He knew what she was feeling. He was feeling it, too. Deep down. A fluid warmth in his stomach, the sweet ache in his chest, the rapid throb of his pulse, and the hum of energy that skated atop every inch of skin. Every bit of him was zeroed in—laser focused—on every bit of her. Without thought or choice. It just was. *Safe?* He shrugged.

Her grip on his shirt tightened right before she pulled him in and stepped closer. Right before she stood on her tiptoes and he, finally, cradled the curve of her cheek in his palm.

"Momma?" Brynn's voice rang out. "Momma! Momma!"

"I'm here." But Skylar's words were too soft, her gaze unfocused as she blinked.

"Momma?" Brynn's voice changed, instantly alarmed.

Skylar pushed away from him, shaking her head and letting out a sigh. Her gaze darted to his, an almost apologetic smile on her face. Was she apologizing for the near kiss? Or the interruption? He was hoping it was the latter.

"She's coming." His mother's voice was calm. "She's just getting little Greer cleaned up."

He saw Skylar glance at Greer and offered, "I've got Greer." Kyle scooped up the baby.

"Thank you." Skylar hurried from the room, her voice strong and loud. "I'm here, Brynn."

Kyle followed, Greer contentedly making noises and staring around her with wide eyes. "Lots to see, right, Greer?" He smiled, earning a toothless grin from Greer in return.

"My knees," Brynn moaned.

Kyle came around the corner in time to see Brynn, holding Mya's hand, looking forlorn as she stared down at the grass stains on her pants.

"They're green." Brynn drew in a wavering breath. "Will the green wash 'way?"

Skylar crouched. "I'm sure it will." She patted her daughter's cheek. "It's just a teensy little grass stain."

"I have just the thing for that." His mother nodded, turning to head into the washroom off the kitchen.

"It's green." Brynn frowned, still fixated with the smudges on her clothing. "Look, Kyle. Green stuff."

"I've had my fair share of grass-stained knees." Kyle smiled. "My mom has some stuff you can put on that and it will disappear. Just like magic."

"Magic?" Brynn repeated.

"Almost." Kyle chuckled.

His mother reappeared, a spray bottle in hand. "Skylar, if you want to change her, I can treat those spots right now before they have a chance to set."

Skylar nodded and stood. "Thank you. Let's get your clothes, girls." She glanced his way.

"Greer is happy as a clam," he said, continuing to bounce the baby. "You need a hand?"

"No," Skylar answered a little too quickly, her gaze lingering on his lips before she spun and led the girls out the front door, and pulled it closed behind her.

"Well." His mother stared after them, a thoughtful look on her face. "I can see why you brought them with you." She turned, smiling at Greer. "They're just lovely. All four of them. Though Skylar..." She broke off, studying his face. "When I lost your father, you three were older. It was hard and I missed him so—I miss him still—but I didn't have three little ones or a little one that can't hear." She shook her head. "I get the sense that she's quite a woman. And, from the little you've said, a woman who could use a fresh start."

He nodded. "She does, Mom. From here on out, she deserves only good things."

The corner of her mouth ticked up. "I know this means the world to Chad. I know he only visited the once but that, and your letters, said all I need to know who he was as a man." She patted his cheek. "I know you must miss him—like Skylar must miss him. It's good the two of you have each other. And those girls, too. You were the two that knew their daddy best, after all. You'll have stories to keep him alive for years to come."

He nodded, the sudden lump in his throat preventing him from saying a word. He hoped that was true. Bringing the girls here would never make up for deserting Chad that day... Nothing could undo that. But he'd do whatever he could to give these girls a sense of who their father was. A good man, a true friend, a loyal and loving father and husband… *The best of us.*

His mother stared up at him, her lower lip wobbling just enough to tell him she was struggling to keep her emotions in check. "I'm so glad you're home, Kyle. It's been too long."

"I know." He cleared his throat, continuing to bounce Greer. "And I'm sorry."

"I didn't say that to make you apologize. You're a grown man—living your life. There's nothing to apologize for." She paused, making a silly face until Greer squealed with glee. "But I'm in no hurry to see you leave, is all." She grabbed Greer's little foot and jiggled.

"I'm not planning on leaving." He smiled down at Greer. "I'm ready to come home. I miss being here and Granite Falls." Until he'd seen Skylar and the girls' living conditions he hadn't realized just how much he loved his home. He had family and roots and the legacy of land to carry on. Now that he recognized how blessed he was, he wasn't about to take it for granted. And now, Skylar and the girls were here too… Nope. He shut that line of thought down. "If that's okay?"

"Of course, it is. Why would you ask such a thing? And Hayden will thank you for it. He's running himself ragged." She patted his arm.

"Says you." He chuckled. "I'll let you know after I talk to him about it."

Her frown was pure disapproval. "You and Hayden and John need to stop letting the past dictate your path forward. You three are my boys. If you were little, I'd make you apologize to each other and hug it out."

Kyle grinned. "I don't see that happening."

Her brows rose. "Don't underestimate the power of your mother, Kyle Andrew Mitchell."

"No, ma'am." He chuckled. "You hear that, Greer?"

Greer stared up at him, smiled, and blew bubbles.

"You look good with a baby in your arms." His mother sighed. "That's another perk of having Skylar and her girls around—practice for a family and babies of your own someday."

The front door swung open and Mya and Brynn came in, assuming a sort of here-we-are pose right inside the door. They'd changed and were both wearing knee-length butterfly-print knit shorts with their bright pink and white shirts. Skylar trailed behind them, pushed the door shut and stood back to watch her girls, wearing an amused smile.

A damn beautiful smile. The sort of smile that woke him up on the inside… He ran a hand over his face. *Of course, the one woman I can picture a future with is the one woman I can't have.* He froze, replaying what he'd just thought. *Where had that come from?* And, more important, was that true? His gaze sought her out until he found her and had his answer. *I'm a damn fool.* A damn fool who would never deserve her.

"We can use the magic spray, now," Brynn said, holding up her stained pants.

"Well, then." His mother nodded. "Why don't you bring those in here, Miss Brynn, and you can help me."

Brynn's eyes went round. "I can?" She glanced at her mother, then Mya. "Mya, too?"

"Of course." His mother waved them both after her, leading the way to her oversize laundry room.

"I hope Brynn doesn't get too carried away with your magic spray." Skylar shot him a look, but was distracted by Greer's excitement as the baby spied her mother. "I can take her now." She held her hands out for Greer. "I know she gets heavy after a while."

"Greer?" He smiled at Skylar. "She's no heavier than a doodlebug."

Skylar laughed. "Doodlebug?" She took the baby, the brush of her silky-soft fingers leaving the hair upright on his forearms. "Are you a doodlebug?"

Greer reached up for her mother, making an assortment of adorable noises.

The back doors opened and Lizzie, Weston, and Hayden came in with all three dogs bringing up the rear. All at once the house seemed busy and crowded. Greer stopped moving, her little eyes bouncing from dog to human to toddler and back again.

"People and dogs everywhere, huh?" Kyle asked.

Skylar nodded. "It's quite a change." She smiled down at Greer. "Isn't it?"

Greer babbled something in answer but before Kyle could clarify whether or not it was a good change, Skylar carried Greer in the direction of the laundry room, the magic spray, and the girls.

"We got your house ready," Hayden said, holding out the key. "You'd left it neat as a pin, so there wasn't much to do."

"It was a little bare, for the girls," Lizzie said.

Kyle hadn't thought that far ahead. "We'll see what's missing and make a trip into town in a day or so. As far as material things, those four were making due with next to nothing." He shook his head. "Thank you. Both of you. I know I sprung this on you and you've got your hands full as it is—"

"We were happy to do it," Hayden cut him off. "We're happy that you're home."

Chapter Eight

Skylar stared out over the night sky, a million diamond stars lighting up the canvas of blue-black. The dim porch light was bright enough to entice moths and beetles, the occasional thump of them hitting the bulb or the flutter of their wings was accompanied by the soothing chirp of the crickets and the regular click of Jet's nails on the boards as he followed her every step.

Greer was in no mood to be soothed. Nope. She was committed to an all-night fussfest.

She'd hoped walking, in the cool evening air, would help. But every time Greer slumped against her in sleep, she'd fight herself awake and begin to cry anew.

"I know it's been a big day," she said, smiling as Jet turned and headed back to the other end of the porch. "Lots of new things. Your sisters love their big new bed." And loved that they got to share. Skylar was equally as thrilled to have a full-size bed to herself. The bedroom they shared was massive and, the best part of it, there were no crates or sleeping bags or lawn furniture in sight. *Not anymore.* "New people. New places. Even new smells…" It was true. The Hill Country smelled of green growing things, dark soil, and wildflowers. Flat Brush smelled of dust and oil—being smack-dab in the middle of oil-drilling territory.

"Is that a bad thing?" Kyle's voice startled her so much that she jumped, almost tripping over Jet, before she steadied herself.

"You shouldn't do that." She sucked in a deep breath. "Sneaking up on me like that."

"I'm sorry." He walked onto the porch, running a hand over his face. "I figured you'd heard me—that I was what had woken her up."

She shook her head, wishing his sleepy voice didn't send a shudder down her spine. "I thought she woke you."

He stepped forward, placing his hand on Greer's back. "She'd never do that."

"No?" She couldn't shake the surge of warmth that rolled over her when his hooded gaze met hers. But, even then, she noted the dark patches under his eyes. "You look tired."

He shrugged.

Skylar patted Greer, knowing he'd never admit she or the girls were to blame—even if it was the truth. Things had been on overdrive since they'd climbed into his truck and left Flat Brush behind. After last night? The hospital and the hotel... Had that really only been last night?

"What?" he asked. "What does that look mean?"

"I was just... So much has happened in such a short time." She paused, staring up at him. "You have plenty of reason to be tired, Kyle." She cleared her throat and added. "Once the girls and I are in a position to find a place of our own, you'll have all the peace and quiet you deserve."

He frowned. "You and Greer aren't disturbing me, Skylar."

The way he said her name sent a jolt from the top of her head to the tips of her toes. *Stop being ridiculous.* Obviously, Kyle wasn't the only one overtired. Still, reacting to him this way only strengthened her determination to get out on their own. "That's because she's being relatively quiet tonight, trust me." She kept patting Greer's back. "You don't think you'll want to have the guys over for cards or a football game? Or...or a lady friend, even."

Kyle chuckled. "A lady friend, huh? Other than you and the girls?"

"That is not the sort of lady friend I was referring to." She walked around him, resuming her pacing. She wasn't going to spell it out for him, they both knew what she meant. But she didn't like the odd twist in her stomach when she thought about Kyle entertaining *that* way…

"And that look you're wearing now? I'm not sure I want to know what you're thinking?" Kyle asked, leaning against one of the stout beams supporting the wraparound roof. "That's some look."

"No look." She tried to brush aside his question and rein in whatever expression was catching his attention. Someone as handsome and young and healthy as Kyle Mitchell should be dating and partying and living it up instead of keeping her company in the dark of night while she walked a colicky baby. Not that she minded the company.

Of all the things she'd missed most at Frank's, it was company.

"You've got a shadow." Kyle nodded at Jet, moving along closely at Skylar's side.

"I guess he couldn't sleep either." She glanced down at the dog and chuckled. "They do toss and turn, don't they?" she asked Jet, his tail wagging in answer.

Brynn and Mya had patted the middle of the double bed they were sharing until he'd jumped up. But her girls were full of wriggles and squeaks and, after they'd dozed off, he'd jumped down to sprawl on the floor between the two beds.

"I'd hoped Greer would fuss herself out," Skylar said. "But I rolled over to see Jet staring, eyes fixed on me, until I got up. Once I was up, he followed me to the crib and hasn't left my side since."

"Guess he's figured out who his people are and how to take care of them." He crossed his arms over his chest, looking rather pleased. "He's a smart dog."

Skylar nodded.

"I remember the day Chad and I spotted him." Kyle squatted, clapping his hands until Jet came to him. "He was skin and bones—covered in sand fleas and limping something horrible. But Chad broke off a piece of jerky for him and that was that—Jet never left his side." He gave Jet a good scratch behind the ear. "He's true-blue. Like Chad." His voice grew gruff, the slight shake of his head making Skylar pause.

What was *he* thinking?

Greer chose that moment to yawn, wriggle, squawk, and stare up at her with wide, startled eyes.

"Did you scare yourself?" Skylar asked, laughing softly as Greer's little eyes closed. She adjusted her daughter, her tiny head resting against Skylar's shoulder. "You can sleep now, sweet girl. Momma and Jet…and Kyle are all here to watch over you." She instantly regretted including Kyle. That, this, had to stop. For now, they'd be roommates, of sort. But once she found someplace else, they'd go. A place to live *and* a car. And Mya's surgery? She didn't want to wait on that…

"There's that face again." Kyle was watching her closely.

"My brain doesn't want to turn off." She hedged. "All the things I need to do. All the things I want to do—for the girls."

"And yourself?" he asked. "You're allowed to do a little something for yourself, too."

"I don't need or want anything." She shrugged. "When do I start my job?"

"You need to call Buzz Lafferty first thing in the morning. Good guy. We went to high school together."

"Buzz?" Skylar asked. "Military?"

He shook his head. "He came to school start of junior high after spending the summer with his grandmother. He said she was on his case about taking care of himself and got sick of his messy hair so she gave him a buzz cut—so close, it was Christmas before he had any real hair back on his head."

Skylar smiled, shaking her head. "Poor kid."

"Nah, he's got a great sense of humor. You'll like him." His gaze shifted to Greer. "She out?"

"Like a light." Skylar nodded. "Finally." She sighed—then jumped at the press of Kyle's warm hand against her back.

"Guess she needed some fresh air." Kyle's voice was pitched low, his gaze fixed on Greer.

But Skylar couldn't get past his nearness. When they were close this way, it was almost like Kyle had cast some invisible net—one she couldn't escape from. Not that she wanted to. If anything, she wanted him to pull her in, closer and closer...

She hadn't realized she was staring at him until he was staring back, eyes blazing and jaw locked. His hand remained against her back but his touch was tense now—more braced than supporting.

She'd pondered their almost kiss more than once. What would have happened if Brynn hadn't called out? She would most definitely have kissed him… that much, she knew. But would he have kissed her back? There'd been a conflicted look on his face— like there was now—that made her uncertain.

Of course, he was uncertain. She swallowed. Their situation couldn't be any more complicated. Well, it could. If she kissed him. If she kissed him, a line would be crossed and then…then what? There was no going back.

Now that he was out of the military, he had a new life to start—rebuilding relationships with his brothers and doing his part on his family's huge ranch. This couldn't have been what he'd imagined. Being saddled with Chad's widow and three little girls. Moves and hospital visits and long car trips and screaming babies… Not the more promising way to spend the first month of his new life.

He'd honored his word—and then some. She would be forever grateful to him. Her gaze swept over his face. Even in the dim light, his features were strong and manly. His thick brows, angular jaw, and full lips…

"I'm not sure what's going on in that head of

yours, but it doesn't look good." His voice remained low, a gruff whisper on the night air.

"I'm…I'm tired." She stepped away.

"And?" he pushed, one eyebrow rising high. "I get the feeling there's more to it than that."

She shrugged.

"Don't want to talk about it?" he asked.

"No." She sighed.

"You don't think it would help?" he asked, looking genuinely concerned.

Admitting that she was weighing the pros and cons of kissing him probably wouldn't help. Not in the least. She pressed her face to the top of Greer's head, covering her smile. "I don't think so."

His eyes were intently searching—so much that, for a moment, Skylar worried he might actually be able to figure out what she'd been thinking. *Don't be ridiculous.*

And yet…the longer his gaze held hers, the thinner the air between them became. She was acutely aware of each breath she took—of each breath he took. The warmth of his hand against her back radiated across her skin and caused the slightest shudder.

With a slight shake of his head, his other hand came up to cradle her cheek.

The urge to lean into his touch rolled over her, building and rising until there was no other choice.

"I want to kiss you, Skylar," he whispered. "I don't think I've ever wanted anything so much."

She swallowed.

He continued, "But I—"

She pressed her lips against his, silencing whatever reason, likely a good one, that they shouldn't do this. She knew they shouldn't but... He wanted to kiss her. More than anything.

And if she wasn't so caught up in the feel of his lips on hers, the brush of his breath on her cheek, and his soft groan when the kiss deepened, she'd have told him that she knew exactly how he felt. If there was one thing she'd wish for, it was this: kissing Kyle Mitchell until she couldn't remember why it was a bad idea.

Kyle was overcome. This was wrong.

This was Skylar.

Chad's wife.

Chad's widow—thanks to him.

She'd never want him—not once she knew he'd abandoned Chad on the day he died. She'd hate him... She'd hate him even more for *this*.

The realization was as effective as a kick to the gut. Coldness seeped in, warring with the throb of want his body refused to turn away from. With a shudder, he ended the kiss and stepped back. "I didn't mean to do that," he managed.

"You didn't do anything." She blinked, looking as stunned he felt. "I did."

He ran a hand over his face, doing his damnedest not to note the flush on her cheeks and the fire in her eyes. Not to reach out and stroke the softness of her lips…

Skylar blinked rapidly, the rise and fall of her chest slowing the longer they stood staring at one another, lost in their own thoughts.

He was a fool. A damn fool. "Still, it shouldn't have happened. The last couple of days have been one thing after another…" He paused, searching for the right words—any excuse really—to ensure this never happened again. No matter how much he might want it. Or want her. "We're both tired and not think-ing clearly… Or this wouldn't have happened." He could only wish that was true.

"You're right." She nodded, her gaze falling from his. "This… I'm so sorry. I was just… Well…" She shook her head, her gaze falling from his. "But I'm sorry."

"No." He held up his hand. "How about we both agree to forget this ever happened? Pick up tomor-row morning and chalk this up as a dream or some-thing…" As if that was remotely possible.

She nodded.

"Good." Not good. How was he ever going to look at her without thinking about how soft her lips were and how sweet they felt pressed against his.

"I should… Greer's finally sleeping." She headed toward her door, Jet following along closely. "I'll say good-night."

"Get some sleep." He forced himself to smile,

forced himself to act like his whole world hadn't just been tilted on its axis.

But once the door closed behind her, he leaned forward to grip the handrail of the porch.

What am I doing?

Then again, it was not like he had a choice. *No, damn it, that's not true.*

He might not be able to stop the pounding of his heart or the tenderness she stirred but he could damn well stop himself from doing anything about it.

He stared out into the blackness, knowing sleep was more impossible than ever. Sleep, for him, was a rarity anyway. Normally, his nightmares woke him. Not a nightmare so much as memories. Hellish and inescapable and all the worse because they were real and there was no changing the outcome.

And every damn night he was stuck right back in the middle of it all.

The day Chad died.

Waking up in the infirmary with Jet at his side and knowing something was wrong. Running down the hall—an endless hall—and out under the cloudless sky and blistering sun just in time to see the Humvees roll in. Things slowed then, magnifying every detail until he could taste the dust from the spray of the tires and feel the triple-digit heat searing his skin. The urgency with which everyone was moving slowed more and more… By the time Chad was pulled from the rear of the vehicle, everyone around Kyle was almost at a standstill. He moved normally, pleaded for them to hurry—to do something while Chad was still breathing.

Kyle pushed off the railing, the fury and self-loathing all but crushing his chest.

He'd left Chad alone, made Skylar a widow, and now he thought it was okay to kiss her? He had no right. None. It wasn't okay. It was anything but okay. What he was thinking and feeling was *wrong*. He'd promised Chad he'd take care of Skylar and the girls—not try to take his place.

He ran a hand over his face, headed inside, and turned on the ancient laptop he'd left behind.

Taking care of the girls meant taking care of Mya. Skylar was eager to get her in to a hearing specialist—someone who could assess whether or not Mya was a candidate for a cochlear implant.

I can do that.

He opened the internet, the connection slow going, and started researching options. Around three in the morning, his eyelids closed on him.

He woke three hours later, to the tug of a little hand on his sleeve.

"Kyle," Brynn whispered.

Kyle sat up, the crick in his neck and dull throb in his back from sleeping hunched over the table instantly eased at the sight of Brynn's sweet smile. "Morning, Brynn."

Brynn smiled. "Morning. Momma made pancakes."

"She did?" He yawned, rolling his head.

"Want some?" she asked, stepping back and waving him toward her. "Momma said come on."

Kyle repeated, smiling, "She did?"

"Hurry hurry." Brynn nodded, grabbing his hand and tugging until he'd stood and followed her down the open airway, to the add-on kitchen and eat-in dining room.

Sure enough, there was Skylar flipping pancakes on an electric hot plate.

Greer sat in her infant car seat, braced securely on top of the table, while Mya stood on a stool beside Skylar, watching everything her mother did closely.

"He's here, Momma," Brynn announced.

"You didn't wake him up?" Skylar asked, turning. But she took one look at him and sighed. "Brynn, honey, did you wake him up? Poor Kyle needs his sleep."

Brynn's lower lip flipped out.

"No, I was waking up." Kyle jumped in, that lip flip reaching right inside his chest and giving his heart a hard and fast tug. "She didn't wake me." He winked at Brynn.

Brynn grinned.

"Uh-huh." Skylar didn't buy it, but she didn't argue. She turned back to the pancakes. "The kitchen is stocked with enough for a nice breakfast and lunch but I should probably head into town for groceries before too long." She paused. "Or we…since I don't have a vehicle. Yet."

He liked the determination in her voice. He liked the way Greer lit up and cooed, more like squealed, when he took her little foot and wiggled it. He liked the way Mya waved and Brynn took his hand to lead him to a chair at the table.

He liked all of it.

Being here, with them. It felt like home.

And that was the problem.

"I did some research last night," he said, wishing he'd shaved or changed his shirt or generally cleaned himself up a bit. "On doctors—for Mya."

Skylar turned, spatula upright, to look at him with those big brown eyes. "You did?"

"Figured I should do something productive with my time and since this was something that needed to be done… I hope you don't mind." He wasn't sure what else he'd been planning to say. Once Skylar started smiling at him that way, her smile was pretty much all he registered.

"Momma's pretty," Brynn said. "Her smile."

"She sure is," Kyle agreed. "How do you say pretty?"

Brynn shrugged and both he and Brynn turned to look at Skylar, expectant.

"I'm not sure." Skylar turned back to the pancakes, sliding a stack from the hot plate onto one of the plates waiting on the counter.

"Sounds like we need to find out." Kyle stood. "Can I help?"

"No." Skylar handed him a plate. "Thank you.

We've got this." She smiled at Mya. "Mya likes cooking."

"These look good." He made a big production out of rubbing his stomach until Mya was laughing. "Thank you," he said, signing for Mya.

Mya nodded.

A pancake breakfast meant puddles of syrup, laughter, and Jet cleaning up dropped bits of food within seconds of it hitting the floor. Thanks to the girls, the dog had plenty to eat.

Afterward, Kyle cleaned up—insisting Skylar sit still while he and Brynn hand washed the few dishes they'd used.

"We're taking turns, Momma," Brynn said.

It was hard for Skylar to sit—he could tell. But all the more reason for her to do just that. When was the last time someone had cleaned up? Or cooked for her? Frank didn't look like the sort to pitch in and take turns. Frank Kline was a selfish bastard...and not worth wasting energy on. Besides, Kyle wanted to enjoy this morning—enjoy the girls and Skylar and the simple pleasure of one another's company.

"Done?" Brynn asked, bringing him back to the present. His kitchen—full of laughter and busyness.

"What do you think?" Kyle asked, looking at Brynn.

Brynn stood on the stool, her wide eyes sweeping the kitchen for anything they might have missed.

"Your cup?" she asked, grabbing on to his arm to step down.

"I think Kyle might need more coffee," Skylar said, her gaze fixed on him.

"I think Kyle does need more coffee," he agreed.

"I'll get it," Brynn offered.

Kyle scooped her up, off her feet, and spun her around. "I appreciate that, Brynn, but if you got burned by my old coffee, I'd never forgive myself."

Brynn was giggling and breathless. "Okay."

He set her down and headed for the coffeepot. From the corner of his eye, he saw Mya flipping through the pages of a colorful illustrated book titled *Basic Sign Language for Communication*.

He poured himself another cup of coffee and sat beside Mya, reading over her shoulder.

It was straightforward enough stuff. A picture, the word, then the sign. As bright as Mya was, he was pretty sure she wasn't reading. But, for the most part, the pictures did the job.

"This is from her old audiologist," Skylar said, Greer propped in her lap. "It's well-read."

"Nice doctor," Brynn said from the floor. She lay on her stomach, face-to-face with Jet—whispering to the dog. "Aw-di-owl-o-gist."

Kyle nodded. "Sounds about right to me."

"He had lollipops," Brynn said, smiling.

"That was a treat." Skylar nodded.

"Lollipops, huh?" he asked. "Your daddy loved lollipops, too. Did you know that?"

Brynn sat up, shaking her head.

"He always had a little bag of them—the little ones that tasted real sweet. Pineapple, root beer, cherry, all sorts."

Skylar nodded. "We mailed a bag with every care package. Do you remember?" She waited, her smile almost slipping when Brynn shook her head. "Well, we did. And he loved getting the care packages we sent him."

"Can we send one to Daddy in Heaven?" Brynn asked.

Kyle stared into his coffee cup, feeling like an ass for bringing up Chad. If he'd stopped and thought things through, he'd have realized she was too young for this. At the very least, he should have asked Skylar for permission.

"Sorry," he murmured, his gaze meeting Skylar's.

Skylar placed her hand on his. "Don't be. I want them to know their father. You spent more time with him than…than anyone. Me, included." There was no bitterness in her voice. Only sadness.

"Can we, Momma?" Brynn repeated, stroking Jet's head—who'd moved closer for that very purpose.

"I wish we could, Brynn, honey." Skylar smiled. "But I bet he's watching over you right now."

Brynn looked up at the ceiling, turning a doubtful gaze their way.

Kyle had to chuckle then.

The knock on the door was unexpected. All at

once, Jet barked, Greer squealed, and Brynn jumped up—jostling Mya in her seat and triggering tears.

The door opened to his mother.

"I am so sorry." His mother immediately crouched between Mya and Brynn. "I'm sorry," she repeated, adding the sign for *I'm sorry*, too.

Mya wiped the tears away with the back of her hand and said, "'Kay." She smiled at his mother, scooched over in her chair so Brynn could climb up beside her, and the two of them went back to studying her book.

"Good job, Mom." He grinned. "With the signing. I'm impressed."

"Well, I can't bear for Mya to feel left out." His mother brushed aside his praise. "I'm not too old to learn something new."

Skylar smiled. "You're very thoughtful, Jan."

"Not at all." His mother wasn't one for flattery.

"And for stocking the kitchen, too. We had pancakes for breakfast," Skylar added.

"I was wondering if you'd eaten." His mother took in the clean kitchen in wonder.

"Brynn and I washed up," he said.

"Well now. I guess you did most of the work, eh, Brynn?" His mother winked at the little girl.

Skylar laughed along with his mother. He wasn't sure why they both thought her joke was so hysterical, but he let it go. Laughter was a good thing and something Skylar and her girls had too little of.

"I wanted to see if you'd like to go into town with

me?" his mother asked. "We can go to the grocery store and, if you'd like, there's a lovely little resale shop downtown that might have a few things the girls might enjoy?"

Kyle watched the indecision on Skylar's face. "If it's easier, you can leave the girls with me." He meant it. "I know they've been cooped up in the car a lot the last few days."

Skylar stared at him as if he'd grown another head. "No, no, I couldn't ask you to do that, Kyle."

He sighed. "You didn't—"

"I appreciate it but..." Skylar shook her head. "It's me. I don't feel settled enough to leave them. I know that might not make any sense—"

"It does," he cut her off. Of course, it did. "Well, then, you need an extra set of hands? I'm in need of a few things myself—one of them is a razor." He ran his fingers over the stubble lining his jaw.

"You're welcome to come," his mother said. "We'll take the big van. Hayden was going to the feed store and the lumber yard and he was dropping Lizzie and Weston off at the King Frosty in town. I thought we could have lunch out?" She paused, lowering her voice. "They just added an indoor play place."

Kyle's enthusiasm for their trip into town was fading by the minute. "Oh, gosh, how delightful."

Skylar's laugh was pure and free. And the fact that she kept laughing until she'd wiped an actual tear from her cheek filled him with all sorts of pride.

He'd done that. He'd made this beautiful, composed, independent woman laugh until she cried. He had the feeling today was going to be a good day. How bad could an indoor play place be?

Chapter Nine

Skylar enjoyed every minute of the ride from Mitchell Ranch to Granite Falls. To her, it felt like Mother
Nature had put on her fanciest clothes to make a good
impression. From the crystal blue sky with popcorn
clouds to the fields and roadsides dotted with red and
blue and yellow… And green. Green everywhere.

"You were right," she said to Kyle.

He kept his eyes on the road but answered, "I usu-
ally am. About what?"

She laughed. "The green."

"So bright it almost hurts your eyes." He nodded,
glancing her way. "I was worried I'd misrepresented
things and you might be disappointed."

"Disappointed?" She stared out the window,

watching as Kyle steered the large crew cab ranch truck across the wide four-lane bridge elevated high over a surprisingly wide river. "What river are we driving over?"

"The Colorado River. Granite Falls Lake is a reservoir of the river. The dam, Gresham Dam, was built by the Corps of Engineers—one of the work projects following the Great Depression. Of course, it was overhauled in the 1950s."

"Of course," Skylar teased, shaking her head.

"Are you teasing me? Most folk would love their own personal tour guide to give them the who's who and what's what for these parts." Kyle paused. "Come to think of it, I'm probably a little rusty on most of it."

"Well, if you are, I wouldn't know. You sound like an expert."

"That's me." He chuckled. "Glad my mother decided to take her truck. That way if we decide to go down to the shoreline to feed the ducks we can. If you think they'd like it?" Kyle asked, coming to a stop at a red light midway across the bridge.

"I'm sure they would." So would she.

"If you and the girls would like, we could take out a little fishing boat? Not today—but next time we head into town." He waited for her to nod before adding, "Might even bring my fishing pole. Catch and release, of course. Wouldn't want to upset the girls."

Every single time Kyle said something like that— something thoughtful and sweet and selfless—

Skylar's heart took flight. It wasn't intentional. If she could choose not to react to him, she would. But she was beginning to accept that reacting to him was as instinctual as breathing...

"Ducks today. Fish next time." He glanced in the rearview mirror and smiled.

That smile. She drew in a deep breath. "Let's see how tired we all are when we're done with that list." It wasn't exactly a no, but it wasn't a yes either. One thing was certain: spending more time with Kyle would only...encourage these feelings for Kyle. Considering the effect his smile had on her, she should be going out of her way to spend less time with Kyle Mitchell.

"Sounds fair enough." He made a face in the rearview mirror, earning giggles from the backseat.

"Momma, Momma," Brynn announced. "High up."

Skylar turned, patting her daughter's knee. "We are. Isn't it pretty? Look at all the water."

Brynn wasn't so sure she liked what she saw.

Mya, whose seat was buckled in behind Kyle's, was staring out her window wide-eyed and smiling.

"Fish?" Mya asked, peering at Skylar.

Skylar nodded.

"Big fish," Kyle said.

"Big," Skylar repeated, holding out her hands for scale.

"Big." Mya nodded and went back to looking out the window.

Skylar smiled. "There are times I've almost forgotten what her voice sounds like." She swallowed down the lump so thick and hard it hurt. "She's careful now, about who she talks in front of." She risked a look Kyle's way.

He was smiling from ear to ear. "I get the feeling I've been accepted. Brynn makes sure to feed me and helps me clean up. Mya talks and laughs at me. You...cry on me."

"And Greer adores you." The words were out before she'd considered them.

"I knew it." He winked at her.

The bridge road turned into Main Street. According to Kyle's ongoing narration, Granite Falls was a Main Street city, the central road cutting right through downtown and becoming an interstate highway ten miles on the other side of Granite Falls city limits.

It wasn't just the region that was beautiful, the town was, too. Kyle said it was one of the fastest-growing regions in the Texas Hill Country and Skylar could see why. Main Street was lined with picture-window storefronts, quaint hand-painted signs, black wrought iron streetlamps, and cobblestone sidewalks.

"It's...it's like a Norman Rockwell painting." Skylar smiled, laughing when a perfectly restored 1950s' Chevrolet passed them by.

"One thing about Granite Falls, it's constant." Kyle's attention strayed to the sidewalks. "There was a time that consistency was boring and I couldn't wait to get out of here. But now, well, there's a comfort in finding a place—for all intents and purposes—unchanged."

Skylar nodded. "It's good to have a home base."

Kyle looked at her then, almost apologetic.

"What?" she asked.

"That was careless." He shook his head. "Here I've been going on about running away from a home I should be thankful for and…"

Skylar understood then. "We don't have a home base?" She sighed, staring out at the town. "Maybe we do."

"Momma," Brynn called out. "Where we going?"

"We're going shopping." She smiled into the backseat.

"For food?" Brynn asked, bouncing her legs.

"And some other things, too." Until they spoke to a doctor about Mya and the cost of the surgery and follow-up care, Skylar wanted to be as frugal as possible. "When we're all done, we're going to have lunch with Jan and Lizzie and Weston, too."

"Weston is a baby," Brynn said. "Not like Greer."

"He is older than Greer. But he's also younger than you are," Skylar agreed. "You know what?"

Brynn shook her head.

"He thinks you and Mya are super cool big girls." Skylar watched her daughter process this information.

Brynn nodded. "He's right."

Skylar heard Kyle's chuckle and smiled his way.

"Can't color though." Brynn sighed.

Skylar glanced at Kyle. "She can't let go of the coloring thing," she whispered.

"He did do a number on that page." Kyle's gaze shifted to the rearview mirror again. "I appreciate that she takes pride in her work."

They'd just parked the truck and were unloading the girls when a woman came barreling across the street, laughing and clapping her hands.

"As I live and breathe," the woman said, gleeful. "If it's not Kyle Mitchell, in the flesh." She launched herself, her slim arms twining around Kyle's neck, and her red lips locking with his.

Skylar wasn't sure how to react or what to do except stand there, holding on to her girls' hands and wishing she was anywhere else instead of here, witnessing this. Kyle hugging the woman—hard—as he spun her around. And kissed her back, full on the lips.

"I'd heard you were home, of course." Her arms remained around his neck. "Your momma and my brother and Eileen Doherty. No such thing as secrets in Granite Falls."

"I remember," Kyle agreed. "Something else that hasn't changed, I guess."

"Nothing ever changes in Granite Falls—you know that." The woman pressed her hand against his cheek. "It is so good to see you."

His smile faded a little, his gaze falling from hers.

"Well…" She released him and stepped back,

turning her gaze on to Skylar and her wide-eyed girls. "You must be Chad's widow? And his girls?" She paused. "I thought there were three."

How did this woman know who she was? Or who Chad was? Or how many children she had? *Who* was she? "Greer is still in her car seat." Skylar spoke. "Girls. Hold hands and wait right here." She waited for Brynn to nod before she grabbed the front pack out of the backseat and clipped it on before unbuckling Greer and securing her into the carrier.

"Isn't she just the cutest?" the woman said, stooping forward to smile at Greer.

Greer wiggled and kicked.

"So happy." The woman laughed. "When I heard what you'd all been through, I was astounded. I'm so glad Kyle brought you home with him. Since he and Chad were like brothers, that makes you his sister." The woman shot Kyle a look. "He's never had a sister—before now."

All I'd been through? Skylar tried to ignore the cold knot tightening in the pit of her stomach. Kyle had told someone about Flat Brush and Uncle Frank and Chad; there was no other way for anyone to know any of this. He'd told someone and that person had told someone and now this woman knew? He'd said everyone knew everything about everyone in Granite Falls but she hadn't thought she'd be lumped into that. Now... Well, she couldn't shake the sense of betrayal coiled in her chest.

Kyle's quick and awkward back and forth look between her and the mystery woman didn't help Skylar's growing confusion and agitation. The mystery woman who had perfect hair—not a lopsided ponytail. She wore tan ankle pants and a cute red-and-white-polka-dot ruffle top that hugged curves Skylar would never possess. Unlike Skylar, this woman didn't have a hole under one armpit—or the faintest lingering stains of strained peas on the hem of her well-worn T-shirt.

"I'm sorry." The woman seemed to pick up on the awkwardness. "Where are my manners? I'm Cassandra Lafferty. But everyone calls me Cassie. You're going to be working with my brother, Buzz, aren't you? At the vet clinic."

"Oh, well, I don't—"

"You'll love him," Cassie gushed. "Everyone loves Buzz. He's a barrel of laughs. Kyle couldn't have rescued you at a better time either. Buzz needs all the help he can get at the clinic. I only work there a couple of hours a week, next door at the grooming parlor." She hooked arms with Kyle. "Kyle and I have been sweethearts since, oh goodness, we were knee-high to a grasshopper? Isn't that the saying?"

Kyle's discomfort continued to grow—a telltale red creeping into his cheeks.

"How sweet," Skylar muttered, pleased that she managed to keep the emotional whirlwind taking place on the inside invisible to the outside. She'd get through this. It'd be okay. In the span of three minutes, Skylar had been excited about her job and the move and…everything. But that was before she found out she'd be working with Kyle's sweetheart and Kyle's sweetheart's brother and, most important, that Kyle Mitchell *had* a sweetheart.

As far back as Kyle could remember, Cassie had been the equivalent of a human bulldozer. An upbeat, funny, and sweet-natured bulldozer—but a bulldozer all the same. If he was going to get a word in edgewise, he was going to have to be assertive.

"Cassie, this is Skylar." He turned, wishing Skylar wasn't so good at masking her thoughts. "Skylar, this is my *friend* Cassie." He knew Cassie was teasing. Yes, they had been sweethearts when they were kids but that was ancient history. They'd remained friends for years—partly because he and Buzz were good friends and partly because Cassie wouldn't have it any other way.

"Who dat?" Mya asked, a small frown on her face.

"A friend of Kyle's." Skylar pointed at Cassie, then Kyle, and signed "friend."

Mya nodded, but she still wasn't smiling.

"Cassie and I have been friends since we were kids," Kyle said, needing to set the record straight.

"More than that," Cassie cut in and smiled up at him. "We were married once, too."

Skylar made an odd sound then, shifting from foot to foot and looking at anything but him. "Well…" She offered a slight smile to Cassie. "I'm sure you have lots to catch up on. I'm going to take the girls inside." Skylar led the girls across the sidewalk and inside the Good As New thrift shop his mother thought might have a few things for the girls.

"She's lovely," Cassie said once Skylar and the girls were inside the shop. "A little quiet."

He nodded. "Not everyone is as chatty as you are, Cassie. Didn't anyone ever tell you that?"

She laughed. "Maybe. Once or twice." She paused, glancing at the shop door. "The little girl can't hear?"

"Lost her hearing when she caught meningitis last year." Kyle shook his head. He needed to remember that everything he said would likely be repeated. *Cassie had just proven that.* Skylar wouldn't appreciate other folk knowing or getting involved in her business. It sounded like his mother and Eileen, the foreman's wife, were already sharing more than they should. He'd seen the way Skylar's mouth tightened and understood her anger. This wasn't gossip. This was her life.

"Mrs. Doherty said they were living in poor conditions and you basically rescued them—without a second thought."

Kyle sighed. "That sounds like her." Bobby Doherty was the ranch foreman and a good man. His wife was a character. She was kind and thoughtful but she was also somewhat of a gossip. And since Bobby and his wife, Eileen, shared pretty much everything with each other, it was a near guarantee that anything Bobby knew, Eileen did, too—and went on to share with her bunko friends on Thursday evenings. "All I did was give Skylar an option that wasn't available to her before."

Cassie smoothed a hand over her chestnut-brown hair. "You always had a way with words, Kyle Mitchell."

"How's Mike?" he asked. At least that's what he thought was the name of Cassie's last boyfriend.

"Mike? Mike Smith? Or Jones? Or whatever his name was?" She laughed, but it wasn't a real laugh. "Well, last I heard, he'll be serving a minimum of ten years for a pharmaceutical scam the government didn't like too much."

"Sounds like there's a story there?" He shook his head. "I'm guessing the engagement is off?" he asked, managing to get the words out before he was laughing.

"Ha, ha, very funny." She sighed. "Laugh all you want. Even if Mike hadn't turned out to be a criminal, it wouldn't have worked." She shrugged. "That was strike two for me. Next guy that comes into my life better be the one or I'm out of luck." She winked up at him.

He shook his head. Cassie was an unabashed flirt and a tease—but she was a good friend.

"I might have said this already but…I'm glad you're home." She tilted her head. "You should come to dinner. We have a lot to catch up on. Buzz, too, of course."

"Maybe in a couple of days, Cassie. Once Skylar and the girls get their bearings. I feel responsible for them."

"That's a lot of responsibility." Cassie glanced toward the storefront.

Kyle nodded, then shrugged. "Maybe. But I don't mind."

Cassie studied him for a long time. Her brows slowly rose and her eyes went owl-like until she said, "Kyle Mitchell, have you found your lobster?"

"My what now?" he asked, beyond confused.

"Your soul mate." Cassie rolled her eyes.

Kyle chuckled. "I've never heard it put that way before, Cassie."

"That was a dodge, plain and simple." She was smiling now. "You've got it bad."

"The only thing I've got is a lunch date with my mother at the King Frosty and a triple-bacon cheeseburger." He sighed, knowing what he had to say next would only fuel Cassie's line of thinking. "I'd appreciate if you didn't share *your* lobster theory with anyone. Like you said, no one can have secrets here and I don't want people talking—making Skylar feel awkward or uncomfortable or having people imply that there's anything untoward going on here." He frowned. "There isn't."

"Okay." She nodded, placing one hand on his arm. "I'm sorry. I was teasing. Of course I'd never spread rumors—not about you anyway. You're too important." She patted his arm. "As your first wife, I feel duty bound to protect your good name."

He had to chuckle. "I can't believe you brought up the whole wedding thing."

"Backyard weddings are the best, even when you've got a rag-doll bridesmaid and a dog…"

"Zeus," he said.

"Zeus for a groomsman. Buzz married us, remember? That was when Buzz still thought he wanted to be a pastor so he'd get to tell people what to do and eat a lot of home cooking and everyone had to be nice to him."

"I remember." It was a hazy memory, but a good one.

"Well, I'll let you get to your shopping. If you have time, take Skylar by the clinic before you leave." She shrugged. "Buzz is anxious to meet her and put her to work."

Kyle nodded, gave her a one-armed hug, and entered the resale shop. A quick scan and he found Skylar, bouncing in place to keep Greer happy, while reading over the tag on a small plastic bed.

"Kyle?" A man's voice snagged his attention. "Good to see you, man."

Kyle turned. "Dean." He shook the man's hand. "Running the place now?"

Dean Hodges was one of those all-around solid guys who no one ever had anything negative to say about. He and Kyle had played football together in high school but, once Kyle had left, they hadn't kept in touch.

Dean nodded. "Dad passed last winter and left the place to me." He shrugged. "Family business."

"Sorry about your dad." He'd missed a hell of a lot. Next time he had his mother alone, he needed to get the lowdown on things so he'd be prepared.

"Thanks." He smiled. "What can I do for you?"

"I'm with them." He pointed at Skylar and the girls. "Looks like the girls might have found a few things." Mya and Brynn were having a good time on two beds—Mya- and Brynn-sized beds. *Just what they needed.*

"They yours?" Dean asked. "They sure are cute. Congratulations, Kyle. Family is everything."

"No. No. They're just friends." He nodded. "But you're right. Family is everything. It was good to see you."

Upon closer inspection, Kyle realized they weren't just beds. One looked like a race car and the other a fire truck—and the girls were already climbing in and out, pretending to drive, and having a good old time.

"We getting these?" he asked, smiling at the level of imagination unfolding before him.

Skylar scanned the price tag again. "I don't think so. It can't hurt to let them play for a bit." She glanced at him, then back at the label. "Where's Cassie? I'm sorry. If I'd known… I feel a little awkward—like we were intruding."

"You weren't." He resisted the urge to turn her, so she'd have to look at him. "The thing about Cassie?

She likes to tease. Our *wedding* was back in…second grade?" Was it his imagination or did Skylar look relieved? "I was wearing my astronaut costume from Halloween, if I recall correctly. She wore her mother's robe—and got into a heap of trouble for it, too." He chuckled. "She and Buzz, my brother John and I were a motley crew. Riding bikes all over. Catching grasshoppers. Being kids." He was studying her face. "We are all still friends."

Skylar's posture eased and, for a second, her gaze met his. "You might think you're just friends but I'm pretty sure she'd be happy with more."

Even if that was true, he wasn't interested. "Cassie is…well, she's Cassie. Friends only."

"Beep beep," Brynn said, the steering wheel on the car bed squeaking loudly.

"Watch out, Brynn, don't run me over." He jumped out of the way, in front of Mya.

"Fire truck," Mya announced, patting the bright red plastic bed. "Mine?"

He knew Skylar was struggling with buying the beds. And, from the price on the tag, he suspected it was tied to spending money. But the way Mya's face lit up plus the fact that she used her words made it damn near impossible to refuse the little girl. For him anyway.

He nodded. "Yep."

"Kyle," Skylar murmured, grabbing his arm.

"My mother wanted to get the girls a welcome present. She insisted," he said—which was partly true. His mother said to make sure the girls had everything they needed. If his mother was here, and saw Mya's face, he felt confident she'd see things his way: Mya needed her red fire truck bed.

"Kyle," Skylar tried again. "It's too much."

"A gift. With no strings." He swallowed, seeing the mix of uncertainty and irritation on her face. "If you really feel that strongly about it, I won't push."

But Mya was running her hand along the edge of the bed and smiling from ear to ear—if he had to disappoint her, he'd be devastated.

Skylar sighed, admitting defeat. "This is it, Kyle. No more presents or surprises or doing generous things. Okay?"

"Okay." He gave Mya a wink and a grin. "I'll try to be selfish and demanding from now on."

Skylar laughed. "I don't think you could be either of those things—even if you wanted to."

He liked hearing her say that. "No? Maybe not." He waved back at Brynn, as she honked her horn and spun the steering wheel on her bed car. "I like making them smile. Is that such a bad thing?"

"No." It was a whisper. "I understand. There is nothing sweeter than their smiles."

Except maybe yours. His chest was heavy and warm. "Anything else?" he asked, turning to check out the rest of the inventory—and give him a minute to calm down.

When everything was said and done, the girls had their beds and a wooden chest of drawers Skylar would sand down and repaint. Dean gave them a steep discount and helped him carry everything out and load it into his truck bed.

"You have fun and drive carefully," Dean said to Mya and Brynn.

"Thanks again," Kyle said, shaking Dean's hand.

"Welcome to Granite Falls, Miss Davis." Dean was all smiles for Skylar. "I hope to see you around. If there's anything you're looking for, for the girls, let me know and I'll keep an eye out."

Kyle had no right to get bent out of shape over Dean Hodges's being neighborly. Skylar was beautiful. And single. Why wouldn't Dean notice? Kyle frowned, letting Skylar and Dean chat while he turned to double-check the ties holding the beds securely in place.

"All set?" she asked, opening the back door and letting the girls climb up.

"Yep." He held his hands out for Greer, cradling the baby close while Skylar buckled in the other two. "Happy?"

She turned and stared up at him. "Yes." Her smile damn near blocked out the sun.

He wished he had it in him to resist the pull of those eyes. It'd make things easier if the hum and tug of energy didn't start the moment her eyes locked with his. As it was, he had no choice. Skylar had a hold on him. The real problem was, he didn't mind.

Chapter Ten

Skylar shaded her eyes, watching as Jet trotted ahead of them on the trail that led to the main Mitchell house. It was a short walk from the dogtrot house that they called—for now—their own. The closer they got to the main house, the louder the buzz became. Skylar drew in a deep breath. It was a birthday party and birthday parties meant people and music and being social. It was the social part that they were all still adjusting to.

"What's happening, Momma?" Brynn asked, her pace slowing as the Mitchell backyard came into view.

Balloons, streamers, and festive banners were strung along the roofline of the large wraparound porch. Tables covered in plastic tablecloths with cute little cowboys, horses, cacti, and horseshoes. Folding chairs were grouped around the large fenced back-yard, chairs occupied by a sea of strange faces.

Mya let go of Skylar's hand and stood behind her legs.

Skylar crouched to look her girls in the eye. "It's Weston's birthday today. He is two years old. And since it's his birthday, remember? He's having a party. And we're invited, too." She nodded at the brightly wrapped box Brynn held, smoothing the front of Mya's blue dress. "That's why we bought him that present, remember?"

"For color practice?" Brynn asked.

Skylar chuckled. "That's part of it."

"He needs help, Momma." Brynn peered around her shoulder. "That's lots of peoples."

Skylar glanced back over her shoulder, too. "There's Lizzie and Miss Jan and Hayden—"

"Kyle!" Brynn called out, waving her arm.

Kyle, who'd been talking with a group of unfamil-iar people, turned and waved back. In his starched blue button-down, creased jeans, and tan cowboy hat—he was hard to miss. *So handsome.* With a grin, he said something to the group, and jogged across the backyard to the fence and through the gate—send-ing Skylar's heart into overdrive.

"Look at you all." Kyle pressed a hand to his heart. "Prettiest things in the whole state. And Texas is one big state."

Brynn spun. "Our dresses match. Momma said today is a special 'casion." She tugged on Mya until Mya spun, too.

Kyle nodded and knelt, still smiling. "Pretty," he said, making the sign for *beautiful*.

There was something endearing about the way Kyle focused on his finger placement, the angle of his hand and arm, and the deliberate motions he used. From the looks of it, Mya was pretty enchanted, too. She emerged fully from behind Skylar's legs, walked straight over to Kyle and wrapped her arms around his neck.

The look on his face was almost Skylar's undoing. His surprise quickly shifted into something infinitely sweeter. Kyle understood that Mya's hug was a gift to be cherished. He wrapped his arms around Mya with a tender reverence, tearing at the restraints Skylar had placed on her heart.

Kyle Mitchell was a good man and he loved her girls. That should be more than enough for her. Even if she allowed herself to entertain the idea of giving in to her barely controlled attraction for Kyle, she knew the truth. Any relationship between them would be built upon the promise he'd made Chad—out of obligation, not love. *If* she ever opened her heart to another man it would be knowing he loved her—not because he loved the girls with all his heart or that he felt bound by duty.

Right about then, Kyle's eyes opened and searched her out. Every rational argument she'd made not five seconds before evaporated. It wasn't just that Kyle wanted to share this with her, it was that he made no effort to hide his feelings. The rigid line of his jaw. The slight tightening of his mouth. The flare of his nostrils.

"Mya loves Kyle, Momma," Brynn whispered— not that four-year-olds ever really whispered.

"I know." Skylar hated the waver in her voice.

A waver Kyle heard. His attention sharpened, narrowing in on her face, searching her features… For what?

"And me and Greer and Jet love Kyle, too. We all do, right, Momma?" Brynn gushed, smiling at up at her. "You, too?"

There was no right answer to this question. None. Not answering it was her only option.

"That makes me the luckiest man alive, Brynn." Kyle winked at her. "To have all that love. I'm not sure I deserve it."

Skylar avoided his gaze—desperate to ease the frantic thump of her heart. And the rapid emptying of her lungs… What was happening? Why did he have such a hold on her? And how could she make it stop?

"It's 'cuz you're nice," Brynn said, as if that was the only reason they needed to be so fond of their big, burly, gorgeous, tenderhearted neighbor. "Isn't he?" Brynn asked, looking at Skylar. "Isn't he, Momma?" This time, it was clear Skylar would have to answer.

Thankfully, this was a question she could answer.

"He is very nice," Skylar agreed, hoping she sounded more herself this time.

"I think so, too." Jan's voice was unexpected—not that she'd been hiding.

No, Skylar had been too caught up in Kyle and Mya and Brynn and all the heartfelt tugs and warmth and longing rising up and pulling her under to notice that they weren't alone. Not even close. Jan and Hayden and Cassie all stood at the gate, watching the exchange with varying expressions.

"He has his moments," Hayden said. But Hayden wasn't looking at Kyle or the girls or his mother. He was looking at Skylar like she was a puzzle he had yet to figure out.

"Says my big brother." Kyle stood, lifting Mya up into his arms as he did so. Mya seemed unperturbed, resting easy in his hold—as if it was the most natural thing in the world.

Brynn deserted her, too, skipping across the grass to take Kyle's free hand in hers.

As sweet a picture as the three of them made, she knew letting this go on would be bad for all of them. The more attached they got, the harder it would be to go their separate ways. She couldn't expect Kyle to put his life on hold to be a stand-in father to her daughters. He should have a family of his own. His new life—the fresh start—should be unencumbered by his past. He'd done what he promised Chad, now it was okay to move on. *I guess I need to say as much.*

"Matching dresses," Cassie said. "You three are the cutest."

"They are," Kyle agreed so quickly the other three adults looked all the more curious.

"Come on in," Hayden said as he waved them inside the gate.

Jet trotted past the people and headed straight to Sierra and Charley, sprawled out on a relatively deserted part of the porch. Even Jet had made himself at home here.

"For Weston." Brynn held up the present to Hayden. "To learn to color."

"He does need help with that." Hayden took the box and smiled.

"Yep." Brynn nodded. "He does." The seriousness of her delivery earned a chuckle from both Hayden and Kyle.

"She is just precious," Jan said, hooking arms with Skylar. "And so are you." She stooped, smiling at Greer, strapped into place against Skylar's chest. "Don't feel like you have to keep her all day. I know there are plenty of hands that would be happy to hold her and give your back a break."

Greer squealed, stretching out her legs and flapping her arms.

"I'm betting she's agreeing," Kyle said, watching the exchange.

"We'll see." Skylar dodged, all too aware of the looks she and her girls were getting now that they were mingling amongst the guests. Not just looks, but talk, too—from the looks of it. "We probably won't stay too long," Skylar hurried to add. "Greer gets tired out and the girls still aren't used to so much…going on."

Jan's smile faltered but she recovered quickly. "Whatever you think. A momma always knows what her babies need."

Skylar shot her a grateful smile, took one of Greer's tiny hands in hers, and braced herself to meet what appeared to be the rest of Granite Falls.

Within forty minutes, Skylar had met so many people she was worried she'd forget who was who. There was the Mitchell Ranch foreman, Bobby, and his wife, Eileen. Buzz and Cassie were there. Dean from the resale shop with his mother, Penny. Then there were the newcomers. Trace Dawson, the local game warden, was gruff and stern, barely giving her a nod before hurrying away from the children. Twins Angus and Dougal McCarrick owned McCarrick Cutting Horses and had plenty of stories about their rodeo days with the Mitchell boys.

After that, names and faces blurred together.

It was almost a relief to excuse herself to change Greer's diaper. Jan and Kyle assured her they'd keep an eye on the girls but she still hurried.

"You look a little shell-shocked," Lizzie said. "It's a lot."

"It seems like you're a close-knit community. Not so different from base housing. Military wives tend to bond." *Until I dropped off the face of the earth, that is.* Once that happened, it was easy to lose track of one another.

"I can imagine." Lizzie nodded. "Granite Falls is a special place, I think. The people here are decent, hardworking, put-down-roots, neighborly types. Sometimes a little too neighborly, I suppose." She grinned. "Don't let the nosiness throw you off. People are curious, but no one means anything by it. It wasn't that long ago I was in your shoes."

Skylar nodded but didn't say much as she finished cleaning up Greer and slid her bloomers back into place.

"Is this the place to be?" Cassie asked as she came into the nursery. "It is less crowded. What a great party, Lizzie. Little Weston is loved by everyone."

Skylar still hadn't made up her mind about Cassie. Was the woman truly this upbeat and together or was this all a front? *Or am I just being paranoid because she's gorgeous and childless and has a history with Kyle—making her a much better match for him?*

Where had that come from? She *wanted* Kyle to be happy. She didn't want to be so…so selfish.

"He's pretty irresistible." Lizzie smiled. "But that was before little Greer got here. Goodness, you are adorable."

Greer, who lay on the changing table with her legs pulled close so she could hold on to her toes, smiled up at Lizzie.

"She knows it, too." Skylar had to smile at her daughter's antics. *Shameless.*

"Goodness you are just about the sweetest little dumpling." Cassie shook her head. "May I?"

Skylar saw the smitten look on Cassie's face and nodded. "Watch your hair though. Greer loves to grab."

Cassie scooped up Greer and smiled down at the baby. "She is beautiful, Skylar. All your girls are. It's easy to see why Kyle has fallen so in love with them."

"They are." Lizzie nodded.

"How are you settling in?" Cassie asked. "You made quite an impression when you stopped by the clinic."

Skylar held her breath. "Oh?"

"A *good* impression," Cassie said. "Sorry, I should have said that. My brother, Buzz, is so excited to have some help. His old tech, Ivan, retired about a year ago and he's used a few temps since then but he really needs regular help."

"It was meant to be," Lizzie agreed.

"It seems like it. I admit, it's different." Skylar swallowed against the knot in her throat. "Being here. With people. A job. Everything." There was so much more she could say. For the first time in a long time, she felt a glimmer of control. And yet, she couldn't quite shake the feeling that—at any second—things would come crashing down around her. She'd lived so long braced, waiting for the next *thing*…

"It took me a while to feel at home here, Skylar." Lizzie hesitated. "I'd lived my whole life in

Houston—I was a big-city girl. But Hayden and Weston and Jan welcomed me with open arms into the family."

"You are family." Skylar smiled. "I appreciate everything your family and Kyle have done for me and the girls but…we're not family. I owe you all an incredible debt that, when I'm able, I want to repay."

Silence fell.

"Well, I'd like us to be friends." Cassie's declaration was unexpected. "Kyle is a good friend. You're…a friend of his so—"

"Yes. That's all we are," Skylar said a little too assertively. "Friends, I mean." She met Cassie's gaze, wanting the woman to believe her. Lizzie, too.

"Oh?" Cassie's brows rose. "If you say so."

Lizzie kept her opinion to herself, but her face said it all. She didn't believe Skylar.

Skylar cleared her throat and added, "He's a great guy—don't get me wrong." *He's the best.* "It's just… I don't have the time or the interest in anything more than that."

Lizzie chuckled. "You do have your hands full."

Greer cooed, giving Cassie a broad grin.

"With all this adorableness." Cassie smoothed the wisp of curls on the top of Greer's head. "Just know, if Kyle's not the one, there are plenty of gentlemen in these parts who would gladly catch your eye—when you're ready. I got the impression Angus McCarrick was *very* interested."

If Kyle's not the one… Kyle *couldn't* be the one.

Giving her heart to him would likely see her hurt and, once he realized loving her girls wouldn't hold a marriage together, the girls would be hurt, too. It would be a mistake—one that would end with her being on her own. Again. She'd been through that once. She wasn't strong enough to do it again.

Even as he picked up leftover cups and plates and napkins into the large black trash bag, Kyle was constantly aware of Skylar. He knew she was perfectly capable of handling herself but, if she needed a hand, he wanted to be there for her. At the moment, she was sitting on the porch, coloring with the girls while Weston slumped, sound asleep, against Hayden's large dog Charley. No assistance needed.

Today had been good and not so good. Good because the girls had fun. Once they got comfortable with the crowd, they seemed to enjoy the piñata and cake and scavenger hunt. Not so good because of the amount of masculine curiosity Skylar had received. Between Dean's quiet helpfulness with the girls and Angus's and Dougal's more overt interest in Skylar—Kyle had found his gaze drifting her way far too many times over the course of the day.

"Thanks for helping out with cleanup. I'll trade you." Hayden handed him an empty trash bag. "You keep that up, people won't stop talking."

"People are talking?" Kyle pretended this was news. But he innocently asked, "About what?" for the fun of it.

Hayden shot him a look.

Kyle chuckled, doing his best to act like he hadn't been caught openly staring at Skylar. He had been. One hundred percent. He seemed to be stuck in her gravitational pull... Plus, he'd never seen her with her hair down or wearing a dress... Not that it mattered what she was wearing. To him, she was always beautiful. Hell. He was making excuses? It was simple. No matter how hard he tried not to look, he was going to. She *was* beautiful—even more so when she smiled. Like she was now, listening to Brynn and Lizzie and seeming, at least outwardly, at ease with things.

"What's the holdup with you two?" Hayden asked.

It was Kyle's turn to shoot his brother a look.

"I know you." Hayden wasn't in the least put off. "She's different. The way you look at her, act around her..." He pointed at him. "You're different."

"We've barely known each other for a week." Kyle ran a hand along the back of his neck. "You're seeing things." As brush-offs went, it was pretty lame.

"Sure. Right. Okay." Hayden waited before saying, "We're repairing the windmill in the north field tomorrow. If you're up for it, we could use another set of hands."

Kyle nodded. "I'm up for it." He'd always found peace while working with his hands. It required concentration—enough so that there was no room in his brain for other things. Things like Skylar and

Chad and wanting Skylar and knowing he didn't deserve her...

"Is it Chad?" Hayden asked.

Dammit. It was a little unnerving to realize his older brother could still read him, even after all these years.

"You think he'd have a problem with it?" Hayden pushed.

It was on the tip of his tongue to dodge the question. "Hell yes." He sighed. "Wouldn't you?"

"Not offense but...Chad's gone." Hayden frowned. "I'd think he'd rather you were with Skylar and the girls instead of someone else. He knew you. Trusted you. Put his life in your hands... He'd know you'd take care of his family better than anyone else could." He cleared his throat. "If that's what you want, that is."

Kyle shook his head. *It's not that simple.* Maybe it was the look on his brother's face or the crushing weight of his burden, but the words slipped out before he realized he was saying them. "Chad's death? I wasn't there. I should have been. But I wasn't." He ran a hand along the back of his neck. "I'm the reason she's a widow. I'm the reason she's had to face *everything* alone..." He stalked to the end of the porch, needing space.

Hayden's boots echoed, following him. "What happened?"

Kyle swallowed, staring out over the rolling hills

instead. He couldn't look his brother in the eye. "He went in, blind, because I wasn't there."

Hayden waited, quiet—but there—at Kyle's side.

"We'd gone to this school." He swallowed. "A goodwill mission. Take a bunch of stuffed animals, tell bad jokes, make the kids smile—get the locals to trust us." He gripped the handrail. "Chad missed his girls something fierce. The twins at least. He never knew about Greer." That was a throat punch. "He had a good time. It had been a good damn day."

Hayden's hand rested on his shoulder.

"The next day, the school was shelled and Chad went…" He shook his head again, anger and guilt and grief bouncing off one another. "We'd been playing basketball. I got laid out—busted my head. I was getting stitches while he was running into that damn school… He said he'd heard kids crying, needing help and he had to go in…"

"And he did." It was Skylar's voice. Skylar. Not Hayden.

Dammit. He pressed his eyes shut. *Shit.* He drew in a deep breath and turned to face her. How did you apologize for something like this? "Skylar…" His throat closed off, clamping down so hard he stared at the ceiling overhead until the pressure eased.

"I'll… I'm…" Hayden sighed. "I'm going." He spun on his heel and headed away.

Skylar was close then, the spring breeze awash with her scent. "He went into the school? That's where he stepped on the…" Her voice wavered.

Before they'd shelled the school, land mines had been placed around the periphery—knowing the soldiers would come. They'd used those kids as a trap...

"You think it was your fault?" Skylar asked.

"Skylar, I know it was." He stared down at her then, knowing she'd be angry, knowing she'd be hurt.

"How? How are you responsible for the land mines?" she asked, confused.

"I wasn't there to stop him." He looked beyond her, at Mya and Brynn stacking their crayons on Jet's head—all smiles and laughter. His mother stood nearby with Greer sound asleep in her arms. "He should be here today."

"He should." She nodded, coming to stand beside him. Her hands gripped the handrail so hard her knuckles were white.

Kyle watched the range of emotions shifting across her features. This wasn't the way he'd planned on telling her. He'd wanted to be careful with his words—to be prepared. He sure as hell hadn't wanted to have this conversation on the back porch of his family home while his family and friends were in earshot.

"But he's not," she whispered. "There's no changing that." Her indrawn breath was sharp, catching, before she added, "And it has *nothing* to do with you."

"I should have—"

"Kyle, you think you being there would have stopped him?" She faced him then, her gaze pinning his. "Do you think you *could* have stopped him? You knew him. I knew him. Nothing would have stopped him." She paused, blinking rapidly.

"I could have tried," he ground out.

"If you'd been there, you'd likely have met the same fate." There were tears in her eyes. "He made it back to the base… That's where you spoke to him about me…and the girls?"

Kyle nodded, doing his best to hold back the images. The Humvee, the blood, Chad—in pieces, the chaos and panic and acceptance that this was it. That was the worst of it. Sitting there, letting Chad talk, knowing there wasn't a damn thing Kyle could do to stop the inevitable. "He had to know you'd all be okay." Once Kyle had given his word, Chad stopped fighting. He'd trusted Kyle to follow through.

She nodded, her gaze searching his as she whispered, "And you promised him we would be."

"Yes." He forced the word out.

"Chad knew what he was doing—he had to do it." She shivered, hugging herself. "I don't blame you so, please, stop blaming yourself. You've honored your word to him. More than honored it." Her attention wandered, her eyes scanning the distant hill. "You don't need to take care of us and you certainly don't owe us anything else. You do need to start living your own life—one that's not based on a promise you've already kept." She straightened.

"But I want to—"

"Next week, things will change." She kept on.

"Buzz said I'll get use of the clinic van, so you won't be taxiing me and the girls around anymore. Penny Hodges, Dean's mom, would love to watch the girls three days a week. She's a retired teacher, did you know that?" She didn't wait for an answer. "And Angus mentioned something about a rental house in town… So, soon, we'll be out of your hair."

He wasn't prepared for the disappointment that gripped him. "All that happened today?"

"Like you said, small-town folk take care of each other. Good, right?" she asked, smiling at him. "The house won't be ready for a month or so, but at least you know we won't be underfoot forever."

Which didn't help. If anything, it was worse. It had never occurred to him that she'd leave. Why would she?

"There's no rush." The edge in his voice was sharp. "I mean…" He cleared his throat. "You and the girls don't need to rush off. There's plenty of room and, considering all the changes you've made the last week, take some time and catch your breath." *Don't go.*

"Thank you." She nodded. "You're right. We won't leave right away."

"Momma," Brynn called, waving at her.

Skylar held up one finger. "I'm going to take them home and get them cleaned up. It's getting late and they need dinner, a bath, and bed."

"You need a hand—"

"No. I mean it, Kyle. You don't owe me anything else—that includes your time. Do something for yourself. I don't know. Go out?" She shook her head, nodding toward the girls. She paused then, and turned back. "Have some fun, something that doesn't include diapers or coloring." She smiled. "It's been so long, you might have forgotten how to do that."

He stared after her, grappling with the amount of information she'd just unloaded. Being independent was important to her—but he hadn't realized that meant looking for a new place to live. Was she unhappy here? His place was nothing special but, he'd hoped, it had everything they'd need to be comfortable.

Why was she suddenly so invested in him going out? Did she think that's what he wanted? Or that he'd sacrificed his social life because of them? Or was she tired of him being underfoot? If that was the case, then her interest in moving out also made sense.

He ignored the ache in his chest and focused on cleaning up.

He gave Brynn and Mya good-night hugs and managed a curt nod when Skylar waved before they walked out the back gate and along the path to his home—with Jet trailing behind.

"You done here?" Buzz asked. "I'm heading over to the Watering Hole. Wanna come? Play some pool? Drink a few beers? Take a break?"

"Sure." Maybe getting some distance and perspective would help. Since he'd rolled up in front of Frank Kline's house, he'd spent the majority of his time with Skylar and the girls. Maybe she was right, maybe they did need space… Or maybe it was too late and he'd already fallen for Skylar Davis.

Chapter Eleven

Skylar flipped through the brochure she'd received from the audiologist in Austin. They wanted her to read over everything so she'd be prepared when she and Mya went for the first appointment later that month. The brochure laid it all out there, in black and white. Not only was it a breakdown in how surgical candidates were determined, it went through the cochlear implant process, recovery, device activation, and care of patient and the device. She'd read over it, front to back, several times now—so that wasn't the real reason she was sitting up. The *real* reason had nothing to do with Mya's surgery or her upcoming appointment and everything to do with the fact that it was after two in the morning and Kyle wasn't home.

Every time she thought about Kyle with…with anyone it left a horrible hollowness in her chest. She'd told him to go because Kyle's happiness mattered. He was a good guy. No, he was the best. That's why, even though it would never happen, there was a part of her that wanted his happiness to include her and the girls. Watching him with the girls made *her* happy. It'd been a long time since she'd felt happiness. Even longer since she'd been overcome with longing.

His kiss had woken up a part of her she'd almost forgotten. Now all it took was a casual touch or a lingering glance and she was replaying the feel of his hands on her and the press of his lips… She ran her fingers over her lips. *Oh, stop.* She shook her head. One kiss shouldn't have her weak-kneed and her heart thumping. *I'm a mother three times over.* She needed to remind herself that was the whole reason she was here: Kyle had promised Chad he'd take care of her. *That* was Kyle's motivation.

That was before she'd heard his guilt-ridden confession on the back porch today. He felt responsible for Chad's death. It wasn't true. Chad did what he'd felt he had to do but Kyle couldn't see it that way. If something were to happen between them, even if she set aside his promise to Chad, now there was the added concern that his misplaced guilt was the reason he stayed with her. Guilt or duty… Neither was love.

He should be out having fun. This was good. This

was what she wanted. He had a right to a life of his own, something she and the girls were getting in the way of. How could they not be? Kyle was pretty much the perfect catch—handsome, bighearted, loyal, and kind. But he couldn't exactly meet someone else when he was chasing Brynn around, coloring with Mya, or making faces at Greer.

The memory of Greer cradled in those muscular arms still made Skylar's stomach tighten.

Stop it.

She scanned over the brochure, ran a hand over her face and stood to get a glass of water. At the sound of a truck door and the beat of boots on the wooden plank porch, Skylar panicked. Should she run to her room before he caught her here? What possible excuse could she come up with for being up at this hour? *Other than I'm waiting for him.* The door swung open...

"Skylar?" Kyle paused inside the door, a furrow creasing his brow. "Is Greer awake?"

"She just went to sleep." Which was a lie. Greer had been asleep for hours. "I was...getting some water." She ran her hand over her hair, wishing she'd braided it back, wishing she wasn't in her old cotton nightgown—tingling with awareness. From the dark stubble lining his jaw to his heavy-lidded gaze, Skylar wasn't sure which of his features she found most appealing. *All of them. All of him.* She swallowed.

Kyle pulled the door closed quietly. "She okay?" he asked. "It's late, even for her."

Skylar nodded, shivering at the gruffness of his

voice. If she hadn't been thinking about his kisses seconds before he'd arrived, she wouldn't be reacting like this. As it was, he seemed to tap directly into the hunger she had for him. This longing for him was wrong. She was tired. It was late. And she should say good-night and go immediately to her bedroom... *Immediately.*

Kyle's gaze slipped over her, resting on her bare toes. "You okay?"

She wiggled her toes, her stomach in knots and her throat tight. Was she? She wasn't fine. If she was, she wouldn't be here...in her old-fashioned long cotton nightie, acutely aware of the fact that they were alone. She'd made a choice. Even while she'd rationalized all the reasons they couldn't be and his need for a life of his own, she'd sat up. She'd waited for him. And now...

"Skylar?" His eyes locked with hers.

She nodded. *I needed to see you.* Because she wanted... What? What did she want? *Kyle. I want you.* It was true. With her heart pounding, she met his gaze.

Kyle's jaw muscle clenched, hard and every inch of him seemed to tense.

No. No. Pull it together. Remember all the valid reasons not to throw yourself at him. But that didn't stop the surge of heat that rushed from her toes to her cheeks. "Did you have...a nice time?" *Did you meet someone?* What was wrong with her?

He shrugged, his gaze fixed on her face.

The longer he stared at her, the harder it was to pull air into her lungs. When she sucked in a deep breath, the waver echoed in the quiet stillness of the room.

His eyes narrowed.

"I'm glad you went out. Met some new people, maybe. Not in diapers?" She sounded forced. She could hear it. He probably did, too. "You didn't miss anything here—"

"I wasn't looking to meet anyone." He sighed, running a hand along the back of his neck.

Hearing him say that shouldn't flood her with relief. It did, but it shouldn't. She should say good-night and go to bed. She definitely needed to stop before she made a complete fool of herself. "You don't owe me any explanations or—"

"I might as well make it clear. I'm only interested in one person. One." He swallowed, looking more uncomfortable than she'd ever seen him. "It's you. I only want you."

She hadn't heard correctly. He hadn't said that. He couldn't have. She shook her head. He didn't mean this. But the way he was looking at her made it hard to pull forward his guilt-ridden confession on the back porch or worry over his motivation. What did he mean *interested*? Yes, he was attracted to her— the feeling was mutual. But, beyond that? She kept shaking her head.

"Yes," he said. "I do." He slowly closed the distance between them. "Every time I see you, I want you more." He stopped, staring down at her, letting his gaze wander over her face to linger on her mouth. "I want to touch you—to kiss *you*."

"But…" But what? *Touch me.* Wait. *No.* "I…"

"I won't." He swallowed. "Not unless you ask me to." His jaw muscle tightened again.

The fire in his eyes incinerated every ounce of resistance. She nodded, resting her hands on his chest. "Kyle, please kiss me—"

He reached for her and pulled her tight against him. A muffled groan escaped him, right before the first brush of his lips. She was clinging to him then, gripping the front of his shirt and pressing herself closer. His hand slid up her spine to cup the back of her head, holding her there as his mouth fitted more firmly against hers.

She didn't need to breathe. Or think. All she wanted was to get lost in the feelings he stirred. Being wrapped up in his arms blotted out the rest of the world. There were no questions or concerns or fear, there was only an all-consuming need for more. More of his touch and kiss… More of Kyle.

Her hands slid down his chest and around his waist. She wanted to explore the ridges of his back and soak up his warmth. He felt so good. But his kisses distracted her. His lips were soft but firm, commanding but coaxing, and seductively relentless. When their breaths mingled and the slight stroke of his tongue teased along her lower lip, her breath hitched.

One large hand came up to cradle her cheek, his thumb tracing along her jaw while he tilted her head back and deepened his kiss. From the tickle of his breath against her cheek to the sweep of his tongue against hers, the only thing keeping her upright was his hold.

He broke away from her. "Do you know how long I've been wanting to do that?" he all but growled, his breath ragged and harsh. "I see you and it's all I can think about." His fingers ran through her long hair, smoothing it from her shoulder and down her back. "Wanting you."

At the moment, she knew exactly how he felt. She was aching for him. Craving him, was more like it. So, so much. His kiss lit a fuse she had no interest in snuffing out.

"If you keep looking at me like that, I'm going to keep right on kissing you." His hands cupped her face.

"Okay," she whispered, all but humming with want.

"Skylar..." He broke off.

As much as she wanted him, it wasn't easy to say "Don't stop." She rose on tiptoe, reaching up to tug his head down to hers. Desire pulsed low in her belly.

"Kissing you?" he asked, hesitating before their lips touched. "What are you asking for, Skylar?"

Kissing wasn't enough. It was a good start but... They both knew what she was saying. But Kyle, being Kyle, wanted her to say it—so there was no misunderstanding. Her heart was all but thumping out of her chest now. "I want to be with you. Tonight."

Kyle swallowed the groan her words stirred. Did he want to take Skylar to bed? Hell, yes. He'd never yearned like this before. Skylar shook him something fierce. But wanting something didn't make it right. No matter how much he wanted her. *Dammit all.*

"But…" She shook her head. "If you don't want to—"

"I do." Which probably wasn't the best thing to say if he was going to stop this. He trailed his thumb along her jaw.

"Good," she whispered. With her eyes blazing and her cheeks flushed, she was pure temptation.

"You're sure?" he pushed, hoping she was strong enough to do what he couldn't.

She nodded.

That was it. He was done for. He gave in, pulling her against him and nuzzling her neck. There was no stopping this. Needing her. Wanting her. Tonight, he'd give her everything he had. He'd show her she was who he wanted. Her. And no one else. He couldn't stop himself from wanting her, that was true. But there was an ache in his chest now, too. An ache he suspected had nothing to do with wanting her.

Her broken moan had him leading her from the kitchen—pausing just long enough to grab the baby monitor—through the door to his room, tripping over jeans and boots, before falling onto the tangle of sheets and blankets on his bed.

The minute her arms twined around his neck and she was warm and soft beneath him, the rest of the world slipped away. Skylar was in his bed. Her hands slid from his neck, down his chest, to free the buttons along the front of his shirt. Her featherlight touch against his bare chest sent a shudder through him. The brush of her fingertips, trailing along his chest and abdomen, emptied his lungs. She had no idea how much she got to him.

He shrugged out of his shirt and bent forward to kiss her.

Skylar came alive under him. Her hands stroked along his arms and shoulders before taking her nails down his back. Her knee came up, pressing against his hip, baring her leg to him.

His mouth never left hers as his hand slid along her thigh, soaking up her shudder and moan. There was nothing as arousing as knowing he caused that reaction. He was making this beautiful, passionate woman gasp and cling to him. He wanted to take her higher. He wanted to make her lose control and fall apart.

She was silky soft beneath him. The higher his hand traveled, the higher the hem of her white nightgown. He'd have taken his time exploring her with his hands and eyes, but Skylar's soft "Please" changed his mind.

She helped him remove her gown before pulling him on top of her.

It was the best sort of shock. Skin to skin. Her softness pressed tight against his chest. She rained openmouthed kisses along his throat and shoulder until he couldn't take it. His hands slid up, along her sides as he stooped to nuzzle the swell of her bare breast.

Her nails raked through his short-cropped hair, her breath rasping as he drew one pebbled nipple into his mouth. She arched up and into his touch. Her head fell back, her long dark hair spilling across his rumpled white sheets.

He paused, braced over her, to look his fill. She was wild and passionate and…his. He hadn't expected that surge of possession.

Her eyes fluttered open and sought him out.

"You're beautiful," he said, shaking his head. "Damn beautiful."

"It's dark," she whispered.

He was so surprised, he laughed. "It's not that dark."

"You are, too, you know." She sighed, her gaze traveling along his shoulder, across his chest, and down his stomach. "You need help with those?" she asked, eyeing the waistband of his jeans.

He pushed off the bed and stood. Until now, he'd never thought of taking off his pants as a turn-on. But that was before he'd had someone eagerly staring at him—the way Skylar was looking at him right now. By the time he kicked off his jeans, he was on fire. She was propped up on her elbows, one hundred percent focused on the rock-hard evidence of just how much he wanted her. He wanted her something fierce.

She rolled up onto her knees and moved to the edge of the bed, her eyes fluttering shut as his hand slid around her waist to grip her hip. He hooked his other arm around her waist and lifted her, tossing her back onto the bed and coming down on top of her.

This time, *she* was laughing.

And he loved it.

He kissed her, gently tugging on her lower lip, at the same time her legs parted in invitation. The simple act was the most seductive thing he'd ever experienced. He wanted this woman, wanted to be a part of her. His breath came out on a growl. He stared into her eyes, steadying himself.

Her fingers tightened against his back as he moved into her. He was slow and careful, letting each new sensation roll over him and pull him under. He was drowning in her eyes—drowning in her— and he welcomed it. Once he was buried deep, he kissed her, doing his best to keep control.

"Oh, Kyle," she murmured, arching against him as her hands gripped him to her.

As one, they began to move. The shift and glide of skin on skin turned their fire for one another into an out-of-control blaze. Kyle wasn't sure how long he could hold back, pleasure rolled over him—

making his thrusts deeper and faster and more urgent than ever.

Skylar stared up at him, so damn lovely she took his breath away.

If he'd had any breath in his lungs, that was. He didn't. He couldn't. The pressure building inside his chest was powerful. His lungs throbbed and his heart pounded and he didn't want this to end.

When Skylar's head fell back against the mattress, Kyle kept moving. He absorbed it all—the slim column of her throat, her gasping breaths, and the broken groans that spilled from her lips. He was shaking, fighting for control, fighting to hold on until she'd climaxed.

"Kyle… Oh, Kyle…" Her knees pressed against his hips and her fingers bit into the skin of his back as she stiffened and arched, straining against him. She met his gaze then closed her eyes tight, burying her face against the tangled sheets to muffle her cry of release.

His release hit hard, the roar rising up inside him smothered against her throat.

He was breathing hard, propped over her on his elbows, when he felt the sweep of her fingers along the side of his face. He caught her hand and pressed a kiss against her palm before he rolled to her side.

Other than the sound of their breathing, it was quiet. Outside, the crickets chirped and a spring breeze blew as if nothing had changed. Inside… Well, Kyle was pretty sure everything had changed.

For him, at least. Whatever this feeling was, it was new and strong and clear and all about Skylar. He'd never been in love. Before Skylar, that is.

Skylar. He studied her profile in the dim light. Her eyes were closed and the rise and fall of her chest was slowing—her breathing growing steady once more.

Was her heart beating like his? Pounding?

Part of him wanted to ask her, to put it all out there and see what happened. But the other part balked at the idea. Tonight had been one hundred percent unexpected. He'd had a few beers, beaten Buzz at pool, and thought about Skylar the whole damn time. So, finding her still awake, almost as if she'd been waiting for him, had been one hell of a surprise.

He wasn't foolish enough to think she'd been waiting for him. She'd been headed to bed after walking the floor until Greer had fussed herself out and things had just…happened. Things that couldn't be undone.

Things like losing his heart to Skylar Davis.

"Skylar?" he whispered.

She turned toward him, her eyelids heavy and her motions sluggish.

"Sleeping?" he whispered again, content to lie there.

She shook her head but her eyes drifted shut.

It took some maneuvering, but he untangled the sheets and blankets and wrapped them up, pulling her against him. She fit there, against his side—like she was made to do just that. Maybe she was. He pressed a kiss to her temple and closed his eyes. He didn't have high hopes for getting much sleep but he didn't mind.

Six hours later, Kyle woke up with a smile on his face. Not only had he slept like a log, there was a new sense of optimism for the future. He stretched and rolled over...

Skylar was gone—not surprising since he could hear the morning chatter from the kitchen. The girls were up, so Skylar was up.

He hurried to shower and dress then headed into the kitchen, eager to see Skylar. As much as he'd like to believe she'd had the same sort of epiphany he'd had, he wasn't going to hold his breath. She'd been in love before—been married... And he was no Chad.

As soon as she saw him, Mya waved.

Kyle waved back. "Good morning."

"G'morning," Brynn said, scooping up cereal. "Sleepyhead." She giggled.

He glanced Skylar's way and paused. Coldness seeped into his bones, clamping down on his stomach, and instantly dashing his sense of optimism. "Everything good?"

Skylar didn't look at him. "Wonderful."

Right. Maybe she was feeling shy? He hoped like hell that was it.

"Can I talk to you for a minute, Kyle?" she asked.

Not shy then. This wasn't good.

Skylar scooped up Greer. "Finish eating," she said

to Brynn then tapped Mya's shoulder and nodded at her cereal.

Kyle followed her onto the front porch, stooping to give Jet a rub behind the ear—and buying time.

"I… This is going to be hard." Skylar broke off. "But I'm going to dive in. Okay?"

No. Not okay. He was pretty damn sure he didn't want to hear what she was about to say. "'Kay," he managed, coming to stand before her. Staring down at her put knots in his stomach. She was doing her best to avoid his eyes—keeping her expression blank and remote. Nothing like the passionate woman he'd had in his bed the night before.

Greer cooed, grabbing his attention. Her gleeful smile tugged at his heart.

Skylar cleared her throat. "You know last night was… Well…"

Amazing. Wonderful. "Good?"

"Physically, maybe." Her gaze darted his way, then away. "Last night was a mistake. Kyle, you have to see that. You said you… The attraction is there but… That's just it—attraction. I don't want to jeopardize our friendship." She closed her eyes, the words coming out in a rush. "I regret…*everything*… I was tired and emotional and…and *so* lonely. And well… well, I used you to ease my loneliness. It was wrong. I'm so sorry. If I could undo last night, I would."

He was pretty sure she'd said everything he'd never wanted her to say. Hell, no one ever wanted to hear one of those things. All together? It was a knee to the groin.

"Please tell me I didn't ruin our friendship." She was bouncing Greer, her brow creased. "You've become…my best friend… My *only* real friend. Someone I can count on… I don't want to ruin that."

What the hell was he supposed to say to that? I love you? That wasn't going to change how she felt. She was worried about losing his friendship. Professing his love was an altogether different thing. Now she was braced and wide eyed, waiting—almost fearful. "No. Nothing's been ruined." He shook his head, clearing his throat. "We'll always be friends."

She drew in a deep breath and nodded, but she still wouldn't look him in the eye. "We're okay?"

"We're okay." He stood there gripping the porch railing long after Skylar had carried Greer back inside. He'd fallen in love for the first time in his life and had his heart pounded to dust in a span of hours. Unfortunately, he suspected the recovery period was going to last a hell of a lot longer.

Chapter Twelve

Over the next two weeks, Skylar threw herself into her new life. Overall, things seemed to fall into place. Penny Hodges, the retired elementary schoolteacher, instantly clicked with her girls. Not only had the older woman gone online to learn some basic signs to communicate with Mya, she had daily activities and mini field trips around town on the days she had the girls. Penny had become the grandmother her girls had never had. And since her grandchildren lived several states away and only visited once or twice a year, Penny was eager to play grandmother to her girls. Thanks to Penny, she was able to work Monday, Wednesday, and Friday at Granite Falls Veterinary Clinic and Hospital with Dr. Buzz Lafferty.

Dr. Buzz, as his clients called him, was a character. It didn't matter where he was in the clinic, Skylar could hear him. He had a booming voice and a slightly over-the-top personality that somehow made him charming—not irritating. The instant Skylar shook his hand, she'd known they'd get along just fine. He was all business, exactly the way she wanted things. And since the business often required them to go to their patients, he'd entrusted Skylar with the clinic van—a van that just happened to have enough room for all her car seats.

Between paying Penny and rent—she'd insisted on paying rent—she was managing to save a little. That, and the monthly check from the government, was how she'd pay for Mya's surgery. Mya had her assessment appointment next week, and then she'd know if Mya was a candidate and, if she was, when the procedure would happen.

Even though things were going well, Skylar was struggling. She missed Kyle. Desperately. She was falling for him. Hard. But the idea of engaging in a purely physical relationship wasn't something she could do. There was no denying she'd lost her head. Did she regret it? Yes—now she knew how it could be between them. And no—for one night, she'd shut out all the reasons they couldn't be together. She'd been playing a dangerous game. She'd known how conflicted he was, and still slept with him and wound up hurting herself in the process.

Lucky for her, he seemed to be as intent on avoiding her as she was on avoiding him. Between Penny, Jan, Lizzie, and Weston, and even Hayden, it was rare that she and Kyle were ever alone together. When they happened to run into each other, they did their best to act the same—but there was no denying the strain between them. The girls noticed his absence and missed him. *I miss him, too.*

She glanced at the clock. Wednesday meant five o'clock closing time for the clinic. Penny would bring the girls over soon, they'd load up the van, and head home. But tonight, she'd told the girls they were going to King Frosty for dinner and some fun in the play place. It would be nice to take a break from cooking in the small kitchen—but it would also ensure she wouldn't run into Kyle.

Too late.

Kyle stood outside the clinic, a bouquet of flowers in his hands.

Flowers?

She smoothed the navy scrub top she was wearing and straightened her ponytail, surprisingly excited—and nervous. He'd brought her flowers? This was bad. This was good. Her stomach flipped when he paused, his face lighting up as the girls arrived with Penny. He stooped, giving Mya and Brynn each big hugs, listening as Brynn chattered and carefully watching as Mya signed that she'd made cookies and pet a cat and gone for a walk in the park. If he didn't understand, he didn't let on. Instead, he answered, speaking and signing, "Sounds like a busy day. Did you have fun?"

Brynn nodded. So did Mya.

Skylar watched the exchange, clutching a stack of manila patient folders to her chest. That smile was her kryptonite. One smile and whatever logical arguments she constructed to remind her that the two of them couldn't happen went out the window.

"Everything okay?" Buzz asked, pausing by the counter. "Skylar?"

She jumped, the rush of heat flooding her cheeks a dead giveaway that her face was likely bright red.

"Aw." Buzz glanced out the window. "You two…" He shrugged. "You know what I mean?"

She frowned. "We're friends."

He didn't bother masking his disbelief. "That's what Cassie said. But I figure that's just wishful thinking on her part." He sighed. "My sister has had it bad for Kyle since she was, oh, about five years old. But if you say so, I guess it's true."

"Well, they know each other. Being friends is a good way to start a solid relationship. It's nice." Cassie and Kyle made sense. *They* had a history. She and Kyle didn't. They'd barely known each other a month—Chad's letters notwithstanding. *And I slept with him.* The thought popped up, surprising her, and making her cheeks go hot again.

"Or not." Buzz made a face.

"You wouldn't want Kyle for a brother-in-law?"

she asked, the words almost getting stuck in her throat.

"Nope." He chuckled. "We've been friends too long. I don't want to get stuck in the middle or having to choose sides when they fight."

"Why would they fight?" She carried the files to the filing cabinet, trying not to overthink what Buzz was saying or watch the incredibly sweet exchange still taking place between his girls and Kyle.

"That's what couples do." Buzz sounded incredulous, like everyone knew that.

"Is it?" She peered over her shoulder at her boss, noting the tightening of his jaw. Her relationship with Chad had been easy. Of course, he'd spent more time gone during their marriage than home, but she'd like to think their relationship would have stayed that way. Easy. Uncomplicated. The exact opposite of whatever was happening between her and Kyle. *Enough. Nothing is happening.* She'd made certain of that. Her heart twisted, an unexpected pain radiating throughout her chest. "I'm almost done here."

"I'll lock up," Buzz said, that easygoing smile back in place. "Well, look who's here." He waved as the girls came through the door, Penny pushing Greer in her stroller.

"Hi, Doc Buzz," Brynn said.

Mya waved.

"Hi, Momma." Brynn ran to her, hugging her around the knees.

"I'll see you Friday?" Penny asked. "I don't want to be late for my hair appointment."

"Yes, thank you, Penny." Skylar smiled. "I hope they were good."

"Angels. As always." Penny smiled, blew kisses at the girls and left.

Brynn tugged on her pants. "Momma, Momma, look! Kyle's here."

"I see that." Skylar swallowed, hating that her smile faltered when her eyes darted Kyle's way. Kyle. Looking gorgeous and fit in his black button-up, jeans, and cowboy hat and holding the most beautiful bouquet of flowers… She drew in a deep breath. "Hi."

Kyle nodded, his gaze sweeping over her face. "Skylar." The way he said her name was criminal, his velvet-rich tone soothing.

Her gaze fell to the flowers, torn between hope and dread. She couldn't accept them. But her girls were watching—

Kyle shifted the flowers. "Is she here?" Kyle asked Buzz.

"Yes." Buzz eyed the flowers. "I was running out of ways to keep her here. She's still in the salon." He waved Kyle after him. "See you Friday, Skylar. Good night."

She? In the salon. *Cassie…* The flowers were for Cassie. "Sure," she murmured. "Good night."

Kyle waved. "See you later, girls."

"Goin' for ice cream," Brynn announced. "Can you come, too?"

Skylar scrambled to respond, fully aware that Kyle and Buzz were waiting for her to say something. "Oh, Brynn… Kyle has plans."

"What?" Brynn asked, frowning, staring at Kyle in disappointment.

"Grown-up plans." Skylar crouched, lowering her voice. "Maybe next time. He's busy, Brynn—"

"I'm never too busy for ice cream," Kyle argued. "I'd like to come, if you're okay with it?"

To her horror, her eyes were stinging with unshed tears. Angry or sad or frustrated tears—it didn't matter. She was not going to cry. "Are you…are you sure?" She stood, looking at the flowers.

Kyle stared down at the flowers. "These are…" He shoved the flowers at Buzz. "Here. Take a Benadryl."

Buzz held the flowers at arm's length and scowled. "Thanks."

"You're welcome." Kyle chuckled. "A little Benadryl won't hurt you. It's a lot better than getting on Cassie's bad side."

"I owe you." Buzz nodded. "See you Friday, Skylar. Enjoy your ice cream." He carried the flowers through the door that connected the clinic to the pet-grooming salon Cassie ran.

Skylar wasn't sure how to react. What had just happened?

Her face must have said as much because Kyle said, "It's Cassie's anniversary—the day she left her basta…" He glanced at the girls. "Her ex-husband. Buzz forgot, until now. Likes to make a big deal out of it since it was a…bad situation and she had the courage to leave." He shrugged. "Buzz is allergic to chrysanthemums and daisies—those are her favorites, apparently." He paused, watching her closely. "He couldn't get away and asked me to help him out." He held up his finger. "Since I was coming to give the girls a new coloring book Lizzie bought to replace the one Weston used, I was happy to pick the flowers up. But it looks like I left the coloring book in the truck."

"I love coloring," Brynn gushed. "Mya, too."

"I know you do," Kyle said, winking at the girls.

Skylar was staring at him and she couldn't stop. She had no reason to feel such relief—none. But, she did. Kyle hadn't brought flowers to Cassie. He'd been helping out a friend.

Just like he'd helped out Chad—by taking care of *her*. Because Kyle had promised that he would. And Kyle was a man of his word.

Kyle squirted a dollop of ketchup into each of the twins' dinner basket. "Good?"

Brynn nodded. "Thank you."

"Thank you," Mya said. "Yum." She used a French fry to scoop up some ketchup and took a big bite.

"Yum is right," Kyle agreed, grinning. "You think Greer will like ketchup?" He did his best to spell out "ketchup" for Mya, then "like," and pointed at Greer.

Mya nodded.

Brynn shook her head.

He had to chuckle then.

"Guess we'll have to wait and see," Skylar said, smiling at Greer, who was practicing standing on Skylar's lap. "You'll be gobbling up fries in no time, won't you?"

Kyle had picked up on the special tone of voice Skylar used and how animated she got when she talked to the girls. "Look at you," he said, leaning close to Greer. "You're getting so big and strong."

"Isn't she?" Skylar nodded. "You'll be chasing Jet in no time, won't you?" She turned, at ease and smiling and so damn beautiful she took his breath away.

"Well, lookie here. If it's not the lovely Miss Skylar and her adorable brood." Angus McCarrick leaned against the booth, giving Skylar a charming smile. "If I didn't know better, I'd think you were a happy family." He leaned forward, making a face at Greer—who giggled. "Lucky for me, I know better. What are you lovely ladies having for dinner?"

Brynn held up a French fry.

Mya held up her chicken strip.

"Looks good, looks good." Angus nodded. "And what about your beautiful Momma?"

"Salad," Brynn said. "No French fries."

"Poor Momma," Angus said, giving her an openly appreciative once-over.

"It was a very good salad," Skylar said, completely oblivious about Angus's open admiration. "I will be having ice cream."

"A woman who has her priorities straight. I like that." Angus grinned. "It must be my lucky day, finding you all here. I was planning on stopping by the clinic."

"Oh?" Skylar asked, looking up at him. "For an appointment? You should call first thing in the morning. I think we can come out and look at your horses on Friday morning."

Angus chuckled. "I was coming to see you."

Skylar blinked, her eyes going wide. "Oh."

It wasn't exactly the sort of reaction a man hoped for but Kyle thought it was hysterical. He sat back and crossed his arms over his chest, trying not to smile.

"You see her now," Brynn said. She used her French fry to point at Skylar.

Kyle knew where this was going and he didn't like it. Not one bit.

"I do." Angus winked at Brynn. "I guess now's as good a time as ever—"

"It is?" Kyle mumbled, running a hand across the back of his neck. He hadn't meant to say anything out loud but it was out there now and both Skylar and Angus had heard him.

Angus's attention shifted to him then, his eyes narrowing as one dark brow arched high. "No?"

Kyle risked a glance Skylar's way. Skylar, who was red cheeked and flustered but trying not to acknowledge how uncomfortable the situation was rapidly becoming. He shot Angus a tight smile and shrugged.

"I'll stop by and visit at the clinic on Friday, Skylar. Maybe I can talk you into some fries for lunch?" Angus chuckled. "Enjoy your ice cream, ladies."

"Bye." Brynn waved. "He's nice, Momma." She went back to eating her fries.

"He's...something." Kyle didn't bother to hide his irritation. He'd known Angus for years. Angus McCarrick was exactly the sort of guy Skylar should avoid. He wasn't looking for a family—he was looking for a good time.

"The accent's nice." Skylar shrugged, then laughed. "And he definitely doesn't lack confidence."

"What's so great about his accent?" Kyle asked, offering her a French fry.

Skylar bit her lower lip, then took the fry. "It's... different."

"Different?" he snorted. "Anyone can have an accent." His attempt at a Scottish accent was painful to his own ears.

Brynn and Skylar both stopped eating to look at him.

"You sound funny," Brynn said, wrinkling up her nose.

"No good?" he asked.

"No." Skylar shook her head.

"I should take my French fry back," he teased, grinning at Skylar.

Skylar immediately ate the fry, her face full of mischief.

And just like that, Kyle was reeling. That look. That smile. The spark in her eyes. He was pretty damn fond of every single thing about Skylar Davis. If he was staring at her, he couldn't help it. She was the flame and he was the moth, drawn in—even if he wound up burned in the process.

Skylar's gaze swept over his face slowly—as if she was taking inventory. When her attention zeroed in on his mouth, his blood warmed and headed south. Her lips parted then, the shudder of her chest making him bite back a groan of frustration.

Two weeks.

Two damn weeks of them dancing this dance. Of avoiding one another and making sure they were never alone. For what? She'd made it clear she wasn't interested in anything more with him. Attracted to him, yes…

Mya patted the table, waiting for him and Skylar to turn her way before she signed, "Ice cream, please?"

"I'm on it." Kyle stood. "Who wants what flavors?"

Ice cream was a whole other matter. Mya wanted a sundae—no chocolate sauce, no butterscotch, and no coconut, of course. So, basically, it was vanilla ice cream with a whole lot of strawberries and strawberry juice and whipped cream. Brynn wanted strawberry ice cream with chocolate sauce in a big cone. He and Skylar rotated sipping their chocolate malts with the constant cleanup of chocolate-and-strawberry drips and ice-cream puddles. And when the ice cream was gone and Brynn and Mya were looking heavy lidded, Kyle waited for them to get their faces and hands wiped clean with Skylar's ever-ready wet wipes, then scooped them up—one in each arm—and carried them outside.

Skylar followed, carrying Greer, her gaze bouncing his way again and again. "You've got them?"

"I've got them." His heart nearly burst when Mya rested her head on his shoulder. "They weigh next to nothing." He nodded as they passed two blue-haired ladies whose names he couldn't remember. "Light as a feather."

"I'm no feather," Brynn said, giggling.

"You sure?" he asked, lifting her up higher. "I think you might be."

Brynn kept giggling.

They reached the Granite Falls Veterinary Clinic and Hospital van Skylar had been driving around for the last couple of weeks. He'd done his best to keep his distance—he needed time to regroup and process their last run-in. He missed her, he missed the girls, but his heart wasn't used to feeling... Not like this anyway. But today, seeing the way she reacted to those flowers, he couldn't shake the feeling that—maybe—she wasn't being one hundred percent forthcoming with him.

"This is quite a tank." He stood aside while she slid the door open.

"It is." She nodded. But she looked so pleased he suspected she'd have been happy with just about anything if it gave her a sense of freedom and independence. "I'm turning wide and parking away from everything and being extra careful." She climbed into the van and put Greer in her car seat.

He set Brynn inside the van. "Oof. Maybe you are heavy." He pretended to be stretching his arm out.

"You okay?" Brynn asked, her little face creased with concern.

"I'm teasing, Brynn." He hugged her. "I'm fine."

"Kyle's big and strong, Brynn. You can't hurt him." Skylar nodded, securing the buckles on Greer's car seat, and climbed out of the van. "Climb on up."

"Okay." Brynn climbed into her seat and buckled herself. "Good?"

Skylar checked the clasp. "Good."

"Big and strong, huh?" Kyle asked.

Skylar didn't take the bait.

"Big arms," Brynn said. "Like Weston's green man super-he-whoa toy."

"Green man…?" Skylar asked, smiling. She turned, tilting her head, and giving him a head-to-toe inspection. "Almost. His pants aren't purple."

"He not green," Brynn pointed out.

"That, too," Skylar signed slowly, explaining everything to Mya.

Kyle watched as a little crease formed between Mya's brows.

"No," Mya said. "Pretty." She made the sign for his name, followed by the sign for *beautiful*.

Kyle smiled. "I don't think I've ever been called pretty before."

"Are you blushing?" Skylar had laughter in her voice.

"No." He was.

"Mya." Skylar helped her into her seat and with her buckles. "Ready?" She waited for their nods and closed the door. "Well…"

"I'll see you at home." He resisted the urge to smooth the long strand of hair that had slipped free of her ponytail. "Do I really look like the a superhero?"

"No." She laughed.

"Because I'm not green and I'm not wearing purple pants?" He crossed his arms over his chest, waiting.

She kept shaking her head, still smiling. "I'm not sure you could pull off purple pants."

"Is that a challenge?" he teased.

"No." She held her hands up. "Don't you dare waste your money on purple pants."

"Who says I don't have a pair in my closet?"

Her eyes widened. "You do not."

He paused, shrugged, then confessed, "No. I don't."

She laughed again.

"I like hearing you laugh, Skylar." He did. It made something deep inside him go soft and warm. A place he hadn't known existed until Skylar.

Her laughter stopped and her smile wavered. "I should get them home." She fumbled through her purse for her keys and made her way to the driver's door of the large van.

"See you in a bit." He headed down the street to his truck with a spring in his step. It might have started out rocky but, he hoped, everyone seemed to have a good time. He sure as hell had. He hadn't realized just how much he enjoyed spending time with them—he'd missed them. He nodded as the van drove by, Skylar at the wheel, and turned the corner to his parking spot. The last thing he'd expected was to find Angus McCarrick leaning against the hood of his truck.

"I figured I'd cut right to it." Angus shook his hand. "If you've got a soft spot for the woman, then I'll walk away. But—"

"Then walk away," Kyle said, regarding his key chain.

"I thought so." Angus chuckled. "Can't say that I blame you. She's a looker."

Kyle nodded, meeting Angus's gaze. "And the mother of three."

"I noticed." He shrugged. "Good girls though. Not the sort that talk back or cry all the time. I thought, maybe, I'd give it a go. I like the idea of a big family. Someday."

Kyle smiled.

"But I won't." Angus shook his head. "For now. You drag your heels too long, well…" He touched his fingers to the brim of his cowboy hat. "Don't drag your heels too long."

Message received. The drive home gave him time to realize his blunder. If he'd thought before he'd spoken, he'd never have revealed his feelings to Angus. Granite Falls was a small town—gossip was a way to pass the time. He'd just handed Angus some prime-time gossip. As much as he'd like to think Angus would keep their conversation to himself, Kyle knew the man loved to spin a yarn. Which meant Kyle only had one choice—he had to tell Skylar how he felt before someone else did.

Chapter Thirteen

Skylar glanced out the large windows of the Mitchell Ranch house. A spring storm had rolled in during the early morning hours, knocking out power to Kyle's home. Jan had arrived within minutes of the girls waking up, inviting them up to the main house until the power was restored.

Greer lay on a thick play mat in the middle of the room, wriggling and squirming and making so much noise that Jet, Charley, and Sierra were all nearby—ears perked up, watching.

Weston, Mya, and Brynn were playing with blocks. According to Brynn, Weston could play with blocks much better than he could color.

"It's the little things, isn't it?" Jan asked, sitting in the rocking chair next to Skylar.

"It is." Skylar nodded, sipping her coffee. "Thank you again for letting us come visit."

"The door is always open, Skylar. You don't need an invitation, you hear?" Jan waited for her nod before she went on, "Kyle mentioned something about a big doctor appointment for Mya coming up?"

"Yes. It's a preliminary consultation. There are a few tests to see if Mya is a candidate for the surgery." There was nothing Skylar could do about the outcome, but that didn't mean she wasn't worried. Mya was so smart; she was picking up signs with ease. And yet, Skylar knew things would be easier for her daughter if she could hear. Either way, her little girl would be fine.

"Oh, so there are things that would prevent her from having the…the…" Jan frowned. "What are they called?"

"Cochlear implants." Skylar smiled as the brick tower came tumbling down amidst peals of laughter and clapping. "See if you can build a taller one this time." She used her hands, making sure Mya understood.

"Okay, Momma," Brynn said.

Mya nodded.

Skylar studied Mya's smile, her easygoing nature. She'd lost so much of her shyness since they'd come to Granite Falls. She wanted her little girl to be confident and happy—with or without the surgery. "It's rare, but yes, sometimes the surgery and implants aren't recommended. Sometimes the scans and tests indicate that even if they have the procedure, it might not work."

"Well, I am happy to watch Brynn and Greer when you go to your appointment." Jan rocked slowly, watching her grandson. "I have no doubt Brynn will keep Weston in line and Greer will entertain the dogs the whole day."

It was pretty adorable to see Greer's blanket surrounded—at a safe distance—by three large dogs.

"There are times, like now, when I can't quite wrap my head around how much everything has changed," she confessed, glancing Jan's way. "Everything."

"Good changes?" Jan asked. "Well, even good change can take some getting used to."

Skylar nodded. "The girls seem to have adjusted just fine." She was the one struggling. Not with everything, of course. She had a roof over her head, food, clothing, a job, and a way to get around... But the night she'd spent with Kyle had made her painfully aware that something was missing from her life. A partner. Someone to love. *Kyle.*

She shook her head, tightening her grip on her coffee cup.

"I'd best get some lunch thrown together." Jan pushed out of the rocking chair. "Hayden and Kyle will likely be stopping by to eat. Those boys can eat, let me tell you."

"Can I help?" She trailed after Jan into the kitchen—the large open great room and kitchen making it easy for her to give Jan a hand while having full view of the kids.

The two of them worked in tandem, making a hearty chicken soup and fresh-baked rolls, chatting and laughing the whole time.

"I do wish Lizzie was here." Jan pulled a stack of bowls from the cabinet. "She loves to cook. But that girl has more talent in her pinkie finger than anyone I know. The new high school was being finished just about the time she visited Hayden. Once those two laid eyes on each other, it was clear to see where things were headed." She went around the table, putting bowls on the place mats. "I'd like to think she's as happy with her new career as the head of the fine arts department as she is with Hayden."

Jan was content to keep the flow of conversation going. From Granite Falls's yearly festivals to this weekend's rodeo to the controversy over the old clock tower being moved to the fun the girls would have in the creek when the summer got too hot. Skylar listened, making up a bottle for Greer, and chopping up some fruit and vegetables for Weston and the girls.

"Mom, something smells good." Hayden came in through the garage door. "You must be in hog heaven," he said, spying the kids.

"I am." Jan smiled and then she turned and put her hands on her hips in frustration. "And I'll stay that way as long as you boys remember to leave those muddy boots in the mudroom."

"Yes, ma'am." Hayden chuckled. "You hear that, Kyle. You're gonna want to strip down a bit. Kyle might have fallen into the tank up by the high field."

"Fallen?" Kyle pulled off his rain-spattered cowboy hat and shook his head. "Pushed, is more like it." He hung it on one of the pegs lining the wall in the mudroom.

"And it was funny as hell, too." Hayden laughed, hanging his hat.

Skylar watched the brothers, smiling. As wet as Kyle was—and his plaid button-up shirt and blue jeans looked soaked through—they were laughing and joking the way brothers should. Seeing them this way, it was hard to imagine that they'd ever had a strained relationship. She hoped, with all her heart, that was all behind them now.

Jan shook her head. "Might as well throw that in the wash." She pointed at Kyle's button-down brown plaid shirt, which was streaked with mud. "I'm surprised at you two. Acting like children."

Neither of them looked the least bit repentant.

Kyle looked… Well, he looked big and strong and manly and so handsome her insides grew liquid hot.

"Skylar." Hayden nodded. "Your girls wearing Weston out, I hope?"

"I think it's mutual." Skylar pointed at the tower they were working on, almost as high as Weston now. "They've been very focused."

"Look at that." Hayden knelt, clapping his hands.

Weston jumped up and ran across the room, throwing himself into his father's outstretched arms. "Dadda." He pressed a kiss to Hayden's cheek. "Hi."

"Hey, little man." Hayden kissed his son. "That's some tower."

Skylar risked a glanced Kyle's way, the sight of him slipping out of his soaking shirt enough to grab her full attention. His white undershirt clung in all the right places. But as he was tugging off his button-up, the undershirt pulled up just enough to expose the carved musculature of his abdomen.

Kyle chose that moment to look up. At her. *Of course.* Right when she was ogling his exposed bare skin… Thoroughly.

She blinked, turned and headed for the play mat. "Hungry?" she asked Greer, beyond flustered.

Greer cooed and kicked, reaching up.

"I'll take that as a yes." Skylar scooped her baby daughter up, laughing as all three dogs followed them into the kitchen. "Your security detail is on top of things."

"They know who needs protecting." Kyle moved closer, making a funny face at Greer and tickling her feet.

Any chance of Skylar not noticing the stubble on his jaw or his delightfully earthy scent went out the window as he stepped closer. "Can I?" he asked, holding out his hands for Greer.

Greer kicked and squealed enthusiastically.

"I'm not sure she'd like that," Skylar teased, shifting the baby into his arms.

Kyle cradled Greer against his chest. "Your momma thinks she's funny." He bounced her, making faces.

If she'd been distracted before, she was mesmerized now. Tight white shirt. Bulging arms. Loving smile. Greer, so little, cradled so tenderly. He shouldn't look this good. He shouldn't be this…this good.

"You ready for your bottle?" Kyle asked Greer, his gaze meeting Skylar's. "I got this, if you want to eat?"

She nodded, suspecting words would give away all the things she was thinking and feeling and wanting.

Beyond Kyle, she'd developed a real fondness for the Mitchell family. They'd welcomed her with open arms and treated her as part of the family. The girls loved being here—Weston and the dogs and Jan's ready supply of fresh-baked goodies helped with that. It felt good to sit around the table and listen to Kyle recount the morning's barn repairs. Of course, he added a little extra drama for the kids, smiling broadly when they laughed at his story.

When she was done eating, she took Greer so Kyle could eat. "Thank you," she said.

"My pleasure." He grinned. "Greer likes hanging out with me."

"Oh, she does?" Skylar stared down at her sleepy-eyed daughter. "Do you, Greer? Do you like Kyle?"

"She loves him," Brynn said.

"Hear that?" Kyle puffed out his chest, like a proud peacock. "She loves me."

"I love you, too, Kyle," Brynn said.

Mya held up her hand, signing, "I love you" and smiling broadly.

"Three against one," Kyle said.

Skylar laughed. "Fine. They love spending time with you."

He nodded triumphant.

"Great. Glad that's taken care of. I'm going to eat my lunch now," Hayden grumbled. "Before it gets cold."

"They love spending time with me?" Kyle's voice was low, almost a whisper. "What about you, Skylar?"

She wasn't sure how to answer that because she wasn't sure what he was really asking. All she knew was that he seemed to be searching for something, that he seemed entirely focused on her. "I…" She swallowed. *I love spending time with you, too. I love you.* Did she? Really love him? She cared a great deal for him but… Was she? In love with Kyle?

"Skylar?" He frowned. "What is it?"

"I need to change her before she goes to sleep." She ignored the flash of disappointment on his face and carried Greer to Weston's nursery, thankful for the moment's retreat. When she'd told Kyle they could only be friends, she'd meant it. It was the right decision—for both of them. Their future couldn't be built upon a promise he'd made to Chad, no matter how noble that may sound. She needed to remember that, before she said or did something she'd regret.

Kyle finished off the water in his canteen and peered up at the windmill. "Looks good." It'd taken a lot of sweat and teamwork, but they'd finally finished replacing the broken blade.

"Yep." Hayden wiped his brow with the red bandanna he had tucked into his back pocket. "I heard something in town this morning." He paused. "Well, Lizzie heard it and told me. Teacher's Lounge gossip."

"Sounds exciting." Kyle shot his brother a disappointed look. "Why would I care—"

"It's about you." Hayden slapped him on the shoulder. "You and Skylar."

"What about us?" He frowned. "Why can't people leave well enough alone?"

"Hold on. According to Lizzie, you said something to Angus." He tucked his bandanna into his pocket. "Something about staking your claim to Skylar."

"Oh, that." He avoided his brother's eyes. "Yeah, well… He was going to ask her out."

"And that's a problem because the two of you are just friends?" Hayden started packing up tools into the toolbox in the rear of the ranch truck.

"No… Yes… Hell if I know." He shook his head. "I think—no I'm pretty damn sure I know how I… what I want."

"So, you tell Angus? Not Skylar?" Hayden stared at him over the truck bed.

"Angus was laying it on thick. I was buying some time. The plan was to tell her before word got out." His sigh was bone deep. "I'd assumed I'd get more than ten hours."

"You have been gone awhile." Once Hayden took a look at him, his smile faded. "She doesn't blame you for Chad's death."

"Maybe not." Kyle stared up at the blue sky. "But I do." He shook his head.

"Then it sounds like that's where you need to start. With yourself." Hayden slammed the toolbox shut and pushed his hat back for more shade. "When I met Lizzie, my past came back with a vengeance. It was going to break me, break us, if I didn't face it and let it go."

Kyle stared at his big brother. "I hope all the… stuff with me and John didn't have anything to do with it. I'm sorry for that, Hayden." He waited for his brother to look his way. "It took a few close calls and a whole lot of missing home for me to realize you were trying to protect us. I know that now. And I'm sorry."

Hayden nodded, clearing his throat. "Thanks." He cleared his throat again. "I'm sorry, too. I did overstep. I missed Dad so damn bad but I…I was never angry with you."

"Just sad." Kyle gripped the truck bed, wishing there was a way to go back and change things. "I miss him, too. And John."

Hayden's jaw tightened. "Haven't heard from him in a few months. He's pretty good about sending Mom a line or two, giving her the what and who but none of the where or why."

"Sounds right. He'll come around." At least Kyle hoped he would. It was hard to say with their little brother.

Hayden didn't look convinced. "You think?" One brow rose.

Kyle laughed then. John had been born stubborn. Even as a toddler, he'd dig in his heels and say no just to be contrary. It'd been cute when he was little, not so much when he grew up. Add Ed fueling his hostility and resentment for Hayden, and their home life had gone to hell pretty damn quick. Their mom, a lot like Skylar, had been so devastated over losing their father that she'd been desperate for companionship. Ed had been there, waiting in the wings, to swoop in and take over—a life of plenty without needing to do any of the work. Ed was why they had all enlisted. Each of them was looking for distance and space to heal.

"The rodeo's this weekend. Why not ask Skylar to go?" Hayden asked. "Lizzie and I are going. You know Mom and Penny would be happy to watch the kids."

"Like…a date?" Kyle frowned. "Did I mention how hung up she is on the whole friend thing?"

"Tell her a group of us are going." Hayden stepped away from the truck and scanned the ground for anything they might have missed.

"Is there a group of us going?" He pushed off the truck bed and walked the periphery of the windmill, pocketing two long screws and a sheared-off drill bit.

"Maybe. I haven't heard back from everyone." Hayden stared up at the windmill. "Not too bad." He pulled his bandanna out and used it along the back of his neck. "If you want my advice—" Hayden broke off and waited.

That told Kyle everything he needed to know. Hayden wasn't going to offer it up anymore, not unless Kyle asked. He didn't want his little brother to feel bulldozed or bossed around.

"Let me have it."

"Keep it simple. Tell her, straight out, how you feel." Hayden pulled the truck keys from his pocket. "None of these fireworks or flash mobs at the rodeo or any of that nonsense."

The image of the good people of Granite Falls doing a flash mob had Kyle in stitches. "Thanks for that imagery."

Hayden grinned. "You know they'd do it. It wouldn't be pretty—but they'd do it."

"I'll consider it my backup, backup plan." He paused. "I'll add another backup for good measure."

The sun was on its way down when Kyle parked in front of his house, tired but determined. Hayden had been right, he needed to work through the guilt and fear that haunted his dreams each night. But he had a plan. One he hoped would help him find peace—or come to terms with the past. As he walked up, he could hear the cheerful voices of the girls and smiled. Brynn was singing—loudly—and Jet was howling along with her.

The door opened and Skylar, a bag of trash in her hands, stepped onto the porch. "Oh, hi." She paused, a slow smile forming as their eyes locked.

"Evening." He took off his hat. "Sounds like you've got a real humdinger of a concert going on."

"Humdinger? I don't know what it means, but it does sound right." She smiled. "Long day?" She nodded at his dust-covered boots and jeans.

"Long, but good. Nothing like fixing something—then watching it in action." He grinned. "Of course, it's not always fixed the first time."

"Momma?" Brynn called out. "Who's there?"

He saw Skylar hesitate. Like she didn't want to tell the girls he was here, and he didn't want to complicate things for her. "I'm headed for the shower." He smiled as he moved past her, then paused. "Hayden wanted me to see if you were free to go to the rodeo tomorrow? A group of people are going. Mom and Penny will watch the kids."

"You're not going?" she asked.

"I'm not sure yet." Since he'd decided tonight was the night to tell her how he felt, he'd see how that went first. "But you should go. The rodeo is a lot of fun. You'll meet people." Everyone would be there. Including Angus. *Dammit*. He damn near had to go—to run interference if nothing else.

He'd opened his door when he heard Brynn say, "Kyle! You home!"

He took a deep breath, turned and crouched—ready when she came barreling across the porch and into his arms. "I'm all dirty."

"I have bath later," Brynn said, her little arms twining around his neck.

"I heard you singing." He savored her hug.

Mya came tearing across the porch then, launching herself into his arms and knocking him back and onto his rear. "Sorry," Mya signed. "Okay?"

He nodded, laughing. "I'm fine. You're strong."

Mya laughed, too.

He stood, dusting himself off. "I didn't mean to interrupt your dinner. Or your singing, Brynn. You keep that up and sing me to sleep, okay?" He made a big production out of stretching and yawning.

"You tired?" Brynn asked. "I'll sing you to sleep."

"Night?" Mya said, her voice the sweetest sound.

"Night, girls." He winked. "Give Greer a kiss from me, will you?"

"'Kay," Mya signed, "night," then blew him a kiss. He grabbed it and winked.

Skylar's smile was forced and brittle but she said, "Night, Kyle. Get some sleep."

With another wave at the girls, he went inside, and closed the door behind him. He listened as the girls told Skylar they were sad and wanted him to come for dinner.

I want that, too.

But first things first. He took a fast shower, donned clean clothes, threw an old sleeping bag over his shoulder, and slipped out the front door—tiptoeing so he could sneak away.

The path he took was familiar, winding along the fence line, then back into the dense underbrush, through the spindly cedar and tall Spanish oak trees to the base of what he and his brothers had dubbed Mountain Top. It was no mountain. But the hill was steep to get up—a challenge when they were boys. Between the dark and the crumbled limestone beneath his boots, it wasn't exactly easy. But once he'd reached the top, he was glad he'd spent the effort.

He spread out the sleeping bag and lay flat, staring up at the stars. "Same stars we'd look at…" His voice echoed in the quiet. "Hi." He shook his head. "It's me. Kyle…" How many nights had they been holed up somewhere with the stars overhead? Telling tall tales and doing their best to keep their nerves steady when every shadow posed a potential threat.

"Here we are again." He blew out a long, slow breath. "Chad, I'm sorry. I know I said it then but…

I'm saying it again." He was equal parts embarrassed and desperate. What did he have to lose? He pressed his hands against the sleeping bag, fingers flexed. "Skylar says it's not my fault. And I want to believe her but…we both know things would have played out differently if I'd been there.

"She doesn't believe that either. She seems to think you'd made up your mind and there was nothing I could have done to stop you." He fisted his hands. "Maybe she's right. She sure seemed to think so. But you being there and me here…it eats me up every damn day. And I have to let go." He took another deep breath. "I miss you, man. Skylar and the girls. They are something. And I wanted to tell you that I get it now. How they were the most important thing in the whole world for you? I get it. And though I'll never deserve them, and I'll never take your place, I will love them that way. More than anything in the whole world." He cleared his throat but the pressure didn't ease. "I guess I wanted to promise you that, if she'll have me, she and the girls will never want for a thing." He stared up at the diamond-crusted sky. "And they'll know every single day that they are loved—both by you and by me. Because they are."

And just like that, there was nothing left to say. But he stayed there, watching the sky and breathing in the clean and quiet that surrounded him. Exhaustion pressed in on him until he was forced to close his eyes.

When he drifted off, he didn't know, but his sleep was deep and peaceful.

Chapter Fourteen

"It was nice of Jan to loan me the boots. It looks like they're required attire." Skylar glanced down at the surprisingly butter-soft leather boots she wore.

"For rodeo, yes. You're in Texas, Skylar—you have to own at least one pair of cowboy boots." Lizzie did a little-skip-ball-step dance move then held her booted foot out.

"I won't lie, this is way outside my comfort zone." She stared down at the outfit Jan and Lizzie and Penny had put together for her.

"You look amazing," Lizzie assured her. "And it was fun getting you all dolled up. The makeup. Your eyes look *huge*. The hair. You look like a rodeo queen. You did have fun, didn't you? I mean, we all did. Now I feel bad."

"Yes, it was fun." At first, it wasn't. But then, she'd gotten caught up in it all. Getting dressed up, putting on makeup, using a flat iron on her hair, and laughing with a bunch of women—it had been years since she'd done something like it. This was the first time she'd gone out in brown leather cowboy boots, a blue chambray shirtdress tied with a beaded leather belt, and a brown cowboy hat. It was a little much for her but the other women—and Brynn and Mya— oohed and aahed so much she'd decided to go with it. She wanted to look pretty, for herself—not for any other reason or person. *Yeah, right.* She wanted to look pretty for herself *and* Kyle. "It's been a while since I've had a night off."

"Too long, I'm betting. Tonight, you can relax and have fun—no worries about the kids or anything else." Lizzie hooked arms with her, steering her toward a food booth with a short line. "If boots are required rodeo attire, this is required rodeo eating."

"Funnel cakes. Oh, yum." The powdered-sugar-covered confection smelled divine. "Another thing I haven't had in years."

They got their funnel cakes and headed to the stands, where Hayden was saving seats.

Her gaze scanned the crowd but there was no sign of Kyle's broad shoulders or his tan cowboy hat. There'd be nothing to distract her from the rodeo…

or her funnel cake. There was no reason to feel disappointed. So why did she?

She took Hayden's hand and climbed up the steps to their row. The wooden bleachers were filling up and, from what Skylar could tell, everyone knew everyone. She said hello to Dean, who sat on the row beneath them, while trying not to dump powdered sugar all over his head as she balanced her plate on her lap.

Dean wasn't the only familiar face. Trace Dawson, the game warden, was there. He and Hayden spent a good deal of time talking about the wild hogs causing all sorts of trouble. Skylar had no idea there were wild hogs in Texas—or that they were such a nuisance.

Cassie showed up, Angus and Dougal and Buzz in tow. The four of them wedged in on the bleacher above where she, Lizzie, and Hayden were seated. The more people that sat, the louder the chatter. Skylar gave up trying to have a conversation with anyone for fear of shouting. Instead, she broke off a piece of her funnel cake and stared down at the arena.

On the far end, different pens corralled horses, bulls and steer. A sea of cowboy hats moved, busy doing whatever it was they were doing.

"Not riding tonight?" Hayden asked Angus.

"Still healing." Angus touched his chest.

"What happened?" Skylar asked, curious.

"A bull and I had a disagreement. I was on his back. He didn't take all that kindly to it," Angus said, leaning toward her. "I got knocked off and stepped on, broke my clavicle."

"That sounds incredibly painful." She shook her head.

"It's all part of the fun." Angus winked.

"Getting stepped on by thousand-pound animals and breaking bones?" Cassie asked. "Sign me up."

Skylar laughed.

"You look extra nice tonight, Skylar. You make one mighty-fine cowgirl." Angus shook his head, smiling broadly. "Where is Kyle? I figured he'd be here tonight."

That was a bizarre leap. She realized Cassie, Angus, Dougal, and Buzz were all looking at her, waiting for her to answer. "Um, I don't know?"

Angus sighed, crossed his arms over his chest and shook his head. "Damn fool."

Cassie elbowed him, hard. "Shush. Eat your nachos."

Buzz chuckled. "Something tells me he'll turn up…any minute now."

"He's right there," Dougal said. "Now things will get interesting."

Don't look. Don't stare. The minute her eyes found him, she almost dropped her funnel cake. He was, without a doubt, the most handsome man here. He was talking to a couple, laughing, his good-natured self. Like everyone else, he'd dressed himself up a bit. A pearl-snap button-down navy shirt. Black jeans that fit so well it made it hard for her to breathe. His black cowboy hat, that was new, sat at the slightest angle on his brow.

He shook hands with the man, hugged the woman, and turned toward the bleachers.

Her nerves stretched taut as her heart thudded in welcome. Why did she have to fall for him? Why not Angus? Why not anyone else? Someone who could love her free and clear, without his conscience tying him to her?

Kyle saw her and froze. It wasn't subtle. Someone slammed into his back—but he didn't move or acknowledge it.

"There it is," Angus murmured.

Skylar exhaled slowly, making her chest collapse in until the pressure made her light-headed. Her heart, as always, took off. It thumped so hard and fast there was a chance everyone could hear it, even over the noise of the crowd.

"Kyle!" Hayden waved his hand.

"He sees." Cassie sighed. "Believe me, he sees."

Was it good that he was here? Bad? Both? *Breathe.* He should be here. This was his home. These were his friends. And she was one of them. She needed to stop being so focused on her own feelings and start acting like a friend would. Whether or not he loved her, she loved him. Fine. That's the way it was. She'd get over it and, in time, her heart would recover. But if she kept jumping and avoiding him, she might cause permanent damage to their friendship. She couldn't bear the idea of losing Kyle altogether.

Angus whistled, long and loud—startling her so much that her funnel cake went flying. A fine dusting of powder sugar rained down before the plate, and the crispy fried dough, landed on Dean's head.

She jumped up. "Oh, Dean! I'm so sorry."

"It's okay." Dean laughed, brushing the powdered sugar out of his hair. "It surprised me, too."

Angus was practically rolling in the aisle, he was laughing so hard—so were Dougal and Buzz.

Skylar gave them her mom face, shaking her head, before she dug through her purse for her wet wipes. "Here." She handed the pack to Dean. "I'm so sorry, Dean."

"Don't you worry about it, Skylar." Dean held up the wet wipes. "Thank you for these, but I think I'll wash up." He stood, dusting off his pants and sending up an avalanche of powdered sugar, then walked down the steps and out of the bleachers.

"Poor Dean," Lizzie said, but she was smiling. "Let's hope the mosquitos aren't bad tonight."

Skylar frowned and sat, instantly searching for Kyle. He was gone. Where? And why?

"He'll be fine." Angus kept laughing. "It's a little sugar, not gasoline or cow sh—"

"We get it," Cassie cut him off. "I'm sure he knows it was an accident, Skylar."

The music started and a line of women on horseback rode into the arena, holding the Stars and Stripes high. Skylar watched, surprisingly moved by the show of patriotism. When the announcer thanked the service members, veterans, and their families, a lump rose up in her throat. A young woman sang the national anthem and, as the final notes spilled into the air, everyone rose to their feet clapping, cheering, and whistling.

They were sitting down when Kyle appeared again, a funnel cake in hand.

"It looked like you lost yours," he said, smiling the smile that stoked a fire low in her belly.

"If she doesn't want it, we'll take it," Angus called.

Skylar took the funnel cake. "Thank you."

"Can I?" he asked, nodding at the sliver of space on the bleacher beside her.

She nodded, not in the least prepared for the instant wave of sensations his nearness caused. He was a warm blanket, a fierce hug, and an electric shock all rolled into one. She wasn't sure whether to lean into him or scooch as far from him as possible... Considering how sandwiched in they were, the latter wasn't an option.

"This keeps getting better and better," Angus murmured, followed by an "Ouch, woman."

Skylar looked back to see Cassie smiling broadly and Angus rubbing his upper arm, scowling.

"Did I miss anything?" Kyle asked, pointedly ignoring what was happening behind them.

"We were waiting for you." Angus leaned forward. "Then Skylar threw her funnel cake at Dean and you showed up."

Skylar was so surprised, she laughed. "I did not—"

"Covered him, from head to toe," Angus continued.

She kept laughing, shaking her head. "Poor Dean…" Kyle's eyes, one brown and one blue, were watching her closely.

It didn't matter that they were surrounded by people and noise, all Skylar could see was Kyle. Every little feature seemed to come into sharp focus. The way one corner of his mouth tipped up higher than the other. The crinkles at the corners of his eyes when he smiled. The scent of leather and aftershave and…Kyle. She knew that scent, loved that scent. She loved everything about Kyle Mitchell. Who was she kidding? She was one hundred percent, head-over-heels, madly in love with him. All she had to do was survive the night without every citizen of Granite Falls realizing it. Or, more important, Kyle realizing it.

Kyle's plan wasn't working. He'd meant to keep it light, to laugh, and not get too hung up in how he felt about Skylar. And then he'd seen her. How was he supposed to pretend that she wasn't something special when she looked like…this?

Things got worse, and better, when she grabbed on to him during the bull riding.

When calf roping started, she leaned in so he could explain the rules. And the whole time, he was thinking how damn cute she looked in her cowboy hat... And how much he wanted to kiss her.

When there was a break, Skylar, Lizzie, and Cassie all made their way out of the stands—leaving him to deal with Angus.

Angus didn't wait. "So, you're telling her tonight, are you?"

Kyle glared at him.

"I'm thinking the dance is the perfect place for a potential suitor, like me, to step in." His accent thickened. "I'm light on my feet and rather dashing—or so I've been told."

Dougal snorted. "She's been making eyes at Kyle, here, all night."

Had she?

"I don't mind a little challenge." Angus crossed his arms. "If Kyle isn't going to be a man, then I will."

Buzz was laughing, hard.

"Really?" Kyle asked.

Buzz held his hands up.

"What now?" Hayden asked, eyeing them warily. "Or do I want to know."

"Angus is pressuring Kyle to make a play for Skylar, is all," Dougal said, shoving a handful of popcorn into his mouth.

"Oh. Well...that'll liven things up." Hayden sipped his beer.

Buzz was laughing all over again.

"Thanks for having my back, big brother," Kyle

snapped. Albeit, a half-hearted snap. "What's the rush?"

"I'm not a patient man," Angus pretended to whisper to no one in particular.

"That is very true," Dougal agreed, eating more popcorn.

"The better question is, what's the holdup?" This came from Buzz.

Kyle stood. "I'm getting a beer. Anyone want one?" He didn't wait. "No, okay. I'll be back." He climbed down the bleachers, ignoring the roar of laughter from the stands at his back.

He bought his beer and a bag of kettle corn then walked by the stock pens, pausing to look over tonight's bronc rides.

"Feeling nostalgic?"

Kyle turned to find Cassie, Lizzie, and Skylar walking toward him.

"Did you know Kyle used to ride?" Cassie asked the others.

"That was a hell of a long time ago." He turned from the pen, propping his arm on the pipe fencing. "I'm a lot smarter now. And a lot older."

"I knew John was into rodeo." Lizzie was looking into the pen. "I can't quite wrap my head around it. Riding on one of those?"

One of the horses reared up, ears flat, and kicked out at the horse next to him, making Skylar take two steps back.

"My point exactly," Lizzie said, shaking her head.

"He used to be a bit of an adrenaline junkie." Cassie stood beside him, staring up at him. "Fearless and tenacious. If he wanted something, he went right out and got it."

"All that?" Kyle's brow rose. "Some might say young and stupid?" His gaze darted to Skylar, but she seemed fully entranced with the horses.

Cassie shrugged. "I told Buzz I'd get him a beer and some nachos." She waved and sauntered off, glancing over her shoulder at him as she walked away.

What was that all about? The music picked up and the emcee gave a five-minute warning, so they headed back to their seats. He was all too happy to explain the rules to Skylar and answer her questions and share his kettle corn. Being with her felt good—natural and right. The sort of thing that wasn't meant to be rushed. But all through the bronc riding, calf roping, and barrel racing, Kyle felt time slipping away. Once the rodeo ended, they'd go to the dance—a dance Angus had deemed the right time to make his move.

"Should we head home?" Skylar asked when they were clearing out of the stands. "I've never left the girls this long."

"Do you want to go?" he asked. He had been looking forward to dancing with her. It would give him the excuse to hold her and, since he'd first laid eyes on her tonight, he'd been aching to have her in his arms. "There's a dance. Some live music. It's a good time." *A good time to tell you I love you.*

"Oh." Her gaze shifted beyond him to Lizzie and Hayden.

His brother had his arm around Lizzie, leading her toward the open-air stage on the other side of the field. The thump of a drum had started, making Cassie and Dougal take a quick spin.

She watched, a smile forming. "For a bit? Maybe?"

"Okay," he agreed. "If you're not having a good time, I'll take you home."

She nibbled on the inside of her lip, drawing attention to her mouth. "Okay."

The okay took a minute to register—he'd gotten distracted. He knew all too well how that mouth felt, how good she tasted.

"Kyle?" she said, staring up at him. Her cheeks flushed a deep red.

"Sounds good," he rasped. "Let's go."

It took a minute for Skylar to relax. Lizzie got her a strawberry margarita, which likely helped. When the music was in full swing and the floor was full of spinning couples, he made his move.

"Want to dance?" he asked.

Skylar stared at the whirling couples. "I don't know how to do that."

"We don't have to do that." He chuckled. "We can two-step."

"Don't listen to him," Angus stepped in. "I'll show you how it's done. Come on, Skylar." He took her hand and spun her. "Let your hair down and have some fun."

Kyle watched, silently cursing himself, as Angus led Skylar around the concrete dance floor. Her hat went sailing but she was laughing too hard to notice. He didn't miss Angus's triumphant smile as they whirled right in front of him.

I got it. He sighed.

"What happened to you?" Cassie asked. "You're going to let him steal her right out from under you?"

"Cassie—"

"No, Kyle Mitchell, listen to me. I know what a woman looks like when she's in love. It's the way I look every time I look at you." She shook her head, not in the least self-pitying. "And she looks at you that way. She is who you want. Don't you dare give her up without a fight."

Kyle was staring, openmouthed, when the music ended and Angus brought Skylar back to their table.

"Now," Cassie whispered, pushing him in Skylar's direction. "Dance with me, Angus." She grabbed the man's arm and tugged him onto the dance floor.

The music was slow. No spinning. No fancy footwork. Just he and Skylar and all the things he needed to say.

"Skylar?" He held his hand out. "Will you dance with me?"

He'd expected her to hesitate. Instead, she took his hand. "Yes."

On the dance floor, he slid one arm around her

waist and took her other hand in his. Her hand was soft in his rough hold. Soft and warm.

"You lost your hat." And he liked the way her hair fell loose and free around her shoulders. "Lizzie got it."

"Oh, good. It just sort of flew off. Angus is very… vigorous."

He sure as hell didn't like the sound of that. It didn't matter. He had her to himself now, and he wasn't going to give Angus one second more of their time. "Having fun?"

"I am."

"You sound surprised." And happy. That was the best part.

"I am." Her gaze met his, full of mischief and light. "It's nice."

"You deserve a night off." He cleared his throat. "Skylar…" Where to start? He didn't want to mess this up. He wanted her to understand. He needed her to know that he listened to her—that his motivation was his own.

"We don't have to talk." Her eyes went round. "We can just dance."

He shook his head, his gaze searching hers. "I feel like we've been dancing around this for too long as it is."

She swallowed.

"You're right. About Chad." He nodded. "I didn't want to believe it, but it's true. I wouldn't have been able to stop him. But you have to understand, the one time I wasn't there…" He shook his head. "Knowing that doesn't make it any easier."

She nodded. "I know. You miss him. I miss him. But you have to let it go. You have to give yourself permission to move on."

"I am. Moving on." He drew in a deep breath. "You were right about the other thing, too. I have done what Chad asked. I've honored my word to him." This was it. This was him, baring his soul… *This sucks.* "You said I don't owe you anything else. But that's not what this is about, Skylar."

Skylar missed a step, her gaze falling from his and her cheeks flushing. She went from being at ease in his hold, to gripping his arms.

"You okay?"

She shook her head. "I think…all the spinning and the alcohol…" She swayed. "I need to sit. I feel… sick."

He slid his arm around her waist and helped her off the dance floor. "Let's get you home."

"I'm sorry, Kyle. I hate ruining the evening for everyone else." She pressed a hand to her face, fanning herself.

"I'll take you." He smiled down at her, worried. "You're not ruining anything for me. I got to do what I wanted."

Skylar looked like she was going to cry. "If you're sure?"

"I'm sure." He loved her, waiting another night wouldn't change that. But he would tell her. He had to. Once she was well, he'd finish what he started tonight—tell her he loved her and hope like hell, somehow, she might love him, too.

Chapter Fifteen

Skylar rolled over in bed and pressed a hand to her head. Since she'd fallen into bed last night, the pain in her heart had only spread. She hadn't lied about the alcohol and the spinning, it had done a number on her. But it was Kyle who had knocked her feet out from under her.

He'd let go of the guilt about Chad.

He'd accepted that he'd more than fulfilled his obligation to Chad.

He was ready to move on.

She buried her face in her pillow. What was wrong with her? This was what she wanted for him. *Right. Enough.* She rolled over, threw the pillow, and sat up. How dare she wallow? For the first time in a long time, she was in control of her own life. *Focus on that*. She had a job and a vehicle and a home. Next week was Mya's doctor appointment. Life was good.

Because of Kyle.

Thanks to Jan, the girls had their first sleepover. She'd taken one look at Skylar and told her to go to bed—she had things under control. Considering Mya and Brynn and Weston were already sound asleep on a pallet of blankets and pillows and dogs and Greer was sleeping peacefully in Weston's crib, Skylar didn't argue. She'd come home, thanked Kyle, and fallen into bed. Not that she'd slept. Not much anyway.

It was early yet, but she knew the girls would be up and Skylar couldn't leave Jan on her own with them. Watching over them while they slept wasn't the same thing as balancing four kids and breakfast. Besides, being with her girls made things feel better. Some hugs, some laughs—the pain in her heart would hurt a little less.

She took a quick shower, pulled on some old jeans, a Super Mom shirt the girls had insisted she get the last time they were in town, and pulled her hair into a ponytail. After grabbing Jan's boots, she set out.

The sun was rising, the rays growing longer and longer until it had woken up all the colors and textures of the landscape. As happy as she was to have a home close to work and Penny, she'd miss this. Jet would, too. The little house didn't have much of a yard.

The Mitchell Ranch house came into sight, the windows illuminated.

She smiled. *Poor Jan.* The girls woke up happy but they'd never woken up without her being there. She hurried, closing the gate behind her, and ran up the steps of the porch to the back door.

"Morning, Momma," Brynn said, waving the spatula in her hand.

Mya waved, too. "Ma." She was holding a whisk upright, uncaring of the batter running down the handle and up her little arm. "Cooking."

Skylar stopped, taking in the scene. Her girls, covered in flour and smiling from ear to ear. And Kyle…

"French toast?" he asked, his face and shirt dusted with flour. "It's the one thing I know how to make."

"We helping," Brynn said. "Feel better?"

Kyle looked at her then, concerned.

"Yes." Skylar blinked, willing herself not to give in and hold his gaze. "It smells good."

"There's plenty." Kyle nodded at the platter, already stacked high with French toast. "They got excited so…" He shrugged, smiling.

"Good morning," Jan said, carrying Greer into the great room. "We just had a bottle and a fresh diaper."

Greer clapped her hands and reached for her.

"Thank you so much, Jan." She took Greer, cradling her daughter close.

"Don't thank me." Jan waved her hand dismissively. "Kyle came back last night, slept on the couch and was up with the kids before I opened my eyes.

They have been busy." She shook her head at the disastrous mess in the kitchen.

"I'll help you clean up." Skylar bounced Greer, pressing a kiss to her temple.

"We've got this," Kyle argued, frowning. He signed, "Clean up help," to Mya. "Don't we?"

Brynn looked around the kitchen and shook her head. "We need help, Momma."

Mya nodded. "Help." She signed.

Kyle pressed a hand over his heart. "That hurts."

"Do you have a owie?" Brynn asked, leaning forward.

It was all so playful and sweet, Skylar had to giggle. Kyle was amazing with the girls and they adored him. He smiled at her, that eye-crinkling, bone-melting smile that made her heart turn over.

"No owie." Kyle shook his head. "Thank you."

Weston came sprinting into the room then, Lizzie on his heels.

"He doesn't like wearing pants," Lizzie said, running after a giggling Weston with a pair of jeans in her hands. "This is our morning routine."

"Cardio," Kyle said, unperturbed.

Hayden came in then, grabbing up Weston and holding him out while Lizzie slid on his pants. "Teamwork," he said, leaning forward to kiss Lizzie.

"Kiss," Weston said, waiting until both Lizzie and Hayden had kissed his cheeks. "Down."

"Bossy little thing," Hayden said. "Please?"

"Down, please? Please please?" Weston added.

"What can I do?" Skylar asked, amused and slightly overwhelmed by the amount of activity taking place all around her. As foreign as it was, this was what family should be. This was what she wanted for the girls. *Someday.*

"How about we set the table?" Jan asked.

"I'll take Greer," Lizzie offered. "I have to admit, little Greer has me thinking about babies."

Hayden's eyes went round. "What does that mean?"

Lizzie just smiled, rocking Greer as she said, "You see the look on Uncle Hayden's face, Greer? That is called panic."

It was the *Uncle Hayden* that snagged Skylar's attention. She didn't mind it, but… Her gaze bounced to Kyle. Kyle, who was looking at her. He shrugged, smiling.

"How was your first Granite Falls rodeo?" Jan asked.

"Fun," Skylar said, tearing her eyes from Kyle. "I didn't know your boys were rodeo cowboys." She put a plate on each of the place mats.

"I try not to think about it." Jan shuddered. "I'm thankful they made it through, relatively unscathed." Jan launched into one of John's close calls with a bull, a mix of horror and pride in her voice.

"I think we've used all the bread in the house," Kyle declared. "Everyone has to eat five pieces, at least."

Brynn and Mya counted up five fingers and nodded, looking so pleased with themselves that Skylar had to smile.

"Five," Skylar said, nodding. "That is a lot of toast."

"You won't need lunch," Kyle said. "Besides, we're going to need the energy to clean all this up." He turned, frowning as he took in the extent of the mess. "Or we could blow it up and start fresh?"

Jan laughed.

"He has a point, Mom." Hayden shook his head. "How did you get some on the ceiling?"

Brynn looked up, which made Mya look up—so did Kyle.

"Now, that's a picture," Lizzie said, smiling at Skylar.

"That's what I was thinking." The knot in her throat wasn't a surprise. All of this was bittersweet now. If they did move to the little rent house in town, she and the girls couldn't just stop by. It was not like the ranch was a quick drive around the corner. *Might as well enjoy it while it lasts.*

"I'll get the syrup." Hayden held his hands up and slid behind Kyle toward the pantry.

"Very funny." Kyle wiped his hands on his apron, realized he'd only made it worse, and went to wash his hands.

Skylar shook her head. "Come on, girls, let's go wash up so we can eat."

"'Kay, Momma." Brynn jumped off the stool she'd been using, tugged on Mya's print leggings, and the two of them followed Skylar into the guest bathroom.

"Did you two have fun last night?" she asked, signing the question before pumping a squirt of soap into Mya's palm and a squirt for Brynn.

"Yep," Brynn said.

Mya nodded.

"Kyle is sad for you," Brynn said.

"Sad?" Skylar turned on the water. "Why?"

"He sad you weren't here. Cooking." Brynn shrugged.

"He…he said that?" Skylar was pretty sure he hadn't said that.

"He said he missed you," Brynn said. "Didn't he?"

"Miss you," Mya echoed.

Skylar helped them dry their hands and headed back into the kitchen. Once Greer was on the play mat, surrounded by the dogs, Skylar sat between her girls. "You weren't kidding," she said, taking in the amount of French toast on the table. "This is a *lot* of French toast."

"Brynn said it was your favorite," Kyle said. "Everyone dig in."

But all Skylar could do was stare at the toast Brynn stacked on her plate. He'd made French toast because it was her favorite? She didn't want to read anything into this—she didn't want to see what she wanted to see… After everything he said last night… He was moving on. So why was he looking at her like that? Like he cared. Like she was the reason for his smile. Like he wanted her here. If only that was true.

* * *

"Good?" Kyle smiled at Mya, wiping her chin with a napkin.

Mya nodded, her smile sticky with syrup.

"You did good," he signed as he spoke, very aware of his finger placement.

"We'll be eating French toast for a week," Hayden grumbled, sitting back in his chair. "Does this stuff freeze?"

"You don't sound all that grateful," Kyle shot back. "No more for you."

Everyone laughed. More important, Skylar laughed. Every time their gazes bounced off one another, Kyle grew more impatient. He needed to tell her how he felt. He *needed* to know how she felt. There were times he thought there was something there—something she was holding back. But he was a damn fool when it came to Skylar Davis, so there was a high likelihood that he was seeing what he wanted. "You need a ride into town next week, for Mya's appointment?" he asked.

"No." Skylar's brow furrowed, but she avoided making eye contact. "We can just take the van. But, thank you."

"I'd like to go." Kyle set his napkin on the table.

Skylar's eyes pressed tight, her jaw muscle tightening. "Kyle—"

"I want to be there for Mya." He swallowed. *I can do this.* Right here. Right now. In front of…everyone that matters. "And for you."

The table went silent. Even Mya and Brynn seemed to understand that something important was happening.

"I appreciate that but I'll be fine. We will be fine." Skylar's smile was forced and she wouldn't make eye contact.

"You might be, but I'll worry." He cleared his throat. "I know how important this is. Hell, it's important to me." He broke off. "Sorry… Bottom line is I care about you and the girls, Skylar." He took a deep breath. "What I mean is I love you and the girls. I love you."

She faced him, her eyes round.

"Chad told you I'm a man of my word, so here goes." He pushed out of his chair and came around the table to stand by her chair. She was so surprised, she didn't resist when he pulled her to her feet. "You have my word on this, Skylar. Every word. I love you. Not because I promised Chad I'd take care of you. Not because I was struggling with guilt over his death. But because, for the first time in my life, I feel something I've never felt before. For you. I miss you when I don't see you. I look for you everywhere. I'm happy when I see you. I…I need you in my life, Skylar."

Skylar's lips parted but no sound came out.

"If this is too much, too fast, I'll wait." His heart was lodged in his throat, making it hard to finish. "I promise, I'll never give up on you—on us."

"You said…" She shook her head. "You said you were moving on."

"I was working my way there. Here. I was nervous. I've never done this before. Probably shows." He shrugged. "In retrospect, I probably could have done a better job."

She blinked, a long, slow breath escaping.

"My goal was to get here. To the 'I love you' part of it. Because I do." He shook his head. "I know you need your space and you're moving out—"

"Maybe," she whispered.

He placed her hand on his chest, knowing she'd be able to feel just how fast his heart was thundering. "Maybe?"

"I…" She shook her head, then glanced at Mya and Brynn, the two of them watching closely. "I want to do what's best for them. It's not just about what I want. I don't even know if they'd be okay with this."

"Hold up." He drew in a deep breath. "Is this what you want?" he asked, watching her closely.

Skylar hesitated so long, doubt tightened his gut. Her nod almost brought him to his knees.

Kyle let go of her hand, carefully signing what he'd been practicing most of the night. "I love your mom." He waited for Mya to nod, her expression serious. "I want you to stay with me. I want us to be a family."

Mya frowned. "We not staying?" she asked. "Ma? I want to stay."

"Me, too," Brynn sounded off. "Greer does, too."

"Good answer, girls." He winked. "It's up to you, Skylar." He smiled. "Now or later, I'll wait." He cradled her cheek and leaned forward to whisper, "No pressure."

Skylar signed. "Yes, we are staying. With Kyle." She slipped her arms around his neck. "I love you, too. I love you so much."

"Finally." Hayden's reaction caused a ripple of laughter from around the table.

"Hush, Hayden," his mother scolded. "Behave."

"They're having a moment," Lizzie added. "Don't be a stick-in-the-mud."

Kyle was laughing. "Now that everyone has sounded off." Kyle rested his forehead against hers. "Where were we?"

"I was telling you that I love you." There was no denying the warmth in her brown eyes.

"That's one hell of a relief because the only time I've ever felt at home is when you're with me, Skylar."

"Welcome home." She smiled up at him.

He pressed a kiss to her forehead. "I like the sound of that."

* * * * *

**WE HOPE YOU ENJOYED
THIS BOOK FROM**

SPECIAL
EDITION

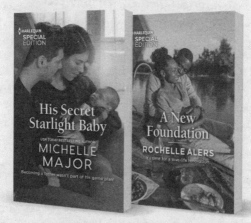

Believe in love. Overcome obstacles. Find happiness.

Relate to finding comfort and strength in the
support of loved ones and enjoy the journey
no matter what life throws your way.

6 NEW BOOKS AVAILABLE EVERY MONTH!

HSEHALO2021

*Uplifting or passionate,
heartfelt or thrilling—
Harlequin has your
happily-ever-after.*

With a wide range of romance series that each
offer new books every month, you are sure to
find the satisfying escape you deserve.

**Look for all Harlequin series
new releases on the
last Tuesday of each month
in stores and online!**

Harlequin.com

HONSALE0521

COMING NEXT MONTH FROM

◆HARLEQUIN

SPECIAL EDITION

#2857 THE MOST ELIGIBLE COWBOY
Montana Mavericks: The Real Cowboys of Bronco Heights
by Melissa Senate

Brandon Taylor has zero interest in tying the knot—until his unexpected fling with ex-girlfriend Cassidy Ware. Now she's pregnant—but Cassidy is not jumping at his practical proposal. She remembers their high school romance all too well, and she won't wed without proof that Brandon 2.0 can be the *real* husband she longs for.

#2858 THE LATE BLOOMER'S ROAD TO LOVE
Matchmaking Mamas • by Marie Ferrarella

When other girls her age were dating and finding love, Rachel Fenelli was keeping the family restaurant going after her father's heart attack. Now she's on the verge of starting the life she should have started years ago. Enter Wyatt Watson, the only physical therapist her stubborn dad will tolerate. But little does Rachel know that her dad has an ulterior—matchmaking?—motive!

#2859 THE PUPPY PROBLEM
Paradise Pets • by Katie Meyer

There's nothing single mom Megan Palmer wouldn't do to help her son, Owen. So when his school tries to keep his autism service dog out of the classroom, Megan goes straight to the principal's office—and meets Luke Wright. He's impressed by her, and the more they work together, the more he hopes to win her over...

#2860 A DELICIOUS DILEMMA
by Sera Taíno

Val Navarro knew she shouldn't go dancing right after a bad breakup and she definitely shouldn't be thinking the handsome, sensitive stranger she meets could be more than a rebound. Especially after she finds out his father's company could shut down her Puerto Rican restaurant and unravel her tight-knit neighborhood. Is following her heart a recipe for disaster?

#2861 LAST-CHANCE MARRIAGE RESCUE
Top Dog Dude Ranch • by Catherine Mann

Nina and Douglas Archer are on the verge of divorce, but they're both determined to keep it together for one last family vacation, planned by their ten-year-old twins. And when they do, they're surprised to find themselves giving in to the romance of it all. Still, Nina knows she needs an emotionally available husband. Will a once-in-a-lifetime trip show them the way back to each other?

#2862 THE FAMILY SHE DIDN'T EXPECT
The Culhanes of Cedar River • by Helen Lacey

Marnie Jackson has one mission: to discover her roots in Cedar River. She's determined to fulfill her mother's dying wish, but her sexy landlord and his charming daughters turn out to be a surprising distraction from her goal. Widower Joss Culhane has been focusing on work, his kids and his own family drama. Why risk opening his heart to another woman who might leave them?

YOU CAN FIND MORE INFORMATION ON UPCOMING HARLEQUIN TITLES, FREE EXCERPTS AND MORE AT HARLEQUIN.COM.

HSECNM0821

Get 4 FREE REWARDS!

We'll send you 2 FREE Books plus 2 FREE Mystery Gifts.

Harlequin Special Edition books relate to finding comfort and strength in the support of loved ones and enjoying the journey no matter what life throws your way.

FREE
Value Over
$20

YES! Please send me 2 FREE Harlequin Special Edition novels and my 2 FREE gifts (gifts are worth about $10 retail). After receiving them, if I don't wish to receive any more books, I can return the shipping statement marked "cancel." If I don't cancel, I will receive 6 brand-new novels every month and be billed just $4.99 per book in the U.S. or $5.74 per book in Canada. That's a savings of at least 12% off the cover price! It's quite a bargain! Shipping and handling is just 50¢ per book in the U.S. and $1.25 per book in Canada.* I understand that accepting the 2 free books and gifts places me under no obligation to buy anything. I can always return a shipment and cancel at any time. The free books and gifts are mine to keep no matter what I decide.

235/335 HDN GNMP

Name (please print)

Address   Apt. #

City   State/Province   Zip/Postal Code

Email: Please check this box ☐ if you would like to receive newsletters and promotional emails from Harlequin Enterprises ULC and its affiliates. You can unsubscribe anytime.

Mail to the Harlequin Reader Service:
IN U.S.A.: P.O. Box 1341, Buffalo, NY 14240-8531
IN CANADA: P.O. Box 603, Fort Erie, Ontario L2A 5X3

Want to try 2 free books from another series! Call 1-800-873-8635 or visit www.ReaderService.com.

---

*Terms and prices subject to change without notice. Prices do not include sales taxes, which will be charged (if applicable) based on your state or country of residence. Canadian residents will be charged applicable taxes. Offer not valid in Quebec. This offer is limited to one order per household. Books received may not be as shown. Not valid for current subscribers to Harlequin Special Edition books. All orders subject to approval. Credit or debit balances in a customer's account(s) may be offset by any other outstanding balance owed by or to the customer. Please allow 4 to 6 weeks for delivery. Offer available while quantities last.

Your Privacy—Your information is being collected by Harlequin Enterprises ULC, operating as Harlequin Reader Service. For a complete summary of the information we collect, how we use this information and to whom it is disclosed, please visit our privacy notice located at corporate.harlequin.com/privacy-notice. From time to time we may also exchange your personal information with reputable third parties. If you wish to opt out of this sharing of your personal information, please visit readerservice.com/consumerschoice or call 1-800-873-8635. **Notice to California Residents**—Under California law, you have specific rights to control and access your data. For more information on these rights and how to exercise them, visit corporate.harlequin.com/california-privacy.

HSE21R

Don't miss the fourth book in the touching and romantic Rendezvous Falls series from

JO McNALLY

JO McNALLY

Love Blooms

It's never too late for a second chance...

"Sure to please readers of contemporary romance."
—*New York Journal of Books* on *Barefoot on a Starlit Night*

Order your copy today!

HQN

HQNBooks.com

PHJMBPA0721R